# Seducing the

# Master

EM BROWN

ISBN-13: 978-1-942822-04-2

## A GENTLE WARNING

This novel contains BDSM elements, themes of submission and dominance, and many other forms of wicked wantonness.

It also contains an imperfect heroine who is strong, assertive, and flawed.

# OTHER WORKS BY EM BROWN

<u>Cavern of Pleasure Series</u>
Mastering the Marchioness
Conquering the Countess
Binding the Baroness

<u>Red Chrysanthemum Series</u>
Master vs. Mistress
Master vs. Mistress: The Challenge Continues
Punishing Miss Primrose
Seducing the Master

<u>Other Novels</u>
All Wrapped Up for Christmas
Force My Hand
A Soldier's Seduction
Submitting Again

<u>Other Novellas/Short Stories</u>
Submitting to the Rake
Submitting to Lord Rockwell
Claiming a Pirate
Lord Barclay's Seduction

<u>Anthologies</u>
Threesomes

For more about these wickedly wanton stories,
visit www.EroticHistoricals.com

# GOT HEAT?

"Ms. Brown has written a tantalizing tale full of hot sex…a very sexy and sometimes funny read that will definitely put a smile on your face."

*— Coffee Time Romance review of*
*AN AMOROUS ACT*

"Darcy's fierce, independent spirit and unconditional loyalty to her family will win readers over, and Broadmoor is a romantic hero to swoon for."

*- RT Book Reviews on*
*FORCE MY HAND*

"Sometimes you just pick up the right book that just hits you and makes you really love it. This was one of those books for me. I just got so into the story and never wanted it to end."

*- Romancing the Book review of*
*SUBMITTING TO THE RAKE*

"HOT AND FUN TO READ!!!!!!!!"

*- Reader review of*
*ALL WRAPPED UP FOR CHRISTMAS*

"This one made me go WOW! I read it in a few hours which technically I probably should have gotten more sleep, but for me it was that good that I deprived myself of sleep to finish this most awesome story!"

*- Goodreads reader review of*
*MASTERING THE MARCHIONESS*

"...sex was intense...thrilling...."

*- Goodreads reader review of*
*CONQUERING THE COUNTESS*

"I loved this book. Clever dialogue that kept m[e] laughing, delightful characters and a wonderful story. I am not generally one who likes historical fiction but this book carried me along from page one."

*- Goodreads reader review of*
*CONQUERING THE COUNTESS*

# Seducing the Master

# CHAPTER ONE

"Impossible," Charles murmured as he leaned against the mantel of the fireplace in Madame Devereux's boudoir and gazed upon the painting above. It was a portrait of the proprietress in her younger days, reclining upon a grassy knoll and surrounded by her favorite flora, chrysanthemums.

He turned to face Joan Devereux, reclining upon her settee, several decades older, a good deal plumper, her complexion far less even but not entirely devoid of the beauty of her youth.

"If Miss Katherine is as terrified as you say," he continued, "a sennight is hardly enough time to transform her into the perfect submissive."

"But, my dear Gallant, there is no other member who can provide a better introduction to the arts of submission," Devereux demurred as she peered through her spectacles at her roster of patrons. "In your early years with me here, you trained many a novice, with splendid outcomes each and every one."

"That was a long time ago. I am out of practice."

The greater truth was that he lacked the inclination for the assignment presented him. *She* still weighed upon his mind.

"But it would seem your time in the Orient has only

enhanced your repertoire. Indeed, you are in great demand. I have had many members inquire after you of late."

Charles returned his gaze to the painting. The young Devereux wore a secretive smile. Some private thought amused her, and she would keep it to herself. He had wondered if the proprietress of the Inn of the Red Chrysanthemum, where pleasures of the flesh were carried to their most wicked and wanton extremes, had had a hand in the return of Master Damien, though such speculation served no purpose. It did not alter the fact that Charles was hers for an entire six-week. He had lost his wager with her and would uphold his end of the bargain, even if she might have deliberately undermined him. She had an interest in preserving the identity of Mistress Scarlet, who, if returned to her former state as Miss Greta, was of less value to Joan.

He had nearly succeeded in restoring Miss Greta to what he believed was her true self. Now, she was lost to him entirely. His letters to her in Liverpool were refused, returned to him unopened. Charles had thought to request a leave of absence from the ministry. If she would not receive his letters, he would go to her in person. But Sir Canning required his presence in London. Charles took some comfort in the prospect that time might afford Greta the realization that she could give herself to him.

Unless she was still partial to Damien.

"Lord Wendlesson insisted upon you," Devereux continued.

Her intended compliment had little effect, and he replied, "You say he is newly married. It would seem the duty of the husband to assume the role of mentor."

"His lordship has been a member here, a master, for nearly two years. He has not the patience to instruct his wife, who has none of his experience."

"I do not mean to evade my obligations," he replied. He accepted he was, in effect, Madame Devereux's indentured servant at the Red Chrysanthemum. If the proprietress desired to make him her own personal slave, he would have serviced her without complaint. And though he had no partiality for his own sex when it came to venereal pursuits, he had fulfilled her first assignment to him by spending the night with a visiting molly. "But I am reticent to interfere betwixt a married couple, and newlyweds at that," he finished.

"Lord Wendlesson would make a terrible instructor. His temperament would stand the both of them in poor stead. It is for *her* benefit that I recommend you. Wendlesson brought her in one evening. I think he thought to titillate her, but she looked quite petrified by the goings on here."

"And he thinks I—or anyone—capable of turning her trepidation into willing submission? In a sennight, no less?"

"He will pay you richly for your services."

Remembering that Damien had offered fifty guineas for Miss Greta, Charles stiffened. "Money does not concern me. I would sooner he make his payment to you for I am in *your* service. I pray you give me another charge."

Devereux pursed her lips. "I have no other at present."

"Then I will await your next bidding. Till then, we may pause the clock on my servitude."

"His wife, though shy, is a lovely little thing. She may make you forget that other one."

He said nothing. He had tried to forget Greta by throwing himself into his work, and his efforts had not gone unnoticed by his employer, the Secretary of State for Foreign Affairs.

"We need to elect you to Parliament, Gallant," Sir Canning had said to him the day after Greta had left without forewarning. "I could have you appointed my Under-Secretary. From there, well, opportunities await."

Sir Canning implied that if he should succeed The Duke of Portland as Prime Minister, the office of Secretary of State for Foreign Affairs would then become available. The prospect of becoming a member of parliament, let alone a cabinet position, had long been Charles' wish. His own father had tried three times, unsuccessfully, to win election to Parliament. Like Canning, the senior Gallant and former Whig had even allied himself with the Tories when the Whigs fell out of favor, but, whereas Canning found success, the senior Gallant always came within a few votes shy of winning a seat.

"I have spoken of you to Sir Arthur," Canning had added, "and he is agreed that you would make a fine MP for the borough of Porter's Hill. He indicated he might support of your candidacy."

Which meant that Charles had as good as won the election, for Sir Arthur, himself an MP, owned nearly half of the tenements in Porter's Hill, purchased with gains from his heavy interests in the East India Company.

Shaking his head, Charles faced Devereux once more. "Even were I keen to undertake the task, not everyone is receptive to the distinctive predilections here. For me to make a determination of her tolerance for the various elements, especially pain, requires more time than a sennight. Nor can I, when all is done, fully impart my knowledge of her capacities to the husband, which is why it is preferable that he assume the role of mentor to begin with. I am not training a sailor, who, once he learns the ways of a seaman, can sail on most ships and be captained by anyone."

Trying a different tactic, Devereux challenged, "Do you doubt your abilities?"

He pressed his lips into a line. In truth, he did. If he had not overestimated himself, if hubris and jealousy had not overwhelmed him, he might not have agreed to that fateful challenge with Master Damien. He might not have lost Greta.

As if worried she might have planted the seeds of doubt, Devereux hastened to say, "I have full faith and confidence in you, Master Gallant. You possess a rare and perfectly balanced quality: a firm and imposing hand coupled with a gentleness that comforts the fair sex."

"You are eager to satisfy this Lord Wendlesson," he said after studying the proprietress.

She shifted beneath his gaze. "Lord Wendlesson is an influential gentleman who will become the Earl of Berksdale. He is also exceptionally generous."

Charles gathered that the man's offer of compensation had extended to Madame Devereux as well. He looked at the bright fire crackling in the hearth as he considered whether or not to assist Joan out of friendship and against his better judgment. Only recently returned to the Red Chrysanthemum, he was unfamiliar with Lord Wendlesson.

She interpreted his silence as a refusal and, heaving a large sigh, said, "For this favor, I would relieve you of further obligation to me."

Looking up, he raised his brows.

"Your service with me would be concluded," she affirmed.

"Servitude. Let us call it what it is."

Devereux stared at him. "Very well. The word has a nice depraved ring about it. If you can satisfy Lord Wendlesson, your indenture with me would be at an end. You would be free to resume your membership with all its ordinary privileges and liberties."

He inhaled deeply. As much as he had reconciled himself to submitting to Madame Devereux, he wanted the freedom. If he did not have to attend to her requests, he could put more of his attentions toward his election to Parliament. Although the support of Sir Arthur would all but guarantee victory, Porter's Hill was not a pocket borough, and Charles would take no outcome for granted. He was determined that Porter's Hill would have in him a fair and dedicated representative.

"I accept," he said to Madame Devereux.

She beamed. "Your success in this endeavor will benefit us both!"

"Miss Katherine is expected shortly," she added as she observed the clock above the mantle. "She has but an hour, for Lord Wendlesson expects to stop here upon returning from his evening at White's."

"He wishes me to complete instruction within a sennight and gives me but an hour of her time? I hope I will be afforded longer on our next occasion."

"I fear Miss Katherine cannot leave the house till her mother has gone to bed."

"Then I cannot have her ready within the sennight."

"You must try. Lord Wendlesson saw your performance with Miss Greta and was quite impressed with how you handled her. He will accept no one else for his wife's instructor. If anyone can succeed with Miss Katherine within the constraints provided, it would be you, dear Charles."

"I will see her tonight, but I will have a word with Lord Wendlesson to temper his expectations before proceeding with any further education."

Devereux sighed. "If you must."

"I insist upon it."

"Perhaps it is wise to do so. You may be able to persuade him to give you more time. I think—I hope—you will enjoy your assignment. I had your interests in mind, too, when Lord Wendlesson and I conferred. It will relieve any preoccupation you may still have of *her*. I am quite convinced that we have seen the last of Mistress Scarlet. Alas, she is a great loss to the Red Chrysanthemum."

He straightened. "Have you…have you heard from her?"

"No. And I have come to know her well in all these years. The fact that I have received no correspondence from her, it is certain she means not to return. Now, aside from Mistress Primrose, you are my greatest asset."

Devereux lamented the absence of Greta but without the depth of grief he would have expected from someone who claimed to value Mistress Scarlet with such gravity. Knowing Joan to favor pragmatism, he did not dwell long on her lack of emotion. Bowing to the proprietress, he took his leave to prepare for his evening with Miss Katherine. He now had reason to approach the assignment with more enthusiasm, and he did not dismiss Devereux's belief that the activity would stay his mind from thinking overmuch of Greta.

As he descended the steps to the second floor, he came upon Miss Terrell at the bottom of the stairs. The nubile blackamoor blocked his path. Her attire was reminiscent of a milkmaid from the prior century, with the corset worn above the garments. Her shift or chemise barely comprised a décolletage, and her supple bosom seemed ready to burst from its confines. The petticoats and skirt rose to her calves, displaying trim ankles, and she wore no shoes at all.

His gaze fixed upon her mouth, remembering that he had kissed those succulent lips and tasted Miss Greta upon them.

"Master Gallant," she greeted with a smile, revealing remarkably white and even teeth.

He was unsurprised that she was genuinely happy to see him. She had made it quite evident during his public display of Miss Greta that she was interested in him.

"Miss Terrell," he replied with a bow, lifting his gaze from her mouth to her large, round eyes. Against her ebony skin, they appeared uncommonly bright.

He expected her to move to allow him to descend the final step, but she remained where she was, pinning him with her stare. He was reminded of a panther stalking its prey.

"Do you stay the evening, Master Gallant?" she asked.

"For an hour." He moved to demonstrate his intentions of proceeding, but still she did not budge, as if she would like nothing more than to have him walk into her. "I am expected."

She raised her sculpted brows. "Indeed? By whom? I thought Miss Greta no longer with us."

He must have frowned or tightened his jaw, for, sensing her error, she quickly followed by saying, "Who is the fortunate one tonight?"

"A new member. Miss Katherine."

Having answered her, he made another move, but instead of standing aside, she leaned in toward him. He already stood a head and a half taller, and the step elevated him such that she looked him straight in the stomach. She tilted her head, and he felt himself caught in her glimmering gaze.

"Perhaps you would entertain a replacement?" she inquired, lowering her gaze to the buttons of his waistcoat so that he could behold the thickness of her lashes.

She was lovely for a blackamoor, though he found her hair far too curly and unruly. Her confidence in her seductive qualities, however, greatly enhanced her allure. He felt a primal response to her nearness. The scent of some form of pomade that she applied to her hair wafted through his nose.

"I could not," he replied.

"There would be no charge. For you, I give of myself gratis."

She looked up once more at him, those plump lips beckoning. His blood pumped more forcefully in certain parts. He would not mind another kiss, but he knew not her age. Unacquainted with Negro features, he feared she might be too young, though she carried herself with the wantonness of a mature strumpet.

Her lips parted and slowly her tongue emerged. The tip of it grazed his button. An image sprang to mind of that supple mouth wrapped about his cock, and he had to, literally, shake the vision from his head. When her tongue retreated back into her mouth, he took the final step, sweeping her with him as he went, and pinned her to the wall, more harshly than he intended.

"A generous offer," he said to her, "but one that I will have to decline. For now."

He knew not why he added those two last words. Perhaps her proximity—he could feel her curves beneath him—had him rattled. Perhaps he meant to soften the blow of his rejection. He should not concern himself too much on the latter. Miss Terrell had admirers aplenty.

Abruptly, almost as if he feared he might be ensnared by her charms if he tarried, he released her and continued on his way without a backward glance.

# CHAPTER TWO

**H**er heart still at a quick palpitation, Terrell watched Master Gallant till he disappeared down the hall. She closed her eyes to more fully evoke how it had felt to be pressed against the wall by him, his warm, hard body hovering over hers.

Ever since she had witnessed his mastery over Mistress Scarlet, she could not rid her mind of him. Over and over, she had recalled how his lips had felt upon her own, how gently he had taken her mouth, as if savoring the sensation, compelling her to do the same. She knew it was the taste of Mistress Scarlet upon her that he sought; nonetheless, he had not hesitated to kiss her, as she thought he might do if he possessed an aversion to blacks.

She had never been kissed like that before. Least ways, not by a member of his sex. She liked that his lips were not as thin as others of his kind. She did not often care for the act of kissing, but his kiss had made molten the stirring in her loins. For an Englishman, he was certainly handsome, with a slender nose and golden locks that sometimes fell over a wide and distinguished brow. Perhaps it was his travels—she had heard he had been in the Orient for some time—but he was not nearly so pale as the other men of gentle society.

Though she deemed him superior in form and

countenance, she considered herself too practical to fall for a pretty face if he had no other qualities to recommend him. A comely visage was often accompanied by tiresome dispositions and a general lack of skill about the bedchamber, perhaps because their easy beauty made them lazy and lacking in motivation to improve their abilities.

Master Gallant showed no such indolence. His performance had aroused her like no other. The man had triumphed over the stoic Mistress Scarlet. Mistress Scarlet, of all people! In her time at the Red Chrysanthemum, Terrell had never seen that woman receive a man, let alone beg him to make her spend. Why Mistress Scarlet would then quit the Red Chrysanthemum mystified Terrell, lest the woman was ashamed of her submission. She should not be ashamed at all to submit herself to such a fine and skilled Master. The manner in which he had bound Mistress Scarlet in rope had been exquisite. Terrell greatly desired to have her own body trussed in such fashion. How she had envied Mistress Scarlet her position, bent over the table with Master Gallant's cock pounding into her.

Even now, she could feel heat and moisture gathering between her legs. She climbed the stairs to the room she shared with another female member. The Inn of the Red Chrysanthemum was an uncommon place. It was part exclusive club, akin to one of those hellfire societies, and part bawdy house. But it was home. In exchange for room and board, she received membership and was expected to satisfy the patrons who had not brought their own partners to play with.

Entering her room and finding it empty, Terrell threw herself upon the bed and lifted her skirts to find her mons. *Lord*, if she could have but one night with Master Gallant... She would allow him to do anything to her. She *wanted* him to do anything and everything to her. Though she had not seen him at the Red Chrysanthemum till recently, he had wielded the flogger upon Mistress Scarlet with great proficiency.

Closing her eyes, Terrell imagined Master Gallant applying the flogger to her thighs, her breasts, and her buttocks. She rubbed herself harder between the legs, dipping two of her fingers into her wet folds and agitating the digits against that naughty little nub. She would have him bury his cock in her cunnie and work her into a frenzy, as he had done to Mistress Scarlet, then she would have him claim her arse.

The thought sent her into shivers as she spent. She eased her ministrations and sighed softly. It would do for now, but she knew only *he* could truly satisfy her appetite.

"Thinking again of Master Gallant?"

Sitting up, Terrell pulled her skirts down past her knees and greeted Sarah, with whom she quartered. Though the two women shared a room, they could not have come from more divergent backgrounds. Once married to a baronet, Sarah had been cast out on her own, along with her newborn son, when she was found guilty of criminal conversation. With her parents deceased and the other members of her family refusing to acknowledge an adulteress, Sarah eventually found herself at the Inn of the Red Chrysanthemum. Now, like Terrell, she received membership in exchange for room and board.

"Alas, it is proving no passing fancy, m'lady," Terrell replied. She always addressed Sarah as "m'lady". Having once been a courtesan to a peer, she knew the world that Sarah had once occupied and the extent of the woman's loss. She admired the quiet dignity with which Sarah continued to carry herself despite her fall from grace.

Cradling her son, now a year in age, Sarah smiled in sympathy. "I think you could not select a finer man to bestow your attentions upon. Many men pass through here, but he is a true gentleman, I think."

"I've no need for *gentlemen*, m'lady," Terrell replied with a smile.

"Ah, yes, I comprehend."

Terrell knew not whether Sarah approved of her brazen wantonness, but as a member of the Red Chrysanthemum, the former could not cast stones. She rocked her boy, George.

"I hope he will sleep soundly tonight," she remarked as she gazed upon his face with a love that would never tire.

Terrell rose to look upon the boy before his mother set him gently on the bed.

"He is a handsome boy," she said, thinking that little could compare to the serenity of a sleeping child.

"And the very image of his lordship," sighed Sarah as she sat down beside him and brushed the forelocks from his brow.

"Are you certain?"

Sarah looked down and away. "It is true I harbored affection for another, but I never broke the sanctimony of the marriage bed."

"Yet you were found guilty."

Sarah pressed her lips into a firm line. "Yes. Yes, I was."

Terrell put a hand upon her shoulder. "It is our lot in life, as women, to suffer."

"I have my son. That is all that matters to me."

They heard a clock in the hallway chime the hour. Sarah rose to her feet. "Do you not see Mr. Worthington tonight?"

"He is returned to the West Indies. I am alone this evening," Terrell said as she sat back upon her own bed. The room being small and the ceiling slanted low, standing felt cramped.

"I envy you then. I am to submit to Captain Gracechurch."

"He is a strapping fellow."

"Yes, and far too fixed upon my breasts. He nearly suckled all the milk from me the other night, such that I barely had enough for George. I should head downstairs. The Captain does not tolerate tardiness well."

After Sarah had departed, Terrell lay upon her bed. She did not envy herself the respite and would have preferred to have a distraction from Master Gallant. As she was in no position to make requests of Madame Devereux, Terrell wondered how she might gain an evening with Gallant. *He* could make the request, for he seemed to be on good terms with the proprietress.

She would simply have to make him desire her as much as she desired him.

George began to cry, though he looked still to be asleep. She went to him and picked him up, rocking him as she had seen Sarah do many times before. His cries diminished to a whimper. She rocked him more and whispered "shhh" till he was quiet and still but for his steady breathing. She could have placed him back upon the bed just then. Instead, she kept the warm bundle in her arms and adjusted the linen about him. How strange the satisfaction from merely holding a babe. Was motherhood so natural a disposition in her sex that she should feel bonded to a child not her own? Or was it her own situation, a womb that could only know emptiness, that imbued such value in that which she could never have?

Even as a young girl she had marveled at the little bundles, the ugliest of which could still inspire awe by the mere proportion of their features. When she was older and nearing the age when she could conceive, she had worked the plantation fields alongside Coral, a mother who always kept her babe with her rather than leave it in a tray beneath an arbour made of boughs with the others, lying like so many tadpoles, naked to the weather and mosquitoes, and tended by the grandee. Though the babe must have weighed upon the mother when she worked in the Great Gang, spending hours upon the knees to dig holes six inches deep and two feet long, she refused to be parted. Motherhood, Terrell learned, gave strength to a woman to endure hardship.

Holding George, Terrell believed she would have done

no less than Coral, though, for better or worse, she would never be tested. She held George a little closer. A soft knock at the door drew her attention from the babe. She placed the boy back onto Sarah's bed.

One of the maids, Tippy, was at the door. "Madame Devereux has a gentleman most interested in you."

# CHAPTER THREE

Charles wondered at the wisdom of his decision as he beheld Miss Katherine sitting upon the four-post bed, quaking behind the bedclothes she clasped to her bare shoulders. It would require more than a sennight to transform the frightened thing to an eager submissive, but he reminded himself that, in the same period of time, he had nearly toppled a veteran Mistress into willing submission.

Nearly.

"Good evening, Miss Katherine," he greeted with a bow. He spoke gently, as if to a child. "I am Master Gallant."

She blinked long lashes over crystalline blue eyes and nodded. As Devereux had said, Miss Katherine was lovely, with long brown locks cascading to her elbows and a heart-shaped countenance with even features. He preferred the vibrant hue of Mistress Scarlet's hair, but he could have landed a far less comely pupil than Miss Katherine. Nonetheless, he did not think she could replace Greta in his mind. Especially as this was the very same room he and Greta had occupied last. With canes, whips, and paddles lining the walls, it was far too intimidating a room for a novice like Miss Katherine. He looked to her and suspected she was completely naked behind the bedclothes. It was unfortunate, for he would have wanted to install her in one of the less imposing rooms.

He also would not have her start her *education* stripped to the buff. Lord Wendlesson must have directed her.

"Do not worry, Miss Katherine," he assured. "Nothing will happen this evening that you do not consent to."

Surprised, her widened eyes grew larger still. He observed her knuckles to have turned white from clutching the linen. One would think the poor petrified thing was about to be burned at the stake. Hoping to impart his composure to her, he rang for the dressing maid then poured a glass of claret. Miss Katherine shook her head when he offered her the glass of wine.

"Drink it," he urged. "It will calm your nerves."

Despite her slender frame, it would likely take more than one glass of wine to settle her, but he kept this opinion to himself. She moved one hand, still grasping the linen, to the middle of her chest. With the other, she took the glass of wine. He cupped both his hands about her trembling fingers and the glass to keep her from spilling the contents. She stared at his hands.

"Allow me to assist you," he said quietly.

With his hands supporting hers, she lifted the glass to her lips and took a small sip. She swallowed and gazed at him with the full force of her large blue eyes. A small creature, cornered by its predator, could not look as helpless as she.

"Another," he directed.

She did as told and took another drink.

"Feeling better?"

She paused, then nodded.

"Let us finish the claret."

Though she did not shake as fiercely as before, he continued to assist her in holding the glass.

"Th-thank you, sir," she said when she had finished the claret.

Glad that she would not be a mute the whole night, Charles gave her a smile and set the empty glass upon the sideboard. A knock at the door indicated the arrival of the dressing maid.

"Tippy," he greeted the young, petite maid. "Please have Miss Katherine dressed."

Seeing Miss Katherine's mouth fall open in fear or disbelief or both, he explained, "I understand your time is limited this evening, and I will not see you delayed."

In truth, he felt she would be much more at ease clothed than naked. After informing her that he would return shortly, he took his leave and sauntered downstairs to consider what he was to do next with Miss Katherine. He could barely remember the last novice he had been with. Most of the women he had known at the Red Chrysanthemum desired to be here. This did not appear the case with Miss Katherine.

Upon passing the room Madame Devereux kept as her office, he noticed the door was slightly ajar. A familiar voice came from within. In the hall, a young page dozed in his chair. Though not one to pry, Charles could not resist pausing before the threshold, attempting to place the voice.

"Fairchild spoke very highly of Miss Terrell," said the man. "He would have kept her as his mistress if he did not fear that his wife would make mischief of the matter."

"And you have no such fear?" asked Madame Devereux.

"My wife passed away two years ago from a tortured childbirth. Fortunately, my son survived. Alas, my wife did not."

Charles could hardly believe it. Sir Arthur had lost his wife in similar fashion.

"I am sorry to hear it. Your poor wife."

"I have had assorted female companionship in the past years, but none have sufficed. Knowing this, and as he is a close friend of mine, Fairchild recommended Miss

Terrell."

"Your friend has exceptional taste, but I must have you know that Miss Terrell is in great demand. She is a rare gem of ebony, you understand, beautiful and more refined than most blackamoors you'd find."

"I am prepared to pay a sizable sum for her favors. No less than a hundred guineas. But I demand her whole attention. I will not have her whoring while she attends me."

"Of course! You will have her utmost devotion!"

"No other man is to go near her. Of that I must be certain or I'll not part with a shilling."

"She is yours and yours alone."

"Good. Then I will see her tonight if I may."

"You are in luck, Sir Arthur. She is unspoken for this evening—a rare circumstance indeed. I will send for her immediately."

The proprietress rang a bell. The page awoke and scrambled to his feet. Charles withdrew and returned up the stairs, surprised that a man of Sir Arthur's standing would dare patronize the Red Chrysanthemum. He also would never have guessed the man to have a taste for black flesh, though Miss Terrell was, as Devereux said, a rare gem of ebony. He was unsure if this newfound discovery of his shared pursuits with Sir Arthur was good luck or a poor coincidence. He was not acquainted with the MP well enough to know how Sir Arthur would react to Charles' patronage of the Red Chrysanthemum.

Tippy had just finished attaching Miss Katherine's embroidered spring garters to her stockings when Charles returned. He had rapped upon the door to announce his arrival, a courtesy a master need not extend, before opening the door. Miss Katherine quickly pulled her gown to her body to cover her shift and stays. The blush spread over her entire physiognomy. Charles considered stepping out, but he had no wish to encounter Sir Arthur. The two men had been in many meetings together, especially after

Charles' return from China, but they had no personal familiarity between them. Even if Charles could call Sir Arthur a friend, he would hesitate to admit his association with the Red Chrysanthemum.

Charles turned discreetly to the door to allow Miss Katherine to finish dressing without his witness. He wondered that Lord Wendlesson did not provide a mask to Miss Katherine. It would not have eased her fears, but it would have provided her some coverage to release her inhibitions.

Many members made efforts to conceal their identities, and in his early years at the Red Chrysanthemum, he, too, had donned a mask to hide his countenance. When it seemed unlikely that he would ever come across anyone he knew, he had ceased employing a disguise. Madame Devereux was cautious with whom she granted membership. Though Charles knew money to persuade her, she had rejected the applications of prospects she considered unreliable, even ones with ample purses. Discretion, being a pillar for the viability of her business, was of utmost importance to her. Members, and the servants as well, did not gossip or speak of the Red Chrysanthemum outside its circle. Nonetheless, with the appearance of Sir Arthur, Charles reconsidered the use of a mask.

"I have but her hair to pin," Tippy informed him.

Turning around, he beheld Miss Katherine in her evening dress. The simple gown with its cap sleeves suited her. Only the fancy embroidery at the hem and about the neckline revealed the gown to be less than ordinary, speaking to the wealth of its owner without ostentation. She reminded him of Miss Lily, though perhaps not as young as the latter but very much the sort of fair submissive that would have interested Mistress Scarlet. He had come across Miss Lily twice since the duel that had won him the chance to claim Mistress Scarlet for a sennight. On both occasions, Miss Lily had cast hopeful glances at him, but, notwithstanding her loveliness, she held little interest for him and would only remind him of his challenge with Mistress Scarlet. With Greta.

Charles took a seat in a stiff wooden chair. The room's furnishings all tended toward the stark. Comfort was not the prime function. He watched as Tippy arranged Miss Katherine's soft, flowing tresses. Miss Katherine kept her gaze steadfastly to the floor. Her profile presented a most pert and charming nose. He reminded himself that this was another man's wife he looked upon, and if Lord Wendlesson was as influential as Devereux said, he would do well not to forget. He shook his head at himself. Perhaps he had been hasty in taking the bait. The assignment was fraught with hazardous complications.

But, if he succeeded, he would be released from his servitude. He suspected Devereux would make him service the mollys whenever possible. That he was partial to the fair sex mattered not to these men. Quite the contrary, his preferences seemed to titillate them, his overt declarations doing nothing to stem their attempts to flirt with him. Though he had no deep aversion to buggery and could find arousal with his own sex, he much preferred the softness of women. He enjoyed the breasts, the supple derrieres, and the moist heat between their legs.

"May I be of further service, Master Gallant?" asked Tippy when she had finished.

Miss Katherine stayed where she was, staring at the ground, one hand clasping the fingers of the other.

"Yes, I should like a bowl of confections, the ones Madame favors," he replied.

Tippy looked horrified. "The chocolates?"

"Yes."

"They are among Madame's most prized possessions. She is not known to share them with anyone."

"Yes, those chocolates," he said, undaunted.

Unconvinced, Tippy did not move and only furrowed her brow.

"I believe she will have good reason to part with a few. Thank you, Tippy."

Though still doubtful, the maid could do nothing but curtsy and attempt to execute her directive.

"Would you care for another glass of claret?" he asked Miss Katherine after the maid had departed.

"Yes, please," she said in a small voice.

He rose and went to pour her a glass. Not wanting to send her home in a state of inebriation, he did not fill the entire glass.

"Please, sit," he said before handing her the claret.

She sat down, her back more rigid than the chair. She took a hearty sip. He took the chair beside her.

"Felicitations to you on your recent nuptials," he said.

"Thank you."

"When was the happy occasion?"

She stared into the claret. "Eight days ago."

*Eight days*, Charles wanted to exclaim. Wendlesson was more impatient than he thought.

"Miss Katherine, I hope I will not disappoint you, but as you are a complete greenhorn here at the Red Chrysanthemum, I intend nothing but a conversation this evening."

She glanced at him. "I should not be disappointed, sir, but my lord Wendlesson—my husband—"

"I will address your husband, but I cannot begin your instruction without first appraising your knowledge and experience of the venereal."

Crimson bloomed in her cheeks, and she took a hurried sip of her claret.

"And you need not speak if the subject greatly discomforts you," he added. "Here, at the Red Chrysanthemum, we employ a word that, when uttered, signifies you no longer wish to proceed. It keeps you safe. Have you a favorite word that we could use for such a purpose?"

She shook her head.

"What do you enjoy, Miss Katherine? Knitting purses, reading poetry, perhaps?"

"I enjoy playing the harp, sir."

He tested the word upon his lips. "Harp. A lovely instrument. Have you a favorite composer?"

"Jean-Baptiste Krumpholz."

*Damnation, that would be harder to say than "harp".*

"How about 'Jean'?" he proposed. "When you wish to cease and desist, you will pronounce the name of your favorite composer."

"Cease and desist what?"

"Anything. For tonight, I mean to ask you a series of questions you may find intrusive and offensive. If you wish me to cease my queries, you need but speak your safety word."

She knit her brows.

"I will stop only upon your utterance of 'Jean'. The word is distinctive, you see. More ordinary exclamations can cause confusion and may not speak to your true desires."

"I see."

"Try it."

"Pardon?"

"I must know that you can and will employ your safety word when needed. If you cannot speak it in a relaxed state, will you do so under duress?"

She stared at him it seemed, for the first time, with curiosity.

"Jean," she pronounced.

"Louder."

"Jean."

"Very good."

Tippy returned and presented him a small bowl. He looked at the two pieces in the bowl and shook his head at the parsimonious allotment.

"Thank you, Tippy. That is all."

After the maid had departed, he turned to Miss

Katherine. "Here. You must try one. They are exquisite."

She looked as if she ought not, but reached for one of the confections. He watched her place it cautiously into her mouth. Her countenance lit up.

"Oh," she gasped. "It is wondrous."

He nodded. "Mrs. Harsthorn here at the Inn makes them from time to time. She is elderly and does very little for Madame these days, but she will always have gainful employment while she can produce these chocolates."

"I have only tasted chocolate in cakes and rolls and drinks before."

He offered her the other piece.

"Will you not have one, sir?" she asked, astonished.

"I am not long returned from China, where I spent a good long year. My appetite for sweets has faded as a consequence."

"Do they not partake of sweets in China?"

"Not in the way we do. Our consumption of sugar would astound them."

She eyed the last piece with obvious interest.

"Please," he urged, and was gratified to see her take the chocolate and enjoy it.

"Thank you," she said when she was done. "This Mrs. Harsthorn would do well to open a confectionery or sell the chocolates alone."

"Yes, she would."

They shared a smile.

"Tell me, how did you come to marry Lord Wendlesson?" he inquired.

"I think our families have talked of our marriage for years."

"Were you delighted when he proposed?"

To his relief, Miss Katherine smiled and nodded. His task would have been much more knotty if she were not partial to her husband.

"Forgive my prying, but it would help if you could provide me a sense of your wedding night. And I pray you be as candid as possible. I render no judgment and inquire merely to ascertain the extent of your knowledge."

She blushed. He waited patiently for a response.

"My husband was gentle, if that is the answer you seek," she replied.

"It is, if it is the truth."

Twirling the stem of her wineglass between thumb and finger, she nodded.

"Was it painful at first?"

"It was all," she cleared her throat. "pleasurable. Only when he, ah, mounted did it hurt."

"Did the pain fade with successive encounters?"

She nodded.

"And the pleasure? Did that remain?"

Again, she nodded.

Encouraged, he asked, "Did you spend?"

"I think I did. Perhaps a little."

"You did or did not. There is no mistaking the paroxysm that takes hold of your body when you spend."

She pressed her lips together and furrowed her brow as if in deep concentration.

"Did all yearning dissipate afterwards?"

"I tired from the exertion. As did his lordship."

"Who tired first?"

"His lordship. Yet, I wonder... He did not seem pleased. I think—I fear I must be a disappointment to him. Do men—are they—do they expect to spend at each encounter?"

She spoke so softly he could barely catch all her words, but he was certain he heard the faint tones of sorrow. He took the empty glass from her and replaced it with his hand, giving her a gentle squeeze.

"You are no disappointment, Miss Katherine."

She looked into his eyes. "I wish to please my husband. I fear, if I do not, he will seek the arms of another. My cousin told me that men need venereal fulfillment as much as they require food and water."

"A quaint exaggeration. Every man is different. Lust, in any man, can change by the season, by day, or by hour. But, first, we must address *your* pleasure."

"My husband's pleasure is my pleasure."

There was a knock at the door, and the maid on the other side announced that Lord Wendlesson had arrived and awaited her ladyship downstairs.

"I fear our time is at an end," he said.

"Have I—Have I failed the first lesson?" she inquired, bewildered.

"Not at all. I only wish we could have had two hours instead of one."

Charles opened the door for Tippy, who had her ladyship's bonnet, cloak and gloves.

"Allow me," he said, taking the articles from the maid, "and please inform his lordship that I wish a word with him."

"I know that I must have done poorly tonight," said Miss Katherine after Tippy had left, "but I will do better the next time we meet. I shall not be as nervous, I think. I promise."

Her eyes pleaded with him before she lowered her gaze. Despite the lack of familiarity between them, he lifted her chin with his thumb and forefinger.

"I have no expectations of your performance," he assured her. "I do, however, wish to address those of your husband. That is all."

Releasing her, he placed the cloak about her shoulders. She said nothing as he handed her the bonnet next, but when she had finished putting on her gloves, he thought a question to be pregnant upon her lips.

"You wish to speak, Miss Katherine?"

"Will you—when I return next—will you always be the instructor?"

"I cannot say for certain."

He did not elaborate that it would depend a great deal upon the outcome of his conversation with Lord

Wendlesson.

"I hope—I hope it will be you."

She bobbed a quick curtsy and stepped from the room. He watched her depart with some grimness. He hoped, for her sake, that Lord Wendlesson proved a reasonable fellow and that he could continue in his capacity as her mentor. Her desire to please her husband was a good start as far as motivation. By stoking her own eros, Charles could add even more incentive for her, but she was still very much a neophyte. If he were a harp instructor, it would be akin to teaching her a sonata when she had only just learnt scales.

He was about to turn back inside the room when he heard his name called out. He paused, as did his heart. It was not the voice he wished to hear.

With great reluctance, he turned back around to face Sir Arthur.

# CHAPTER FOUR

The gentleman rose to his feet at her entry, hunger burning in his eyes as he gazed upon her. Accustomed to seeing the flare of lust in his sex, Terrell kept her composure, but there was something unsettling in the man.

She could not place her unease, for she had never seen the man before or knew anything of him save what Madame Devereux had told her. Perhaps it had to do with the manner in which his arousal *gleamed*, not merely glowed, in his eyes. Though he was comely enough, his features being improved by his superior grooming and the stylish attire he wore, his expression reminded her of the vultures that circled above the cages back in Kingston, where runaway slaves rotted behind bars and beneath the smoldering sun.

"Miss Terrell," the man greeted with a slow, deliberate bow.

His tone did nothing to warm and improve his disposition. She should not be surprised that he felt no need to win her over. He had paid for his privileges. Nevertheless, she would dictate the terms of their engagement.

"Sir Arthur, is it?" she replied, crossing her arms before her, aware of the disparity between their apparel and their stations in life. Sir Arthur had the outward appearance of wealth, for in addition to his finely tailored clothes, he carried a jewel-encrusted walking stick and a pocket watch hung from his waistcoat on a golden chain. She, like a common servant, wore her corset over her gown, the skirts reaching only to the shins to reveal her trim ankles and bare feet. She had a decent muslin that she rather enjoyed wearing, but the men preferred her inferior garments. She believed that they wanted her to look the part of a slave. Within the law, one could sink no lower than lying with a blackamoor, and that titillated them.

"Your humble servant," he said with another bow.

He had pretty manners. These men often did. But their politesse faded quickly in the sack. She glanced about the room. It was the finest one in the inn, save for the chambers of Madame Devereux. He stood amidst plush furnishings in the seating area. Behind him was a four-post bed complete with canopy and the inn's better bedclothes. The implements of the inn's more wicked and coarse activities were stowed discreetly in the armoire and sideboard. A fire crackled boisterously in the hearth though Madame often waited till summer had fully passed before allowing such vibrant fires.

"Please," he said, gesturing toward the settee.

His tone indicated the word to be more command than invitation, but she took her time, as if contemplating her choices. She saw the quick flicker of displeasure in his physiognomy and decided to sidle over to the settee. She had no reason to upset him. He was more handsome than the corpulent Mr. Worthington, perhaps equally full in the purse, and as a Member of Parliament, likely more influential. He certainly carried himself as if he were a man of great importance.

"You would do well to please him," Madame Devereux had advised. "He is willing to pay quite generously for your company."

"And more for my cunnie?" Terrell had replied with

amusement, knowing full well it was not conversation the men sought with her.

"Impish girl. Take care you are not the sauce-box with him. I do not gather he is a man given to drollness, but his temperament is of no consequence. For the amount of money he has offered, I am certain you will suffer his shortcomings. It is not the largesse the Edeltons pay for Mistress Primrose, but it is more than satisfactory. More than satisfactory indeed."

Terrell could not resist a stab of envy. Mistress Primrose, a newer member of the Red Chrysanthemum, had landed herself two gentlemen of the *ton*. Mistress Primrose had a Negress for a mother, but her heritage was mildly apparent, her skin tone being darker than most Englishwomen but lighter than many a mulatto. Taken in by her grandfather, Mistress Primrose had also been raised with some breeding. The death of the grandfather had forced her into her current circumstance, for the rest of the family wanted little to do with her. Nonetheless, she had had advantages that Terrell had not.

But Terrell intended to have those advantages, and men like Sir Arthur were the means to improving her lot in life. Studying the man, she had to agree with Madame Devereux's assessment of his humor. She also agreed it made no difference. The man could be her salvation, her means to a better life than her current occupation at the Red Chrysanthemum. Her previous hope, Mr. Worthington, had said he would make her his mistress. Instead, upon receiving poor news of his plantations in Antigua, he had returned to the West Indies with no promise of when he might revisit England.

"You are indeed a lovely girl," Sir Arthur observed, his gaze settling at the swollen orbs above her décolletage.

He sat close beside her upon the settee, his knee touching her skirts. She suspected he wanted to waste little time before flinging himself upon her, but she would not have it so. She had no intention of lifting her skirts to the man upon their first encounter. He had to make more of an effort to gain access to her cunnie. The more he worked, the more valuable the objective became. The more he yearned, the more the sought-for would fulfill. She wanted him to be painfully cognizant of how much he wanted her.

He leaned toward her till she almost felt his breath upon her. "You are hardly a day over twenty, I gather."

"Are you partial to younger women?" she asked, pinning him with her gaze.

"I am partial to you, Miss Terrell."

She took a deep breath so that her bosom heaved. His gaze returned there.

"You flatter me, Sir Arthur."

"You are worthy of flattery."

He reached a hand, large for a man of his size, toward her breast. But she slid away from him.

"You are in some haste, Sir Arthur?"

He looked surprised and disconcerted but quickly composed himself. He smiled, but there was neither warmth nor amusement in his countenance.

"You expect I am paying for conversation?" he scoffed.

"La, sir! No one comes to the Red Chrysanthemum for talk, lest it be of the criminal sort." She sauntered behind the settee where he sat and draped a hand over his shoulder. "By our membership here, we are kindred spirits, seeking divine corporal pleasure, all manner of pleasure, by testing the limits of our flesh."

He grasped her hand and turned it up to kiss the inside of her wrist. "I confess to being surprised. You are quite well-spoken for a blackamoor."

"I've spent a great deal of time in the company of fine gentlemen such as yourself."

His grip upon her hand tightened, as did his tone. "Let us not speak of these others. When you are with me, I am the only man you need concern yourself with."

"As you wish, Sir Arthur. I will only say this: that I have learned a great deal in my time at the Red Chrysanthemum, and if you will allow me, I will guide you on the most memorable exploration of arousal, unlike any you've ever experienced."

To her relief, he released her hand. He turned to look at her. "You set lofty expectations, Miss Terrell."

She leaned over so that he could view the fullness of her breasts. "I am confident of meeting them—but only if you acquiesce to my guidance."

"You wish to lead?" he asked, his gaze devouring her décolletage.

"I understand that a man in your position may not be accustomed to following, but I assure you, you'll be pleased with the results."

She straightened, taking her beautiful breasts from view.

"Very well," he said. "I will indulge your wish, but know that I am a man accustomed to having his expectations met in a timely manner."

Pleased, she walked past the settee and settled herself in a tall armchair opposite Sir Arthur, tossing one leg over the arm of the chair. He eyed the exposed length of her lower leg. She pulled her skirts to her thighs.

"For tonight," she began, "when you're returned home, I want you to think on me. Recall my vision."

She reached above and grasped the back of the armchair with both hands. "Think long and hard of me as you fondle your prick."

He raised his brows.

"There is no need for shame, sir. All men be guilty of self-pleasure, be they archbishops or kings."

"Careful, Miss Terrell. You speak heresy."

"It is a natural urge in grown men—and women."

Dropping one arm, she slid her hand from her thigh to her skirts, then beneath her skirts. She beheld his eyes widen.

"Do…do you?" he asked hoarsely.

"Do I pleasure myself? Do I fondle myself with wanton abandon?" She closed her eyes as her fingers skimmed the flesh hidden beneath her skirts. She opened her eyes. "Why, quite often, Sir Arthur. Perhaps it would please you to imagine my hand at my cunnie while you stroke your cock."

The veins in his neck stood out. He moved from the settee and sat himself upon a footstool before her. "What need have I to address myself later when I can satisfy myself now?"

She stayed him from throwing himself upon her by pressing her foot to his chest. "Because we desire to double your pleasure tomorrow."

"What if I prefer satisfaction sooner?"

"You said you'd indulge me and give me leave to take pleasure to its greatest heights. Your appetite for me will grow throughout the night. Imagine how your gratification will be magnified when you are finally allowed to feast."

He paused in thought. "Then we are not to engage at all this evening?"

She slid her foot lower, to his abdomen. "Have you ever roasted a pig?"

"Is that a genuine question?" he responded, disconcerted.

"A pig, roasted long hours in its herbs and juices, will produce a most tender meat, succulent and full of flavor. Perhaps you have partaken of such meat and noted how it melts in your mouth, how it delights the senses."

She moved her foot to his tented crotch. "Tonight we begin the roasting. Tomorrow we enjoy the rewards of our patience."

He stared at her slender foot, pressed beside his obvious erection, then spoke in a slow and menacing tone. "If I find you mean only to tease me, Miss Terrell, you will rue having done so. I am not a man to be trifled with."

Unnerved by his threat, she, too, stared at his crotch so

that he might not notice any apprehension in her eyes. Men like Sir Arthur unsettled her. They gave themselves the outward appearance of refinement and forbearance but were as capable of brutish behavior as any coarse ruffian.

Determined not to be cowed by him, she gathered her wits and carefully withdrew her foot. "I'll not promise that you will enjoy every minute of our time together, but the greater the pain, the greater the pleasure. There are many forms of ecstasy, and I would show them all to you, Sir Arthur."

The veins in his neck throbbed and he looked unable to swallow.

Like a queen upon her throne, she gave him her hand to kiss. "Till tomorrow, Sir Arthur."

He stared at the hand but eventually took it and pressed it to his lips.

"You're an intriguing wench, Miss Terrell," he said after releasing her hand. "For your sake, I hope you can make good on your promise."

She wanted to point out that she had made no specific promises to him, but decided not to chance his vexation whilst he seemed inclined to comply with her terms. He stood, gave her a stiff bow, and departed. She did not realize, till after she heard the door close behind her, that she had been holding her breath.

Her hand wandered back beneath her skirts. She would have liked nothing more than to lust after Sir Arthur and enjoy all that she intended for him. He had a mature, square jaw, a fine figure with broad shoulders, but his manners were too cold and left her with much disquiet. She caressed herself, trying to dispel the frost left by Sir Arthur, and her thoughts quickly turned to the one man who could arouse her with ease.

Master Gallant.

# CHAPTER FIVE

Bracing himself, Charles Gallant turned to face the man who had called out to him. Sir Arthur, perhaps the last person he would have wished to see at the Red Chrysanthemum, had descended the stairs and now stood but a few yards from him.

"I thought it was you," Sir Arthur said, pressing the tip of his walking stick into the floor, an indication that he would not, as Charles had hoped, continue on his way.

Charles bowed. "Sir Arthur."

"I must say I never would have expected to find you here," the MP said with what seemed to be mild amusement. "You struck me as somewhat of a puritan."

Not wishing to appear discomfited, Charles squared his shoulders. "Alas, I must disappoint you."

"Not at all, Charles. It is a relief, in a manner. An unwed man who boasts no mistress, not even an opera dancer, prompts suspicion of an unsavory and unlawful nature."

Charles decided not to disclose the fact that many a molly possessed membership at the Red Chrysanthemum. Sir Arthur had perhaps seen Miss Katherine depart the room and, from that, deemed Charles' proclivities the acceptable sort.

"Is this your first visit here, Sir Arthur?" Charles inquired, as if they were easily at White's or Brooks's instead of a bordello that would have made a hellfire club blush.

Sir Arthur looked about them, but they stood alone in the hall. "It is, but I own it shall not be my last. As you know, I am a widower, and it is only natural that I should seek the companionship of the fair sex."

Charles inclined his head in acknowledgement.

"Being without a wife is quite the unexpected hardship. It is worse than being a bachelor, for a husband grows accustomed to having, well…you understand."

"I understand you miss your wife," Charles replied with tact.

"Yes, indeed," Sir Arthur said with disinterest. "Well, while I can choose to court women of our society, I find such associations fraught with tiresome complications. I presume you feel the same."

The membership of the Red Chrysanthemum was not without its women of breeding, a few superior even to that of Sir Arthur, but Charles understood that Sir Arthur sought a woman with whom he could both engage with and dispense of with ease. He did not wish to confirm Sir Arthur's presumptuous inference that the two men shared anything in common beyond the fact that they stood in the same hallway.

The appearance of a third party drew both their attention. Though Charles welcomed the interruption, the Viscount Wendlesson, dressed in the togs of a dandy, reminded him too much of Damien Norrington.

"Master Gallant, you wished to speak with me?" Lord Wendlesson inquired. He looked at Sir Arthur.

"I shall take my leave then," Sir Arthur said to Charles. He bowed and went on his way.

"Lord Wendlesson," Charles greeted and turned back into the room.

Lord Wendlesson followed. Once inside, the man

began an unhappy pacing.

"Katherine tells me—it would seem," he began. "She said very little occurred in her first lesson."

Sensing the man's vexation, Charles went to the sideboard and poured a glass of the same claret he had offered Miss Katherine when she had occupied the room earlier.

"I do not comprehend," said Wendlesson. He stopped and looked at the various accoutrements displayed upon the walls. "You did not introduce the flogger? I understand the cane might be too much for a novice, but perhaps the crop or the paddle?"

Charles presented the wine to Wendlesson, saying, "I did not touch your wife."

"You did not...?" Wendlesson replied, his countenance twisted in confusion. "Did you place her in your rope bondage?"

"I did not. We conversed."

"Conversed?" his lordship exclaimed, flabbergasted. "What the devil are you about, sir?"

"That is what I mean to speak to you of."

"I do not pay you to converse with my wife, sir."

"If you insist upon compensation, you pay it all to Madame Devereux. I refuse to take a penny in the matter. I have agreed to instruct your wife as a favor to Joan."

He wanted to make it clear to the viscount that he was under no obligation to him.

"This is a claret from Gascony. Madame Devereux has family there still. You will find it a near perfect claret," Charles said, presenting the wine once more to Wendlesson, who required it as much as his wife did.

"You toy with me," Wendlesson accused, refusing the wine.

Charles did not respond to the ridiculous accusation. "The purpose of my undertaking has nothing to do with you. My instruction is for the benefit of Miss Katherine— Lady Wendlesson. She is the subject that concerns me."

Somewhat ruefully, Wendlesson said, "Does my wife not please you? You find her revolting in some manner?"

"Hardly. You have a beautiful wife, and I congratulate you on winning the hand of so fair a maid."

With a grunt and nod, Wendlesson finally took the glass from Charles. "She will be the perfect wife when she has learned the ways of the submissive."

"Unlike a claret, perfection in man rarely exists. You only set yourself up for failure if you expect it."

"Are you saying you are incapable of training my wife?"

"Not if you provide me but an hour each evening and for the limited duration of a sennight."

"You require more time with her?"

"And reasonableness from you. It will not help your wife if you were to place undue expectations upon her. Her fear of failing you will only hinder progress."

His eyes downcast in thought, Wendlesson drank the claret.

"How long will you require?" he asked of Charles.

"If you desire a specific result, I cannot name a time. I have had but an hour with Miss Katherine and most of it spent putting her at ease. I have yet to ascertain her aptitude for what you seek."

Wendlesson frowned. "Perhaps you need only press harder. Katherine may appear a delicate flower, but her constitution is strong. She can withstand more than you suspect."

"Is that your conclusion sustained by evidence or wishful thinking?"

The viscount took a step toward Charles. "Do you presume to tell me that I do not know my own wife?"

"In the capacity that you seek instruction in, I will come to know more than you. Will you not serve as her mentor, my lord? I think she would receive her education far better from you."

Wendlesson shook his head and began pacing once more. "I have not the inclination to deal with neophytes."

"Then if you insist upon my services, I will have no interference from you. I will allow her comfort to dictate the pace. You wish, afterall, for her to enjoy the role of submission, do you not? It is *her* pleasure you also seek to fulfill."

"Of course, of course," Wendlesson grumbled. He ceased pacing. "Do I understand that you are interested in representing Porter's Hill?"

Charles paused before replying, "I am."

"The elections of Porter's Hill are often hotly contested. One year there were no fewer than eight and ten men vying for the burgesses."

"You have an interest in Porter's Hill, my lord?"

"I've a cousin who owns a few properties in Porter's Hill. His wife is quite active and has hosted a number of events on behalf of various candidates. She spares no expense. Perhaps I could put in a good word for you."

"Whilst I appreciate the gesture, I would prefer that my actions and acquaintances through this venue not interfere with my activities elsewhere."

"Yes, you would make for a more infamous libertine than Wilkes if your membership here were known."

Charles could not discern if this was a threat. Any member who violated the confidentiality of the Red Chrysanthemum would be banished from the Inn for life, and Wendlesson, an avid member, would surely be cognizant of the rule.

"A risk we all endure here at the Red Chrysanthemum," Charles said, "though the consequences of exposure are greater for men such as ourselves. If I should fail the election due to my association with the Red Chrysanthemum, I have no one to blame but myself."

"I do not mean to suggest that you *would* be revealed. Only that you *could*."

"As could we all."

Wendlesson seemed to accept that Charles had no intention of bartering his services. "I will attempt to grant you more time each night with my wife, but the duration of the sennight must hold. You see, we are to travel to my uncle's estate in the country. He is celebrating his fiftieth birthday, and all the family is expected to be in attendance. I understand you cannot promise a particular outcome within the sennight, but I should like to speak well of you to my cousin and his wife, Mr. and Mrs. Brentwood. You must know of them. Should you meet my expectations, I am certain my recommendation would be sufficient to garner their support, which, for many a candidate, has been instrumental to their victory."

"The incentive is a thoughtful one, Lord Wendlesson, but I require and expect no enticements. Your wife's pleasure is sufficient."

Wendlesson eyed him closely. "Indeed? Surely the charge serves your own interests as well?"

"If I were devoted to seeking my own gratification, I would not be undertaking this assignment. I, too, prefer a more seasoned woman."

"Yes. That is what impressed me: your handling of Mistress Scarlet. I never would have thought her capable of submitting to anyone. You may wish for no reward, Master Gallant, but you cannot prevent me from speaking on your behalf if it strikes my fancy. I think it would behoove my cousin to support a man of your character. I will see that my wife is available tomorrow night for more than an hour. Good night, Master Gallant."

With a bow, the viscount took his leave. Charles leaned against the doorframe and watched the man depart. He had said all he had wished to say to the man but felt little reassurance. That Wendlesson had mentioned the borough of Porter's Hill only complicated matters.

Walking to the sideboard, Charles poured a glass of claret, this time for himself. He would not compromise the integrity of his instruction to Miss Katherine, but if he were clever, he would look for all opportunities to press her progress. He knew of the Brentwoods. His own father, when seeking to represent Porter's Hill, had solicited their support several times. They had backed his candidacy the first time, but after he had lost, they had turned their efforts toward others. Charles had requested a meeting with the Brentwoods and still awaited a response, but, not wanting the interference of the viscount, Charles had not brought this fact to the man's attention. Nonetheless, though it was possible Lord Wendlesson exaggerated his influence, a recommendation from him might pave the way for the Brentwoods' endorsement.

It was just as well that he had had but an hour with Miss Katherine tonight. The morrow portended a long day, filled with meetings, including one with his employer, and he desired to review the documents Sir Canning had requested a final time. Charles also wished to stop by the apothecary of Mr. Barlow to ask after his daughter. Though Mr. Barlow had never asked, it must have been clear to the man by now that Charles had a heavy interest in Miss Greta Barlow.

Charles eyed the implements adorning the wall. He saw the flogger he had used upon her slim body. Miss Greta wanted more flesh, but he had still found her beautiful to behold. Closing his eyes, he could see her bound form kneeling before him, her breasts captured in rope. How delightfully her pale flesh had quivered beneath the tails!

An unexpected click at the door made Charles turn around. He thought Wendlesson to have returned, but the woman upon the threshold could never be mistaken for the viscount. The former was tall and sinewy, a man who had lived past his median year. The latter possessed all the curves and softness of her sex, her youth still apparent in the smoothness of her skin and the tautness of her flesh.

Miss Terrell had accosted him upon the stairs earlier and had made her desires quite obvious. His cock twitched involuntarily at the memory of her tongue protruding from a pair of succulent lips to lick at the button of his waistcoat. But, if he was not mistaken, she was assigned to

Sir Arthur at his request, and the man had made clear his
wish that no other man was to approach her.

"Miss Terrell," he greeted stiffly, hoping his lack of
warmth would send her on her way.

It did not. She gave him a small smile and arched
against the doorway, presenting her waist and hips to him.
He wondered how much of her figure was due to the
corseting. The women of current fashion displayed little
shape at the waist, but he found the disparity between the
width of the waist and the width of the hips to be quite
provocative.

Moving his gaze to what he hoped would be less
enflaming, her physiognomy, though the blush of lust
there proved distracting as well, he asked, "You are in need
of assistance?"

"Indeed I am, Master Gallant." She ran the tops of her
hands up the sides of her neck and then her head, pushing
her thick black hair into disarray.

He looked away from her flagrancy. He had no desire
to deal with her at the moment.

She looked at him through lowered lashes. "And as you
are finished with Miss Katherine—I saw her depart—we
are both of us now alone."

Straightening, he gave her a stern look. "Is Sir Arthur
gone as well then?"

"You know of Sir Arthur?"

"He is not a man to trifle with, especially if you have
accepted his coin."

She moved as if making love to the door with her head
and upper back. "You need not fear Sir Arthur."

"I do not fear Sir Arthur, but I have no desire to
displease the man."

She paused only momentarily, then stretched her arms
above her, pressing the back of her wrists against the door.
If it had arms, it would clasp the wanton little minx to its
frame. Charles took a long swallow of the claret, amazed
that she could lend lewdness to an inanimate object.

"I doubt Sir Arthur concerns himself with you," she said.

"But his interest in *you* is unmistakable. He would not approve of another man's attentions upon that which he deems his."

He finished the claret and retrieved his hat and gloves, a clear signal of his intentions. She noticed but did not budge.

"But he will not know."

"You have no wish to risk his ire, Miss Terrell. I know the man from my dealings elsewhere. He is not a man of abundant tolerance."

"Ah, you are concerned for my welfare, are you?"

He frowned at this unintended interpretation of his words. "Neither would you wish to disappoint Madame if she gave assurances that Sir Arthur would have your fidelity."

Miss Terrell frowned for but a second before saying, "She need not know either."

It was like reasoning with a child, he decided. Her mind was fixed and she would contemplate no contradictions.

Nonetheless, he would instruct her. "How long have you resided here, Miss Terrell?"

She dropped a hand to her head, then lower, skimming her knuckles along the top of one breast before settling at her hip. Though he stood the length of the room from her, he noticed how trim her wrists were, how slender the fingers. As with Miss Greta, he could easily encircle both her wrists in one hand, but Miss Terrell had more substance in other parts. In a challenge of finesse, the odds would likely favor Miss Greta, but if the two were matched in a contest of brute force, the strength and weight of Miss Terrell would prevail.

"A year about," she answered.

"I have known Madame Devereux far longer. She does not forgive transgressions."

His statement gave her pause, giving him time to drape

his cloak over his arm and cross the room, hat and gloves in hand. He came to within an arm's length of her. In thought, she had lowered her gaze, and he noted the lushness of her lashes, the high cheekbones and flawless complexion. He wondered if her dark coloring allowed her skin to better hide discoloration and other imperfections.

"I believe Joan to be quite partial to you," he said more gently. "You could do much to win her favor. Do not let a moment of recklessness squander your prospects with her."

She looked up at him with large round eyes. "You are worth the risk, Master Gallant."

The impact of her stare, the husky quality of her voice, and the conviction with which she spoke made his groin tighten. He had no response for her at first. Despite her youth, she had acquired the arts of a seasoned seductress.

"You know not what you speak," he dismissed, treating her once more like a child. He reached for the handle of the door behind her, but she did not move.

"I am neither child nor dunce," she replied, her plump lips pouting in displeasure.

"No? How old are you?"

"Old enough. I am far more practiced in the ways of a man and a woman than most married women, than the oldest of strumpets."

"How old?" he pressed.

"Twenty. Perhaps nine and ten. I don't rightly know. What does it matter?"

"It is significant enough. I am near ten years your senior."

She slid along the door toward him, covering the handle of the door. "That did not stop you from kissing me."

His gaze fell to her mouth. He remembered that kiss, remembered tasting Miss Greta on Miss Terrell's succulent lips. The blood had coursed strongly through his cock then. It coursed strongly now.

"I've not known age to hinder a man before," she added, and he sensed she spoke not just of her term here at the Inn.

Pulled into her bright eyes of ebony, he thought he saw in their depths years that did not show upon her features, years that belied her youth. In truth, the difference in years, in station, or in color would not have been sufficient to stay him in most circumstances. But he had not given up hope of Miss Greta, and any pursuits beyond his obligations to Madame Devereux would have the air of perfidy to him. Moreover, there were all the arguments he had already presented to Miss Terrell concerning Sir Arthur and her own placement at the Red Chrysanthemum.

Suppressing his curiosity of her past, he said, "That may be, Miss Terrell, but I am not inclined to dismiss our differences so hastily."

She tilted her chin. "Why not?"

"Because the hour is late and I am headed home."

He reached once more for the handle behind her.

"Miss Terrell," he said with exasperation when she did not move.

"I want but one night, Master Gallant," she said. "For one night, bind me with your magnificent ropes, as you had done with Mistress Scarlet. I am yours, entirely, to do as you wish."

"An enticing offer, and one that I am certain Sir Arthur would welcome without hesitation."

"But he has not your skills. With the rope, no one can do what you do."

"Perhaps I will have occasion to provide Sir Arthur a lesson."

The thought made him grimace inside, but he was fast coming to a loss as to what he should do with Miss Terrell.

"That will not suffice," she replied. "You could give him a thousand lessons. He'd not be *you*, and it be *you* I want."

He pinned her with a solemn stare. "Behave yourself, Miss Terrell, or I will remove you by force."

"I should like nothing more than to receive your punishment, Master Gallant."

He inhaled sharply. The saucy jade. Catching her off-guard with a quick movement, he wrapped his arm about her waist and whirled her over to the other side of the doorframe. She landed against the wall with a soft thud. Disengaging himself, he grabbed the handle of the door and pulled, intending to depart without his usual civility.

To his surprise, the door did not open. At first he thought it to be stuck, but then he noticed that the key was missing from the lock. He turned to look at Miss Terrell, whose lips curled in a slight but telling grin.

He could hardly believe the woman—the chit. Did she truly intend to hold him hostage?

"Produce the key, Miss Terrell," he commanded.

She returned a smoldering stare. "Dominate me first. Do unto me as you had done to Mistress Scarlet."

He felt his nostrils flare. He needed no second reminders of *her*, especially from Miss Terrell, who now tested his patience much like Greta had, but for wholly different purposes.

"You think impudence will gain you what you seek?" he asked.

She leaned toward him. "If my impudence displeases you, then punish me for it. Punish me...hard."

He stared at her in disbelief. No woman had ever made such a request of him. He wanted to reiterate that she knew not what she spoke. She had witnessed but one instance of the punishment he had applied to Miss Greta.

As if guessing his thoughts, she added, "I can withstand anything you desire to do to me, Master Gallant."

"That is a bold and foolhardy statement. You know nothing of what I am capable."

Pressing herself back against the wall, she cupped her breasts and caressed her ribs before resting her hands near her crotch. "Prove me wrong. I dare you to."

He shook his head. He was done with challenges.

"I vow I can endure more than Mistress Scarlet, more than any person of either sex. I could be the most perfect submissive for you."

"Unlikely. You have already shown a penchant for misbehavior."

"You could correct my waywardness."

He frowned, because the prospect did not repulse him as he would have wanted it to.

"You need have no reservation with me," she continued. "You would be free to unleash your full strength, to test the breadth of your wicked creativeness."

"You think my ultimate desire is to inflict pain?"

"In return, I promise you the greatest pleasure. No woman can eat cockmeat as well as I. And, while it is true that I have lain with several men, they all vow my cunnie is as tight as that of a virgin."

His blood pumped forcefully through his veins at her words. She cupped her mons through her skirts, and a renewed sense of urgency swelled in him.

"Miss Terrell, this *tête-à-tête* serves no purpose. I bid you desist from wasting your time as well as mine."

Stepping forward, she grabbed the lapels of his coat and pulled herself closer to him. Lust burned like anger in her eyes, calling to a primal part of him that he could not ignore. Her skirts brushed against his legs, and her corset nearly touched where his hardened length was fast becoming visible.

"Then ravage me."

She reached for his burgeoning erection, but, dropping his articles, he grasped both her wrists and pinned them above her head to the door behind.

"Miss Terrell, I am done with this tomfoolery. Produce the key."

He could have threatened to report her mischief to Joan, but he was not inclined to snitch. Devereux was likely to laugh at his inability to handle a young woman ten years his junior. Moreover, the consequences might prove grave for Miss Terrell. He knew not where or how she might survive if Joan cast her out from the Inn.

She squirmed a little in his hold. "I should be happy to, Master Gallant, *after* you have had your way with me. You cannot deny that you desire to do so."

She lowered her gaze to his crotch. He pressed his lips together in a grim line. The scent of the pomade she used in her hair wafted into his nose once more. Their bodies were far too close together for comfort. She slid her leg along his. Holding her wrists aloft with one hand, he cupped her chin with the other and lifted her gaze to meet his eyes.

"The key, Miss Terrell," he demanded, unable to keep the vexation from his voice.

She did not blink and demanded, equally hotly, "*Ravage me.*"

Her words rang in his ears like a song of sirens. The air between them grew thin. With a frustrated grunt, he yanked her from the door and dragged her across the room to the sideboard where he kept the ropes.

"You wish me to truss you, do you?" he asked, jerking a drawer open and grabbing a cord of jute.

Her face brightened upon seeing the rope. "Yes."

He began wrapping her wrists. "And punish you for your impertinence."

"Yes!"

When he had bound her wrists with the rope, he dragged her to a simple wooden chair and bent her over its back. He propped his left foot upon the seat of the chair to hold it down. Bending toward her ear, he asked, "Your safety word, Miss Terrell?"

"I require none."

He would have insisted or provided her one, but if she would persist in such recklessness, then so be it. He was out of patience with her. Straightening, he flung her skirts over her waist, baring her arse. The breath caught in his throat as he beheld the enticing spheres he had revealed: perfectly round, more supple than the backsides he was accustomed to seeing. Others might deem her derriere a bit ample, but, as he palmed a buttock, he felt the promise of such fullness.

She moaned as he filled his hand with her flesh, then yelped when he withdrew his hand and smacked her. The orb quivered only a little, owing to the tightness of the flesh. He thought of making her arse tremble long and hard, as she had requested. He slapped her once more, much harder than he would during the first engagement with a submissive, and elicited another squeal.

"Thank you, Master," she purred.

He groped her buttock, loosening it for the next blow, which he delivered with such force she might have toppled over, had he not secured the chair beneath his foot. She cried out and clung to the ledge of the seat.

"Thank you, Master," she said after a harried breath.

"Will you produce the key now?"

"Is that all you are capable of?" she scoffed.

He delivered several more wallops till he knew her arse to be smarting, though the blush of pain was not as apparent upon her darker skin.

She trembled as she spoke. "Th-Thank you, Master."

His hand brushed against the folds between her thighs. Feeling moisture, he peered around a buttock and saw a rivulet glistening down her inner thigh. The heat rose to his head. He was tempted to touch her *there*, to fondle her and release the desire welled within her. He wondered if Sir Arthur had visited the paradise between her thighs.

The thought of Sir Arthur recalled him. "The key, Miss Terrell."

"No. I want more. If you would sink your cock into me…either orifice would do…"

Astounded, he said nothing. This would not do. He needed that damn key. Reaching through her skirts, he sought her pockets but found nothing. He replaced his foot upon the ground and pulled her up. He should not have given her a taste of what she wanted. He retrieved another length of rope and looped it through the cords binding her wrists. He tossed the end over a beam in the rafters and pulled till her arms reached straight above her. If he intended to punish her further, he would dangle her such that her toes barely touched the floor, but he only meant to render her immobile. After securing the rope, he stepped back to admire her form. She tested her bonds. They held fast.

"It would seem I am at your mercy, Master Gallant," she said, pleased.

"Yes. You would do well to remember not to toy with me, Miss Terrell."

He took a step forward and touched her corset, which laced in the front. He pulled at the ribbon. She inhaled sharply.

"I only ask one thing," she breathed, "that you leave the chemise in place."

It was an odd request, particularly from one who displayed such unabashed lasciviousness, but he had no intention of disrobing her. Without word, he continued to pull at the ribbon till the top of her corset loosened. He could now easily free her breasts from their constraints, and he was not without curiosity to behold the twin beauties. Instead, he slid his hand between the plump orbs and pulled out the key.

She started, perhaps having forgotten she had hidden it there or expecting him to reach for her breasts instead.

"Your first—and last—lesson with me, Miss Terrell, is that I, too, am not to be trifled with."

Walking back to the door, he replaced the key in the lock and picked up his gloves, hat, and cloak from the floor. After putting them on, he tipped his hat to Miss Terrell, who, naturally, had not stirred from where she hung, her arms stretched to the ceiling. Her expression went from surprise to dismay as she realized he meant to leave. She began struggling against her bonds.

"Good night, Miss Terrell."

He opened the door and stepped across the threshold. He closed the door behind him and heard a string of angry oaths from within. Without her proximity warming his body, her scent filling his nose and making his head spin, her brazenness taunting his own desires, he could finally take in a breath of peace. Making his way downstairs, he went in search of a servant and found Tippy.

"In thirty minutes," he told the dressing maid, "no more and no less, Miss Terrell will require your services. She is in the far room on the second floor."

The young maid nodded. "Yes, Master Gallant."

At last, he was able to take his leave of the Red Chrysanthemum. He hoped Miss Terrell had learnt her lesson, but he could not rest easily. She still reminded him too much of one of those black panthers he had observed in the south of China, silently stalking their prey before they pounced.

# CHAPTER SIX

With another oath, Terrell pulled at the bindings that stretched her arms to the rafters. Not surprisingly, the ropes did not give. They would have done so only if Master Gallant had intended she could free herself. His mastery of the ropes would not have permitted carelessness. Nevertheless, she yanked harder, her efforts netting her only a shortness of breath.

Surely he would return and untie her. The teasing man. She rubbed her thighs together. Her wet cunnie still ached, provoked further by her current predicament. She would not have minded her helpless state—indeed, she found it titillating and had been thrilled to see him retrieve the cords of jute—if he meant to deliver her to the finish she sought and longed for. Alas, she suspected *this* was her conclusion. He had pinioned her wrists and tied them to a beam abovehead not to render her defenseless so that he could impose all manner of naughtiness upon her, but to retrieve the key she had stuffed between her breasts.

"Your first—and last—lesson with me, Miss Terrell, is that I, too, am not to be trifled with," he had said.

She scowled at the air yet could not resist a small smile, impressed that he had managed to elude her, as few men could. By denying her his attentions, however, he had, though it might not have been his intention, aroused her craving further. She remembered how, with one arm about her waist, he had whipped her from the door and pinned her against the wall. She had felt his strength and yearned to have the hardness of his body against her. Her arse had only just stopped tingling from the spanking.

Closing her eyes, she tried to relive every blow. He had smacked her hard, as she had desired him to. She had almost asked him to slap her with even greater vigor, for only the sharpest of stings could cool the ardor boiling inside of her.

He had erred. For his touch was exquisite. If he had wanted to dampen her desire, he needed to disappoint her, as all the men, save Isaiah, had done. But Master Gallant was not capable of disappointing. Even now, despite her anger at him, she wanted him. She wanted him to touch her most intimate parts, to calm the flames there with his own heat. She liked to think he had erred because, deep down, he desired her. It was not possible that he could be indifferent. No man had ever proven immune to her.

"Ravage me."

She had never before spoken those words with such sincerity or intensity. She spoke true when she said she would suffer anything he wished to do to her. And yet, he had not accepted her offer. She wondered at the reason. He clearly had more forbearance than expected, but that could not explain all. She suspected he had tender feelings for Mistress Scarlet. Perhaps he still nursed the wound left by her absence.

Perhaps he feared Sir Arthur, though he did not appear to be a man who would tolerate intimidation. How had he even known Terrell was spoken for? Did he truly wish not to infringe upon Sir Arthur's interests or upset Madame Devereux? What could be more compelling than the charms of Miss Terrell?

She would know the answer. Only his complete surrender would satisfy.

Her arms were growing sore, and she tried the bonds once more. She could scream, but it would require all her might to be heard through the closed door if no one was near. At the Inn of the Red Chrysanthemum, her cries would be commonplace and not taken for a genuine plea for help.

She yanked at the ropes, her aggravation returned. Master Gallant was not coming back. What if no one came? Would she hang here the entire night? She had not thought Master Gallant capable of such cruelty. Perhaps she had misjudged him? She shook her head. Her intuition had drawn her to him, not merely for his skills with domination, but because he differed from all the other men of his kind. She could not state why she believed this. Perhaps it was the gentleness she beheld in his eyes of grey and blue. She marveled that they could hold both hues or alternate between one and the other.

"Miss Terrell," Tippy gasped from the doorway. One of the newer maids, she must not have stumbled upon a great many strangeness. She gaped to find Terrell stretched to the rafters, the top of her corset undone.

"Some assistance, if you please," Terrell said.

Tippy nodded and looked about. Seeing a chair, she pulled it before Terrell and climbed atop.

"Oh, hm," she grunted as she studied the rope binding the wrists. "These not be knots I've seen before."

"Is Master Gallant still here?" Terrell asked.

"He left half an hour before."

"If you cannot untie the ropes, then cut them."

"Perhaps if I loop this under…"

The ropes came away with ease. Her arms fell and the blood rushed back to her fingers. Not bothering to lace up her corset, she stood rubbing her wrists. A part of her seethed, mostly because he had not come to free her himself. Instead, she had to be discovered, tied to the rafters, her corset partially undone, by one the maids. But if Master Gallant thought to discourage her advances by this scheme, he was woefully wrong. Instead, her pursuit would find a whole new fervor.

"Did Master Gallant tie you thus?" Tippy asked, puzzled, as she picked up the ropes.

"He was merely demonstrating a tethering trick," Terrell answered, not wanting Tippy to inform Madame Devereux of what had transpired. She laced her corset.

"A lovely gentleman he be," sighed Tippy. "I wouldn't mind him trussin' me up a bit."

The maid's eyes glimmered at the daydream. Terrell, still undecided between being cross with or admiring what Master Gallant had done, gave a wry smile. She may have lost the battle with Master Gallant this evening, but she would yet win the war.

# CHAPTER SEVEN

In the dark quiet of his bedchamber, seated in an armchair far more comfortable than the wooden ladder-back he had bent Miss Terrell over, Charles stroked his cock. Dressed in his nightshirt, he ought to have gone straight to bed for he had a full day tomorrow, but he needed to release the stress of the evening's events, from Miss Katherine to Lord Wendlesson to Sir Arthur to Miss Terrell.

Miss Terrell. He did not even know her given name. Was she truly drawn to him or merely promiscuous? With Sir Arthur's interest, she had no need to seek the attentions of any other man. Sir Arthur was not uncomely and possessed advantages that Charles did not. Most women would have been satisfied to receive the favors of such a man. But Miss Terrell was not. Because she had witnessed, and participated in, his disciplining of Miss Greta. Recalling the scene, he had to admit he had put on quite the performance with Miss Greta, the true foci.

Before an audience of the members of the Red Chrysanthemum, he had had Miss Terrell and another woman, Miss Isabella, undress Miss Greta, caressing the parts revealed, one garment at a time. For her insubordination, he had made her walk the length of the stage with a rope between her legs, her cunnie rubbing against the twine. Afterwards, he had placed a blindfold about her while Miss Terrell tied her to a table. Members were then invited to touch and fondle her.

The memory of it all turned his cock hard as flint and set his cods boiling. Just as the pressure was about to jettison from him, his thoughts drifted to Miss Terrell, and he wondered what would it be like to ravage her as she wished? He imagined her lithe body writhing beneath his as he ground his cock into her. What was it she had said about taking cockmeat?

His load burst forth, coating his hand and soiling the rug below. Shuddering, he lightened his strokes till, gradually, his cock began to soften. He leaned his head back against the armchair and stared into the darkness. That was as far as he would allow Miss Terrell to affect him. His charge was Miss Katherine, and the sooner he completed that assignment, the sooner he could turn his entire attention to the election. He would take another leave of absence from the Red Chrysanthemum. Or forsake it altogether lest Miss Greta returned.

He awoke in the middle of the night to find himself still in the chair. His seed had dried into a tacky consistency upon him. Grabbing linen, he cleaned himself and wiped the carpet. He lit a candle and found the papers he had wanted to review for Sir Canning. They consisted of reports on the Convention of Sintra. After completing the work, he finally climbed into his bed and slept a few hours before the dawn.

After breakfast and consuming an additional cup of coffee, dressed in buff-colored trousers and a double-breasted coat with cutaway tails, he made for the apothecary of Mr. Barlow. To his surprise, a young man greeted him from behind the counter.

"Are you assisting Mr. Barlow?" Charles asked upon approaching.

"Yes. Joseph Turner at your service, sir," replied the young man of twenty or so. "Do you require Mr.

Barlow?"

At that moment, Mr. Barlow emerged from the back of the shop. "Ah, Mr. Gallant. Good morning to you. I recommended the root you provided me, the ginseng, to a Mrs. Penswick, who, like myself, is prone to influenza. She says it has improved her health, especially her lethargy."

"That is good to hear," Charles acknowledged. He glanced at Joseph. "It must be a relief to have another pair of hands in the shop."

"Indeed."

An awkward pause ensued. Charles was about to ask the man how long he expected to employ the young Mr. Turner when Mr. Barlow provided the information he sought.

"My daughter is not expected back for some time. My sister has given birth to her eighth child, and Greta wrote me that she will stay in Liverpool for as long as her aunt requires her assistance."

Charles said nothing at first. The news felt like the final seal upon his hopes that Miss Greta would return to his waiting arms.

"Felicitations to your family," Charles said at last.

"Do you seek a specific tonic or treatment?"

Charles thought of Miss Katherine. "Perhaps an ointment to soothe the skin."

Mr. Barlow presented him an array of choices. Charles purchased the most expensive one, thanked the man, and went on his way to Whitehall. It was still possible that Greta might change her mind and return to London, but if she was the only source of help for her aunt, she might not feel free to leave even if she desired it. He suspected, alas, that Greta did not desire to return. She was hiding from him or from Damien, though the latter was not always to be found residing in town.

For certain she was hiding from her feelings. After Damien had left her brokenhearted, she had sought refuge in the guise of Mistress Scarlet. Now she sought refuge in distance. He only wished he knew what she was so afraid of.

"Ah, Charles," Sir Canning greeted when Charles arrived in the office of the Secretary for Foreign Affairs. Sir George Canning was the senior by ten years. He was possessed of thick straight brows, a tall slender nose, and eyes that reminded Charles of a basset hound's. Prior to his current position, he had served as Paymaster of the Forces and Treasurer of the Navy under Pitt the Younger.

"I have reviewed the letters and they are not as critical of Sir Wellesley as the report from Sir Dalrymple," Charles said, taking a seat before Sir Canning.

"Before we discuss your assessments, which I am certain are all sound, let us address your election. I understand that Mr. Henry Laurel has submitted himself for the open burgess of Porter's Hill."

"I had heard rumors that he might. His time at Eton overlapped mine by a year. He is an intelligent and capable fellow."

"You may know him then to be a protégé of Fox. I have been informed that he has secured quite the base of support. As it stands, he is the only Whig in the race. As such, he is all but guaranteed a good segment of the electorate."

A footman opened the door and announced the arrival of Sir Arthur. Charles sat upright.

"Sir Arthur," Sir Canning greeted. "I had hoped you could join us."

Sir Arthur, his walking stick in hand, took a seat. "We are past formalities, are we not, George?"

"That we are, Reginald. I am certain Charles here will not mind the familiar address."

Sir Arthur turned to Charles. "Yes, I think not. Charles and I have recently discovered a common interest."

"Not gardening? I had thought Sir Barnsworth would be in town before the Season, but he remains in the country while the flowers in his garden are still in bloom."

"Nothing on the order of interest as gardening," replied Sir Arthur as he took out his snuffbox of tortoise shell and inhaled a pinch of snuff.

"The burgess for Porter's Hill," Charles supplied.

"Of course," Sir Canning said. "We, all three of us, share that interest, and it is for that reason I asked Sir Arthur to meet with us. Sir Arthur was instrumental in securing the election of Sir Winslow, the other burgess for Porter's Hill. You are familiar with Sir Winslow."

"I was more familiar with Sir Winslow when he resided in Porter's Hill. He has not lived in Porter's Hill for some time now, and I rarely saw him in attendance at Parliament. The few times I did, he was always asleep and snoring soundly."

Sir Canning cleared his throat. "Yes, well, Sir Winslow is perhaps, well…"

Sir Arthur waved a dismissive hand. "Winslow is in attendance when his vote is required."

He looked at Charles. "Your father was part of the Macartney envoy to China, was he not?"

"He was," Charles replied as he studied the man. Sir Arthur sat in the chair with his right ankle resting upon his left knee, an air of complacency about him as if he owned the room. Charles found it hard to envision the man with Miss Terrell.

"And you yourself are lately returned from there."

"I have been in England several months now."

"I understand, while in China, you managed to travel beyond our factory in Canton. All the way to Japan."

Charles wondered as to the purpose of these statements and kept his responses brief. "I did."

"How did you accomplish this? Foreigners are not allowed outside of Canton."

"Charles is very resourceful," Sir Canning provided.

"I had the benefit of being alone," Charles replied, "without the pomp and fair that Macartney had."

"Nonetheless, the Chinese are not receptive to us. Our

solace is they are no more receptive to the Dutch."

"Knowing their suspicion and aversion, I ensured my demeanor was always humble. And I was fortunate to have befriended a traveling merchant."

"Ah. And did you observe if the Chinese were in want of any goods we could provide?"

Charles raised his brows. "Aside from Indian opium?"

Sir Canning cleared his throat and intended a moderating statement, but Sir Arthur spoke first. Undaunted, he said, "Well, our hand is forced. The Chinese insist upon silver in exchange for their goods."

"Because we have nothing else of value to offer them."

"And now we have. Opium is our trump card, Charles. It will do much to correct the trade imbalance between our countries."

Charles stiffened at the use of his given name. He had little desire to befriend the man. There had been whispers of the man shortly after the death of his wife, but Charles could not remember what the confabulation entailed, only that it was not complimentary of Sir Arthur.

"Surely you are aware the emperor is not pleased with the opium, Sir Arthur," Charles said.

Sir Arthur shrugged. "Do you not agree we should seek greater trade with China?"

"Of course. But this stratagem concerning opium can only lead to a grim end, even war."

"Do you fear a war with China, Charles?"

"Tell me first, would such a war benefit country or Company?"

Sir Canning began coughing, and Charles felt a little sheepish. His employer had invited Sir Arthur with the intention of soliciting the man's support for him, and he had repaid Sir Canning's kindness by risking the minister's ire.

Sir Arthur reclined into his chair, his outward demeanor one of placidity, but his eyes had steeled.

"Your father dreamed of opening China to trade," he

said, as if lecturing Charles. "I think you share the same, and it would provide the two of us yet another interest in common."

This time Charles said nothing. He reminded himself that he had no wish to have Sir Arthur oppose his election. Should he win, Sir Arthur would then be a colleague to him. It was unfortunate their paths had crossed at the Red Chrysanthemum, and Charles had a sinking feeling he would only see more of Sir Arthur in the days to come.

# CHAPTER EIGHT

"Well, what do we intend tonight, Miss Terrell?"

She and Sir Arthur occupied the same room as yesterday. He stood before the settee, both hands resting atop the walking stick he favored so much that it might as well have been a fifth appendage for him.

"Will you sit, sir?" she asked, indicating the armchair she had used yesterday.

With slow deliberation, he flared the tails of his coat and took a seat. He was dressed even more impressively this night. She noted the impeccable tie of his cravat, the lack of a single wrinkle in his trousers, and the fine silk of his waistcoat. In contrast, she wore the same garments but for a fresh chemise. Accustomed to being barefoot from her time in the West Indies when no attempts, not even dampening oneself with water, seemed to relieve the swelter of the summer heat, she opted not to wear stockings and shoes when she could.

Facing him, she settled atop his thighs. He reached for her. His hold felt forceful but awkward, as if he did not know how to hold a woman. Unlike the embrace of Master Gallant. She pushed him away.

"Patience, Sir Arthur," she said. "I have a performance first for you, after which, you shall be rewarded for your forbearance."

"Very well, but make it quick," he said, his eyes aflame with desire. "I have an engagement to dine with a friend tonight."

She leaned upon his chest and toyed with his neckcloth. "You need do nothing. I promise you will enjoy the show."

He raised his brows. "You have had experience on the stage?"

She began to loosen and unwind the linen. "A different sort of stage."

"Were you a dancer?"

"A dancer unlike any you've seen."

Grasping his neckcloth on either side, she yanked his head down toward her bosom. He buried his face in the lush orbs, kissing their tops with reverence and hunger. She slid the neckcloth from around his neck and wrapped it about one of his wrists. He licked and sucked at her flesh, reminding her of a dog lapping at a bone. She slid from his lap, darted behind the armchair, and pulled his arms around the back. He exclaimed in surprise, but she had wrapped the linen about his other wrist. She caressed the length of his arm.

"Fear not," she assured him. "I merely wish to ensure that my performance will not be interrupted."

"If this be some trickery or mischief—"

She tied a knot about his wrists, noting the jeweled rings upon his fingers, a beautiful sapphire among them, then returned to the other side of the armchair. The man did not appear pleased, but he would be distracted soon enough. She began untying her petticoats.

"Tell me of yourself, Sir Arthur. You seem quite an important man, endowed in all ways that matter," she said as the garments pooled at her feet. Men of his sort often liked to talk of themselves.

His breath caught, for her chemise was thin and he could undoubtedly see the silhouette of her legs. "Well, I would be guilty of false modesty if I denied that I am a man of influence."

"You are friend to Sir Fairchild."

"I am, and while he may bear the title of a baronet, I surpass him in many more respects."

She began unlacing the front of her corset. "It be plain you are a man who wants for nothing."

His gaze fixed once more upon her breasts. "My interests in the East India Company have returned a fine sum for me. And there are many men who owe their fortunes or their careers to me."

"Indeed?"

"I own three boroughs, including my own. A fourth, Porter's Hill, is practically mine. These are votes I can deliver to the Prime Minister whenever needed."

"You're a powerful man, then."

"Sir Fairchild cannot claim the same."

She wondered at a man who felt the need to disparage his own friend. Four inches, she predicted to herself. His cock, at its full length, would measure no more than four inches.

"Is this your 'performance'?" Sir Arthur asked when the loosened corset fell to the floor. "I approve thus far but expect the full act has not concluded."

Standing in only her chemise, she gave him a demure smile. "It has barely begun, sir."

Slowly, she began to undulate her body, swaying her hips while caressing herself with both hands. She touched arms, bosom, ribs, and belly. The fire in Sir Arthur's eyes flared. Stretching her arms above, she undulated to a rhythm in her head. Rotating, she presented him her backside. Her hands traveled down her sides and cupped her buttocks.

"My God," Sir Arthur choked.

Turning back around, she loosened the top of the chemise. It slid off one shoulder. She rolled and thrust her hips.

"Your people are possessed of such vulgar lewdness. Such wantonness can only be the work of the devil," he muttered to himself, but his ravenous gaze stayed upon her.

Stepping back, she sat down on the settee opposite him. Reclining, she flared her legs apart and propped her ankles upon the seat on either side of her. His eyes widened at her bawdy position. The chemise fell down her legs and covered the area between her thighs. She continued to caress herself, pushing one hand below her chemise to grab a breast. Her efforts had warmed her body and brought to life a craving between her legs. She imagined Master Gallant sitting before her, bound to the armchair and forced to witness her wanton display.

As she groped and fondled the breast, she reached her other hand to her mound. Sir Arthur, if he were not bound to the chair, might have thrown himself at her.

She made purring sounds and did not need to look at his crotch to know that his cock stood at stiff attention. Her visible hand slid lower. She stroked herself through the chemise. She wanted to bring herself to spend before him but also wanted to save herself for Master Gallant.

Sir Arthur began pulling at his bindings. "Well done, Miss Terrell. A commendable performance. What do you intend for the finale?"

Her mind toyed with the possibilities. "Would you care to glimpse my cunnie?"

His mouth fell open. Parting her legs farther, she inched her chemise up and paused before baring herself.

The veins in his neck extended. "Teasing slattern."

Though she would have preferred not to, she decided she had best satisfy him. She lifted her chemise and presented him the forbidden paradise. He stared at her and looked ready to drool. She replaced her chemise, rose from the settee and sauntered to him.

"Now that you've seen my private, I think it only fair…"

She knelt before him and began to unbutton his fall, freeing his quaint little erection. It was even smaller than Sir Fairchild's, who had not length but some girth. Sir Arthur held his breath as she gazed upon his cock.

"A lovely Thomas you have," she purred, stroking it with a finger.

His breath became shallow. She wrapped her fingers about him and leisurely moved up his length, dragging the tips of her fingers over its crown. She put her forefinger to the underside of his cock and gently caressed an area just below the flare of the head. He groaned and closed his eyes. Wrapping her hand about him once more, she rubbed, twisted, and pulled his member.

Sensing that he was near his peak, she grabbed him more forcefully and pumped her hand up and down his shaft. Within minutes, groaning and grunting, he spent, shooting his seed a surprising distance. Some of his mettle dribbled onto her hand, and she spread it about his quickly softening cock. He quivered and, exhaling a long breath, slumped into the chair. Rising to her feet, she found linen to wipe her hand, then went to untie him. He shuddered once more before attempting to stand.

"I shall call a valet for you," she said.

He grabbed her arm before she could move. "A lovely 'performance', Miss Terrell, but was it necessary to tie me to the chair?"

Once more she was struck by the menacing quality of his tone, but she did not let it affect her. "If you will allow it again, Sir Arthur, I will enlist my mouth for the encore."

His eyes widened. She smiled prettily at him before liberating her arm from his grasp.

She refused to be daunted by this man. He could prove of use to her. While she would have felt safer as the mistress of someone with a more jovial nature, as Sir Fairchild's had been, she believed Sir Arthur to be genuinely flush in the purse. Her youth and beauty would not last forever, and men like Sir Arthur were the only means of securing her future.

# CHAPTER NINE

"**M**y sister could not find employment as a housemaid on account of them teapots," said Sophia, a member of the Red Chrysanthemum, who, like Terrell and Sarah, relied on Madame Devereux for room and board.

"The town is overrun with blackamoors," Sophia continued as Tippy dressed her hair.

Sitting at a vanity nearby, Terrell watched as the maid brushed long, soft locks. They reminded her of Master Gallant's, though lighter in color. After Sir Arthur had left, she had dressed herself. Not surprisingly, the man had shown no awareness that she might require release as well, but Terrell was accustomed to such neglect. Moreover, she fully intended for Master Gallant to address her needs.

"I would sooner brush against a Jew than a Negro," continued Sophia, who was fully aware that Terrell occupied the dressing chambers.

The young woman, a few years senior, had made no effort to conceal her contempt since the day Terrell first arrived at the Red Chrysanthemum. Terrell had sought to fill the position now held by Tippy, but the proprietress saw that Terrell could best be of service in other capacities.

"There won't be a decent wage to be had on account of them," said Sophia. "I wonder that some of them don't work for scraps."

"For certain they work much harder, though they be compensated less," Terrell said with calm.

Sophia glanced over, dainty nose wrinkled in disdain. "*If* they are possessed of a work ethic, and perhaps they must, for even mules and oxen can be made to work. Their coarse natures and inferior minds must put them at a disadvantage."

Terrell said nothing, though she wanted to respond, "If your kind were given to hard work, there would be no need to enslave my kind to toil the fields."

Instead, she replied, "Lucky for me, the men do prefer my coarse nature and inferior mind."

Sophia colored, no doubt remembering the one gentleman who had chosen Terrell over her. "I suppose there are men inclined to fuck even sheep and cattle."

Terrell drew in a sharp breath. Tippy began to cough in discomfort.

"You've done my hair all wrong!" Sophia snapped at the maid. "And I wanted ringlets about my face!"

Before Terrell could respond in kind to Sophia, a slim and finely dressed woman entered. Her light-brown hair pinned in loose curls atop her head, she wore a fur-trimmed pelisse, spotless white gloves, and the prettiest shoes with ribbons.

"Lady Wendlesson!" Tippy greeted. "Er, Miss Katherine, that is. You've arrived early. I shall be but a moment."

"Allow me," Terrell interjected. "What orders has Master Gallant given?"

"Only that she be ready in the small room—the farthest one—on the third floor."

"If you would follow me, m'lady," Terrell said to Miss Katherine.

Her ladyship gave a small nod. Terrell knew the room, which was often reserved for members who planned to stay the night. With only a bed, chair, table, and sideboard, it had none of the furnishings familiar to the other rooms at the inn. Once in the room, Terrell assisted her ladyship with her pelisse and gloves.

"How lovely these are, m'lady," Terrell admired as she fingered the lace trim before placing the gloves neatly upon the top of the table. She had once owned a pair as elegant before circumstances forced her to sell her belongings.

"They were part of my wedding trousseau," her ladyship replied in a small voice.

"Felicitations to you, m'lady."

"Thank you."

Terrell could not discern if the woman was happy about her nuptials but said, "His lordship is a fine man."

Miss Katherine looked down at her clasped hands. "He is."

"If you don't mind me saying, there be a lot of us who would envy your position if we had the right."

"You know my husband?"

"Oh! Not in that way—I don't merit his attentions. But I've seen him about."

Miss Katherine seemed deep in thought. "But there were others...were there many?"

"Not a great many," Terrell fibbed. "His sex, they all must have their *outlet*, you understand. You ought not censure him for the urges common to all men."

"I understand," Miss Katherine sighed.

"His was of a nature that an ordinary opera dancer or tavern maid would not serve."

Her ladyship appeared to wince. Terrell quickly added, "But I do recall the day he informed Madame Devereux that he had married, and I never saw or heard such cheer in him before."

Miss Katherine looked up. "Truly?"

Terrell nodded. "As happy as a man could be on such occasion. Like I said, made the rest of us women envious. We thought for certain we'd seen the last of him. It does signify that he has brought you here and wishes to share the Red Chrysanthemum with you. I know others whose wives are kept at home, oblivious, while their husbands satisfy themselves with the strumpets here."

Miss Katherine brightened at this reasoning.

"And it shows your generous spirit, m'lady, that you've not cast him aside with disdain but seek to fill his need."

Her ladyship took an easier breath but said, "My family and friends should be horrified if they knew."

"Your pleasure is none of their business, if you not mind my sayin'."

"Pleasure? Is it truly pleasure?"

"It is," Terrell answered with such earnestness that Miss Katherine gazed upon her more keenly.

"I'm a member myself," Terrell supplied,

Surprised, Miss Katherine looked her over from head to toe. "Are you no dressing maid?"

Realizing her attire gave the appearance of a peasant, Terrell smiled and shook her head. "The proprietress desires my services elsewhere, but, as Tippy is engaged, I will see to your needs as I am done for the evening. May I fetch you refreshment?"

"A cordial perhaps."

When Terrell returned with the beverage and a bowl of sweetmeats, she found her ladyship sitting on the edge of the bed, her apprehension still palpable.

"It is quite reasonable one should be fearful of the unknown," Terrell said gently as she handed Miss Katherine the cordial. "I was frightened out of wits my first time."

"Your first time here?"

"The first time I surrendered my maidenhead."

"Yes. The pain quite surprised me," Miss Katherine acknowledged. "I knew nothing of what to expect."

"Did your mother not provide you warning?"

"My mother told me nothing. My sisters told me nothing."

"I'm sorry. At the least, once the maidenhead has been surrendered, all else is pleasure, especially if the man be attentive and skilled."

Miss Katherine blushed and drank her cordial. "But the purpose here would appear to be *pain*."

"Ah, yes, but it is pain in the pursuit of pleasure."

"I find it hard to fathom the one can contribute to the other."

"True appreciation can only come from the experiencing of it."

"I suppose. I wish my husband would instruct me in its ways, but I think my ignorance tries his patience, for he has fobbed me off to another."

"Your husband was wise to do so. There is none better than Master Gallant. I've seen many a man through these doors, and there be none like him."

"He was civil and tolerant of me last evening. But I wonder what he intends for a lesson tonight?"

The creak of floorboards outside startled her ladyship. "He is here!"

The two women waited and heard footsteps retreating down the hall. Miss Katherine gave a heavy sigh of relief.

"You fear Master Gallant?" inquired Terrell.

"I fear what he will *do*."

"I suspect he would be gentle at first."

"Precisely! At first! I think my husband is eager I finish my 'lessons' as soon as possible. The two of them spoke yester evening. I am certain my husband conveyed his desires to Master Gallant, and my husband is not a man to be disappointed!"

Miss Katherine looked ready to cry.

"If you wish it, I will stay with you," Terrell offered. "If it would ease your fears, if you should not be ready to feel the fall of the crop or flogger, I will accept it for you, m'lady."

Miss Katherine stared. "Indeed?"

"I am an old hand at this. Nothing Master Gallant can

do will be worse than that which was done to me prior to my time here."

"But my husband will not be pleased."

"I will not replace you as the pupil, but I will assist in the lesson. The perspective of a woman could benefit your progress. Master Gallant might use me for demonstration, and that would bide you more time to calm your fears."

Her ladyship nodded. "I would be grateful for this. Do you expect I should…is there a rate of recompense for your assistance?"

"None, m'lady, but if you should find me useful, I shall not decline a perquisite."

"You are kind to do such a thing."

Terrell felt a little ashamed at not disputing her ladyship's belief that it was kindness that prompted her actions, but she did not feel it necessary to reveal to Lady Wendlesson that Master Gallant, not compensation, was what she was after. Thinking of how Master Gallant would react made her pulse quicken, and for a moment she hesitated to pursue the opportunity she had just contrived. She guessed he would not be pleased at first, but what man would not wish to spend the evening with two women? He would come to enjoy her company soon enough, lest in some manner, he was repulsed by her blackness. She knew many of his kind despised blackamoors yet had no trouble fucking them.

"Better than fuckin' sheep," she had once overheard Mr. Tremayne, the overseer, remark. "Smell a bit better, too."

His friend had disagreed. "After being on a ship full of them black creatures, I can't see them as anything but vermin. God must have cursed them something fierce."

But Master Gallant could not hold such a view or he would not have kissed her, in front of an audience, no less. She had noted the admiration the other members held for him. Did not the fact that he had chosen her provide further validation of her worth, her ability to be as good as any white woman? Better, even. In her short time at the Red Chrysanthemum, she had established herself as good as a veteran, and she would make this known to Master Gallant.

Resolved, she waited with Lady Wendlesson for his arrival.

# CHAPTER TEN

"**M**iss Katherine awaits in the room you requested," Tippy informed him.

Charles nodded as he handed his coat and hat to the page. "Has Sir Arthur been here?"

"He has, and left already."

Glad there should be no chance of crossing paths with the man, he headed for the stairs. One encounter with Sir Arthur was sufficient for the day, though Charles considered afterwards that some repair on his part need be offered.

"Sir Arthur is not a man who takes kindly to being challenged," Sir Canning had said after their meeting. "If you wish to become a burgess for Porter's Hill, I suggest you curry his favor instead of his ire."

As Charles climbed the steps up to the third floor, he put aside his thoughts of Sir Arthur to focus on the matter at hand. Charles contemplated the possibility that Miss Katherine could prove more challenging than Miss Greta. The latter understood the peculiar type of pleasure fulfilled by the Red Chrysanthemum. The former was not yet comfortable in her own body. He preferred to heighten her awareness and ensure her appreciation of her own lascivious desires before introducing more wanton elements. He carried with him a book that he hoped would aid his efforts.

The room he had requested should prove more comfortable to Miss Katherine. If he intended to accomplish the success Lord Wendlesson sought, he needed to do more than converse with her tonight.

After a brief rap upon the door, he entered the room and stopped upon the threshold. He stared. Miss Katherine sat upon the edge of the bed. Beside her stood Miss Terrell.

*What the devil...*

"A good evening to you, Master Gallant," Miss Terrell said cheerfully. "I've offered myself as your assistant for the night."

His frown deepened. "I've no need for an assistant."

"Ah, but as your assistant, I would also be aiding Miss Katherine, and she has accepted my offer."

He looked to Miss Katherine, who kept her gaze lowered. "Indeed?"

Miss Katherine raised her eyes. "If—if you do not think it would infuriate my husband."

Charles said nothing. Lord Wendlesson would more than likely be thrilled that his wife had invited another woman, and Miss Terrell at that.

"I am at your disposal, Master Gallant," said Miss Terrell, her dark eyes boring into him, "and will do anything you or Miss Katherine bid."

He wanted to bid her leave, but if her presence gave Miss Katherine comfort, if Miss Katherine had requested her, then he could not send Miss Terrell away. Miss Terrell had conjured the situation, he was certain of it. How she had managed to ingratiate herself so quickly with Lady Wendlesson mystified and impressed him. The cunning chit.

"Are you certain you wish to have a third party bear witness to our lesson?" he asked gently of Miss Katherine.

She nodded.

"You may stay," he said to Miss Terrell, "but for this

night only. As I've said, I do not require an assistant."

"You may not require, but you may *benefit* from one nonetheless."

She crossed her arms before her. He wanted to drag her out the room then and there and give her a sound talking to—or a sound spanking, the one from yesterday apparently not having sufficed.

"As would I," said Miss Katherine.

"How long have we this evening?" he addressed Miss Katherine.

"Till midnight."

"How gracious of his lordship to extend us half an hour more," he commented unhappily. He would be hard-pressed to accomplish what he wished, especially now that Miss Terrell had interposed herself into the matter.

"May I ask what the lesson this evening entails?"

Her demeanor had changed, he noticed. She was still demonstrably wary and anxious, but she met and held his gaze for far longer than she had yesterday. Perhaps Miss Terrell bolstered her confidence. For that, he began to see possible value in having the interfering jade.

"This evening we but seek your arousal and review the rules common to the submissive position," he answered.

Her countenance turned crimson.

"I do not expect you will require your safety word," he continued. "Nevertheless, do you recall it?"

She nodded. "Jean."

He turned to Miss Terrell. "And yours?"

"I am the assistant, not the pupil," Miss Terrell replied, arching a perfectly curved brow.

"Unlike Miss Katherine, *you* may require yours."

To his satisfaction, Miss Terrell started. Miss Katherine glanced with concern at her new friend.

"I've not had a safety word in some time," Miss Terrell said with a defiant flip of her hair. "You may do your worst, Master Gallant."

He clenched a hand, which itched to show her just how

wrong she could be. "The Red Chrysanthemum requires a safety word of everyone. Do set a good example for our pupil."

Her eyes glimmered and he fully expected her to respond with something ribald or mischievous. More. Flog. Cock. Fuck.

"A simple word, preferably plain and boring," he advised.

"Charles."

He tried not to glare at the woman, given the presence of Miss Katherine. Miss Terrell was testing him, goading him. He thought of tying her between the bedposts and whipping her till she cried her safety word over and over. But that was precisely what she *wanted*. He needed to retain his composure. He lost credibility with Miss Katherine if he allowed Miss Terrell to rankle him.

"Perhaps you can recite the tenets of proper submissive behavior," he said to Miss Terrell. *You've a need to remember them yourself.*

"The most basic principle is showing your dominant the respect due him."

"Dominant?" Miss Katherine echoed.

"He who commands you, who is your superior."

"Not superior in qualities," he clarified, "but only in position and within the context of your carnal bondage."

"Though some men will attempt to claim their superiority in all respects. They think us the weaker sex, but in truth, they are the weak ones."

"How can that be?" Miss Katherine asked. "Their sex is superior in all ways that matter."

"If you would see how women till the fields beneath a sweltering sun from dawn to night, bent in constant labor, some with babes upon their backs—"

He stopped her. "Miss Terrell, if you've a desire to elucidate the philosophies of Wollstonecraft or Bentham, I bid you do so on your own time, not mine."

She looked at him, frowning. By the earnestness in her

tone, he discerned what she had described to be of a personal nature to her, but what little time he had was dedicated to Miss Katherine and her arousal. Tragic images were completely at odds with his purpose.

"Pray, repeat this most basic principle for the submissive," he instructed Miss Terrell. "It bears reminding for us all."

Knowing that he spoke of her, she half-scowled at him. "Respect your dominant."

"What happens if you fail to adhere to this principle?"

"You shall be disciplined."

"How?" asked Miss Katherine.

"That depends upon the wishes of the Master or the Mistress," he replied, "but know that you may employ your safety word on any occasion."

Turning back to Miss Terrell, he said, "Let us elaborate upon this principle. How might you respect your Master?"

"Do as he bids, promptly and without question," she replied.

"Very good. What else?"

"Speak to him with deference. Always."

"And the consequences for impudence?"

Miss Terrell grinned. "Punishment. Which can be most enjoyable."

He gave her a warning look. "Or extremely painful."

"It depends who is administering the punishment. Some Masters have a light hand."

His jaw tightened. Did she think him incapable of meting out pain? He knew not why Miss Terrell riled him, and reminded himself to ignore her antics.

"How else might you show deference?"

"Address your dominant appropriately, as Master or Mistress," said Miss Terrell, "lest you have been told different. For instance, if I am the submissive, I ought not address Master Gallant as *Mister* Gallant. Is that not correct, Mister Gallant?"

A muscle rippled along his jaw. Miss Greta had once

tested him in this manner. He had thrown her into a cage and allowed her to stew there for an hour, and he had a mind to do the same to Miss Terrell.

"As my assistant, you will assume the position of a submissive."

Once more, a small smile graced her plump lips. He wondered if he had played into her hands.

"Yes, Master Gallant."

"Continue," he directed, a hint of exasperation escaping with his command.

"Thank him for everything that your Master does. If he brings you pleasure, if he shows you mercy, if he provides you the punishment you deserve, all these must be accepted with gratitude."

"Thank him for everything?" Miss Katherine asked. "All acts big and small?"

"The criteria for each Master differ" said Charles. "If your husband does not express them to you, ask it of him. It is important that expectations are clear, or you will not be able to perform to them."

"I am allowed questions?"

"You may need to request permission to speak first, but I encourage you to ask as many queries as possible."

"Many dominants require you to assume a proper bearing of respect as well," Miss Terrell added. "I knew of one who never wished me to lift my eyes lest I had permission to do so."

Charles nodded. "You may be required to assume a position of submission upon greeting your Master."

"What is a position of submission?" Miss Katherine asked.

He turned to Miss Terrell and raised his brows. She went to her knees, clasped her hands behind her, and lowered her gaze to the floor. He stared. The prospect of what it would be like to be her dominant tugged at his groin.

Recalling himself, he said to Miss Katherine, "That is

but one example. His lordship should instruct you on what he prefers. Let us practice these rubrics."

At her lack of response, he gestured to the floor. Hesitantly, she rose from the bed, knelt beside Miss Terrell and mirrored her.

"Very good, Miss Katherine."

He walked around the two women. Many a man would envy him his current position with two such beauties kneeling before him.

"I will have your hands clasped behind your backs and your gazes upon me," he directed.

They did as he ordered.

"Now tap the top of your head with your right hand."

The two women exchanged looks but did as told.

"Good. Replace your hand. You may now stand. And hop on your left foot."

"Do you mean to make fools of us?" Miss Terrell asked.

"Permission to speak was not granted, Miss Terrell. The purpose of this exercise is to condition you to follow instructions."

The two women began hopping. He allowed them to hop for a while before saying. "You may cease the hopping and instead wave your arms as if they are the wings of a bird."

Without word, they flapped their arms up and down. It was a ludicrous scene but left no doubt as to who commanded and who followed. After some time, he saw that Miss Katherine began to tire and both of them clearly expected him to call an end to the motion. He did not.

"Permission to speak, Master Gallant," huffed Miss Terrell.

"Denied," he replied with a degree of smugness. She had insinuated herself as his submissive and would endure the consequences. "Lift the arms higher. I want to see them parallel to the ground."

Groaning, Miss Katherine struggled to do so. Miss

Terrell, too, must have experienced soreness in her shoulders but managed to raise her arms the requisite height.

"Come, Miss Katherine," he encouraged. "I've no wish to discipline you tonight."

This proved the motivation she required. With a grimace, she threw her arms into the air and nearly doubled over from the effort.

"Please...Master Gallant," she whispered.

"Once more, Miss Katherine."

She tried but collapsed to her knees.

"Once more, Miss Katherine," he pressed to see if she could recall her safety word.

"I cannot," she gasped.

"Miss Katherine," he admonished as he stood over her. "Please..."

"Once more, Miss Katherine."

Miss Terrell ceased her arm movements. "You ought leave her be."

Whirling around, he faced the meddler. Miss Terrell did not know his motive for pushing Miss Katherine, but she should have known better than to interfere or speak without permission.

"Can you not see the poor thing is exhausted?" Miss Terrell remarked.

She spoke with what sounded to be genuine concern for Miss Katherine. But that did not matter. She had disregarded the principle she was supposed to support and uphold before Miss Katherine.

Now he had no choice but to punish her.

# CHAPTER ELEVEN

Miss Terrell met his unhappy gaze and there appeared a momentary unease in her eyes, but she kept her chin lifted, in defiance it seemed, though, given that Charles was a head taller, she could not have met his stare without looking up.

Still in a poor disposition after his earlier meeting with Sir Arthur, Charles had little patience for Miss Terrell and her mischief. Her intrusion into his affairs with Miss Katherine was unacceptable enough, now she dared instruct him on how to handle his pupil? He considered punishing both women for Miss Terrell's error, but if Miss Katherine found comfort in the presence of the impish blackamoor, and as he still needed to cultivate a sense of ease in the young viscountess, he ought not ruin the newfound bond between the two women.

Drawing himself before Miss Terrell, he said to the chit, "I shall address your insubordination later."

She stared at him with large eyes the shape of almonds. Was it the pronounced eyelids or the contrast of the whites of her eyes to her dark complexion that made them appear so bold?

"Please do," she invited.

His groin tightened, and he decided to turn and look

upon Miss Katherine, who was crumpled to the floor upon her knees. She had not yet employed her safety word, Jean. Though he had not granted Miss Terrell permission to speak, he would have allowed her to remind Miss Katherine that there was a means to putting an end to her suffering. But, despite her tenure at the Red Chrysanthemum, it was perhaps Miss Terrell herself who wanted reminding.

"I've not had a safety word in some time," Miss Terrell had told him. "You may do your worst, Master Gallant."

He should have known, at those words, that Miss Terrell would not prove a shining example of good and proper submissive behavior—though she could be made an example of, and thereby discourage Miss Katherine from misconduct. But punishment was what the minx wanted. He cursed himself. He could not recall being at such a loss as to what to do with a woman. Yes, he could simply send her away, as he had wanted to do moments ago. Miss Katherine might be alarmed at the loss of her shield, but in truth, he was not ready to give in. He was not ready to admit he could not handle Miss Terrell. Especially now that she had challenged him. Miss Terrell needed a lesson as much as Miss Katherine, and who better to instruct her than him?

"On your feet, Miss Katherine," he ordered. He needed to be careful. If he were too harsh, he would obliterate the trust he had established with her yesterday through gentleness.

Miss Terrell bent down to assist, but he thrust his arm between them. "I did not ask you to move, Miss Terrell. Miss Katherine is capable of standing on her own."

The young viscountess pulled herself to her feet.

"Both arms," he said, "straight out at the shoulders."

The two women lifted their arms in compliance.

"Now flap them once more. Without stopping this time. For five minutes"

Miss Terrell blew at a tendril of her hair and rolled her

eyes ever so slightly.

Charles crossed his arms across his chest. "For that little gesture, Miss Terrell, you have earned yourself *ten* minutes."

Frowning, she gave him a hard stare.

He turned back to Miss Katherine, whose arms moved but sagged far below the shoulders. "Higher, Miss Katherine."

She shook her head. "Please, Master Gallant. Will you not have mercy? My arms are greatly fatigued."

"You wish to desist?"

"Yes, please!"

"I can only grant mercy when you demand it."

At a loss, she appeared panicked.

"Higher!" he barked of her arms.

"I demand it, Master Gallant, I demand mercy," she cried.

"Demand me to desist properly."

"John!" Miss Terrell provided. "Or was it Jean?"

Realization dawned for Miss Katherine. "Yes! Jean! I demand 'Jean'!"

With a relieved sigh, he nodded for her stop. With an even greater sigh, Miss Katherine let fall her arms and sat down upon the bed behind her.

"I did not say you could sit," he said.

She jumped to her feet. "Your pardon. Master Gallant, may I sit?"

"You may."

With another sigh, she sank back down.

"Well done, Miss Katherine," he said. "You are proving an apt pupil."

*More apt than this one*, he thought to himself as he stood before Miss Terrell. She continued to flap her arms though the strain was visible upon her furrowed brow. She, too, could have called upon her safety word, but he did not wish for her to use it. Miss Terrell needed to learn a lesson first.

"You boasted you require no safety word," he said, looking upon his pocket watch. "Was that a premature statement on your part?"

Gritting her teeth, she said nothing. Her arm movements made her bosom rise and fall. He allowed himself a quick glance at her décolletage before stepping back and taking a seat in an armchair opposite her. He needed the distance or he might be tempted to do more than have her flap her arms. He might, for example, want to unlace her corset and affix weights to her nipples. Propping an ankle over his other leg, his comfortable position a clear contrast to her situation, he put down his book but continued to hold the pocket watch.

Miss Katherine glanced between them, clearly wanting to plead for Miss Terrell but not daring to.

"Five minutes more," he informed.

The small room was quiet but for the sound of Miss Terrell grunting. Given that her muscles must have been on fire, he suspected the minutes passed like hours for her. If it was punishment she desired, he would deliver it, but it might not be the sort she would enjoy. He wondered what other manner of punishment would suffice. Leaving her to hang in bondage had not deterred her. Nor had the spanking. Perhaps he ought to have used a paddle to her backside. The memory of her charming arse made him shift in his chair. His hand would have liked to connect once more with that smooth and supple flesh.

"Three minutes," he said.

Her lashes fluttered and her grunts lengthened as she struggled to lift her arms. She had mentioned toiling in the fields. Might she have once worked upon a plantation? He knew little of her save that she had been a favorite of Mr. Worthington, a slave owner from the West Indies. He realized her way of speaking differed from any he had heard before in London. Having spent the better part of the last two years in the Orient, however, he had grown accustomed to strange intonations. He had tried his best to master the Chinese language but, while he heard the various inflections in each of their words, he could not perfectly reproduce them.

"Two minutes."

Miss Terrell emitted a growl, but he could see she was determined to see her punishment through. Miss Katherine continued to watch in her nervous way. He had not given up hope of convincing Lord Wendlesson to undertake the instruction of his own wife. Though Charles had not welcomed her interference, perhaps Miss Terrell could be of use. Miss Katherine did not believe pleasure could be had from pain, but Miss Terrell possessed no such doubts. Perhaps the latter, being a woman, could better convince Miss Katherine.

"One minute."

With a grunt, Miss Terrell threw her arms up. Seeing that her limbs quivered, he suspected the muscles of her shoulders burned, but she did her best to execute his orders. He could see how she might make an intriguing submissive. She had a tenacity about her, a fearlessness he had not glimpsed in any other woman—or man. He found himself wondering where she had come from? Was she truly only twenty years of age? And why was she addressed by her surname when all the other submissive women at the Red Chrysanthemum were known by their given name?

He looked at his pocket watch. Her time concluded, he said with genuine praise, "Well done, Miss Terrell."

She was breathing hard and her shoulders sagged, but when she met his gaze once more, her chin lifted, her countenance serene, almost regal, she asked, "Permission to speak?"

"Granted," he replied, replacing his timepiece into the pocket of his waistcoat.

"I await further punishment, Master Gallant."

Taken aback, he said nothing. Miss Katherine looked on with equal surprise.

"You said earlier that you would address my insubordination," Miss Terrell added.

"I did," he acknowledged, and his mind filled with the possibilities.

He could take a paddle to her backside. But that might arouse her. Titillation could not factor into her punishment. Perhaps she would dislike being locked in a cage as much as Miss Greta had. He could make Miss Terrell stand on one foot for a period or make her recite catechisms for half an hour. The consequence needed to be dreary to impress upon her that she would gain nothing of interest by seeking his attention.

But he saw that delicious rump of hers in his mind's eye. There was much he could do. Much he could do indeed.

# CHAPTER TWELVE

"**Y**ou will have to endure the suspense of waiting," Master Gallant told Terrell. "This time belongs to Miss Katherine. You may both of you resume your position on your knees, with your hands clasped behind your backs."

Terrell watched as he pulled at his cravat as if uncomfortable with the neckcloth, but it was also possible that his discomfort was due to her provocation. She wanted to think that might be the case. Did the prospect of punishing her arouse him? He spoke with such calm that she suspected herself to be mislaying hope. Thus far, he had given little indication that she ignited his lust. There were whispers of it, though she could not elucidate why her senses were perked. She knew his sex well enough to sniff their interest, and Master Gallant was not indifferent to her, but she knew not if the passion she aroused the most in him was vexation. She knew not if his desires could overrule his forbearance.

"Miss Katherine," Master Gallant addressed after the two women complied and returned to their knees, "how do you arouse yourself?"

Miss Katherine flushed to the roots of her hair. "Am I p-permitted to speak?"

"When I address you, yes."

"I do not understand."

"How do you stir the venereal in your body?"

Her eyes looked to the far corner, then below as she searched her mind for an answer. "My lord—Master, I do not think I do anything."

"Then what arouses you? What titillates you?"

At a loss, Miss Katherine looked down. "I was not—I was not taught to think of such matters."

"You have not felt the warmth of lust when, perhaps, gazing upon a painting of a nude?"

As he continued to question Miss Katherine, Terrell looked upon Master Gallant with wonder. She found him rather verbose for his sex, but his voice had a sensual quality, and the patience and gentleness in his tone intrigued her. His attention upon Miss Katherine gave her a reprieve. Her shoulders ached from the exertion he had demanded from her—she would have preferred a spanking. Instead, he had made her look ridiculous.

Miss Katherine shook her head in answer to his question.

"Then let us enlist the aid of Mr. John Cleland."

Master Gallant produced a book, *Memoirs of a Woman of Pleasure*. Miss Katherine stared without comprehension.

"It is a novel," he explained, "of an erotic nature."

Recognition dawned upon Miss Katherine. "I thought such books were banned?"

"It was not easy to come by this copy," Master Gallant acknowledged. The discoloration of the pages suggested the book might have been from one of the original printings.

He opened the book to a certain passage and presented it to Miss Katherine. "Read the start of the page and continue till I stop you."

Miss Katherine took the book from him and cleared her throat. "'To slip over minutes of no importance to the main of my story, I pass the interval to bed time, in which I was more and more pleased with the views that opened to me, of an easy service under these good people; and after supper being shewed up to bed, Miss Phoebe, who observed a kind of reluctance in me to strip and go to bed, in my shift, before her, now the maid was withdrawn, came up to me, and beginning with unpinning my handkerchief and gown, soon encouraged me to go on with undressing myself; and, blushing at now seeing myself naked to my shift, I hurried to get under the bed-clothes out of sight.'"

"You read very well, Miss Katherine," encouraged Master Gallant. He had taken a seat in the chair facing the two women, his legs stretched before him. "Pray, continue."

While Miss Katherine continued to read, Terrell took occasion to admire Master Gallant and how well his trousers encased his legs. She knew the shape of his chest, had liked its chiseled but not burly qualities, for she had seen it that day he had bound Mistress Scarlet to the table before an audience of Red Chrysanthemum members. He was a man of privilege, but his fine figure indicated he was an active gentleman, not one given to indolence.

"'No sooner then was this precious substitute of my mistress laid down'," read Miss Katherine, "'but she, who was never out of her way when any occasion of lewdness presented itself, turned to me, embraced and kissed me with great eagerness. This was new, this was odd; but imputing it to nothing but pure kindness, which, for ought I knew, it might be the London way to express in that manner, I was determined not to be behind-hand with her, and returned her the kiss and embrace, with all the fervour that perfect innocence knew.

"'Encouraged by this, her hands became extremely free, and wandered over my whole body…'"

Once more, Miss Katherine grew red in the face.

Master Gallant raised his brows. "Miss Katherine?"

"You-you wish me to read further?"

"Yes. Proceed."

Miss Katherine bit her bottom lip, but read on.

"'…with touches, squeezes, pressures, that rather warmed and surprised me with their novelty, than they either shocked or alarmed me.'"

"Slower."

"'The flattering praises she intermingled with these invasions, contributed also not a little to bribe my passiveness; and, knowing no ill, I feared none, especially from one who had prevented all doubts of her womanhood, by conducting my hands to a pair of breasts that hung loosely down, in a size and volume that full sufficiently distinguished her sex, to me at least, who had never made any other comparison.

"'I lay then all tame and passive as she could wish, whilst her freedom raised no other emotion but those of a strange, and, till then, unfelt pleasure. Every part of me was open and exposed to the licentious courses of her hands, which, like a lambent fire, ran over my whole body, and thawed all coldness as they went.'"

Feeling herself grow warm, Terrell closed her eyes to better envision the imagery that Miss Katherine painted, amazed at how the words made such a scene unfold, as vivid as if she were a *voyeur* in the room with Miss Phoebe and the heroine of the story, Miss Fanny Hill. Terrell recalled her own encounter many years ago with a woman remarkably like Miss Phoebe. A fellow slave on the plantation, Miss Ruth had earned her way into the house.

"'But, not contented with these outer posts, she now attempts the main spot, and began to twitch, to insinuate, and at length to force an introduction of a finger into the quick itself, in such a manner, that had she not proceeded by insensible gradations that inflamed me beyond the power of modesty to oppose its resistance to their progress, I should have jumped out of bed and cried for help against such strange assaults.

"'Instead of which, her lascivious touches had lighted up a new fire that wantoned through all my veins, but fixed with violence in that center appointed them by nature, where the first strange hands were now busied in feeling, squeezing, compressing the lips, then opening them again, with a finger between, till an "Oh!" expressed her hurting me, where the narrowness of the unbroken passage refused it entrance to any depth.

"'In the meantime, the extension of my limbs, languid stretching, sighs, short heavings, all conspired to as-ure that experienced wanton that I was more pleased than offended at her proceedings, which she seasoned with repeated kisses and exclamations, such as "Oh! what a charming creature thou art! What a happy man will he be that first makes a woman of you! Oh! That I were a man for your sake!" with the like broken expressions, interrupted by kisses as fierce and salacious as ever I received from the other sex.

"'For my part, I was transported, confused, and out of myself; feelings so new were too much for me. My heated and alarmed senses were in a tumult that robbed me of all liberty of thought; tears of pleasure gushed from my eyes, and somewhat assuaged the fire that raged all over me.'"

"Once more. Those last few sentences."

Miss Katherine's hands trembled, and a deep blush occupied her cheeks, but she did as told. Terrell could see the passage had unsettled Miss Katherine, in more ways than one. Sensing the same, Master Gallant rose and lowered the book she held.

"What sensations inhabit your body at present?" he asked.

"Sensations?"

"Can you feel the blood course warmly through your loins?"

Her breath uneven, she gave no answer.

"Can you imagine yourself in Fanny's place, being caressed most pleasantly and intimately?"

She shook her head a little. "By another woman? It is wrong."

"It may be wanton, but it is not wrong. Or how would

you explain that you are aroused by it?"

Her mouth fell open in distress.

"Allow yourself these natural urges," he said. "Do not let shame and judgement hamper their beauty. They are pleasant, are they not?"

"A little, I suppose."

"The path they form leads to ecstasy. Does it not, Miss Terrell?"

Distracted by the licentious agitation percolating in her body and lulled into a sensual trance by his speech, Terrell started at the unexpected question directed at her.

"Yes, Master," she replied.

He turned back to Miss Katherine. "When you find yourself in this state, how do you unleash the tension?"

"I-I do not find myself—"

"Do not deceive yourself. You do and you have, Miss Katherine."

She knit her brows and looked down. "Once, before I was married, I did glimpse one of the chambermaids and the footmen in passionate embrace. I did feel a strange distress overcome me."

"And how did you relieve it?"

"I did not. In time, it passed."

"But it returned."

She nodded.

"And you did nothing to address it?"

She shook her head.

He turned once more to Terrell. "What would you have done, Miss Terrell?"

*If the footman were handsome, I might have a go at him myself,* Terrell thought, but not wishing to appall Miss Katherine, she replied, "It would depend, Master Gallant, upon the circumstances."

"Provide one possibility."

"I might pleasure myself."

"How?"

"The places Miss Phoebe touched, I would caress with

my own hand."

He looked at Miss Katherine and gestured to the chair. "Have a seat, Miss Katherine."

Her eyes widened in alarm, as if he had commanded her to undress.

"I merely wish you to be comfortable, as your knees must desire respite," he explained.

Relieved, Miss Katherine took a seat. Terrell could not resist thinking that he would give the only chair to the viscountess, a woman of his kind, while she, the blackamoor, continued to kneel upon the floor.

He stepped to the side so that he did not stand between the two women. "Show us, Miss Terrell."

Unsure she had heard correctly, she made no move at first. "Show you...?"

"Show us how you would caress yourself."

Her pulse quickened. She looked to Miss Katherine, who did not appear as horrified as expected, then looked back at Master Gallant.

"Here?" Terrell asked.

"You may assume any position you find comfortable."

She sat with the bed against her back. Slowly, she brought her knees up and attempted to reach beneath the hem of her skirts.

"Do not hide your treasures," he bid, rather grimly for a man about to look upon cunnie.

She thrilled at the opportunity to display herself wantonly before him but pulled her skirts to her waist with a pace that might have been mistaken for reluctance. With the garments bunched at her pelvis, she widened her legs. Miss Katherine gasped. Terrell wondered how much of her cunnie Master Gallant could see from where he stood.

"You've a lovely cunnie, Miss Terrell."

"Thank you, Master Gallant," she replied. She knew her performance was intended for Miss Katherine, but she was determined to make him wish he was the sole audience. She put a hand between her thighs and stroked herself languidly with the length of her middle finger. From the corners of her eyes, she saw his jaw harden. With a smile to herself, she pouted her lips and emitted small groans of pleasure.

"Are you wet, Miss Terrell?" he inquired.

"Yes, Master Gallant."

"Show us."

She parted her folds with her middle and forefinger, then dipped a digit into the wetness to coat it upon her clitoris.

"And where are the sensations most pleasant?"

She circled her finger about the pleasure bud. Looking at him, she could not believe him unaffected, though he assumed the detached posture of a surgeon gazing upon a carcass.

*This cunnie could be yours for the taking,* she told him with her eyes, *yours to do as you please, to inflict all manner of wicked pleasure.*

Having brought herself to spend hundreds of times before, and with Master Gallant standing but a few feet from her, it would not take long for her to reach that glorious climax. She reclined her head against the bed and arched her back. With her other hand, she groped her own breast. She began to pant and rubbed herself faster.

"Remember to request permission to spend," he reminded her.

"Permission to spend, Master."

"Not yet."

The tension coiled in her groin, and she tossed her head from side to side. She squeezed her breast and resisted the temptation to quicken her ministrations.

"Permission to spend," she appealed.

"Why?"

"Why?" she repeated, puzzled.

"Why should you wish to spend?"

"Because...because I desire it, my body wishes for it. It craves that divine elation, that greatest of carnal joys."

"You've a skill with words, Miss Terrell," he said, impressed. "What if I should deny your request?"

"I pray you would not deny me this."

"Why not? Is your present pleasure not sufficient?"

She shook her head. "I must have its natural conclusion. It, the pleasure, it must come to a peak before it can be released."

"Describe the release."

"Waves of the most incredible ecstasy. My body yearns for this."

"If you had to fondle yourself for hours to reach this climax, would you?"

"Anything. I would do anything for it."

"Are you near to spending?"

"Very near, Master. If you grant permission, I should spend within seconds."

"If I did not?"

"Denial would be torturous."

"Punishing?"

"Yes."

She had to slow her fondling, seek out less sensitive spots, for the slightest touch in the perfect direction would send her over the edge.

"I have yet to discipline you for your earlier insubordination," he said.

She glanced sharply at him. He would not.

He *would*.

But he could not stop her. Her body hung upon the precipice. A few hard strokes and she could claim her satisfaction, whether he permitted it or no.

"But I should like for Miss Katherine to see your dénouement," he said. "For that reason, I grant you permission to spend."

He could not have spoken sooner, for the slightest flick upon her clitoris sent her into shudders. Her head and shoulders jerked forward, and she felt the lovely waves of her paroxysm flowing through her body, trembling her limbs, making her glow upon the inside. She pressed against that potent bud and eked out a few more, smaller spasms. Her head fell back against the bed. Her legs jerked one last time. When the tremors had faded into a simmer, she heaved a contented sigh and allowed her body to grow limp.

"Thank you, Master," she murmured, her lashes lowered as she basked in the serenity of fulfilment. She had enjoyed fondling herself before Master Gallant. Even the presence of Miss Katherine added a different flavor to the titillation. But her cunnie had felt empty. She wanted the deeper convulsions that came from fucking. She wanted Master Gallant. More than ever.

"And now, Miss Terrell," said Master Gallant, "you may attend Miss Katherine."

# CHAPTER THIRTEEN

**D**amnation. His cock was as hard as ivory.

From where he stood, Charles did not have an unobstructed view of Miss Terrell's quim. He would not allow himself a better angle. It was enough to see the concentration upon her countenance, the movement of her arm as she agitated her fingers against herself, the pouting of her lips, and, finally, the eruption of pleasure through her body. The sight of her had heated his blood, and he now viewed the remaining time with Miss Katherine rather as a form of agony. He was not likely to find relief soon enough.

Dragging his attention away from Miss Terrell, he looked upon Miss Katherine. A discernable flush covered her upper body, and she continued to gaze upon Miss Terrell with some awe. He had noticed that Miss Katherine had not looked away once while Miss Terrell fondled herself to spend.

"And now, Miss Terrell, you may attend Miss Katherine," he said.

This jolted Miss Katherine.

"M-Me?" she stammered, wide eyed. "N-No. That is unnecessary."

He walked over to the sideboard and found two scarves of red silk. "But why should Miss Terrell have all the pleasure?"

"But…what…"

"Would you rather pleasure yourself?"

"No, but—"

"Miss Terrell has a very adept tongue."

Her mouth fell open. "A *what*?"

Silk in hand, he returned to Miss Katherine. "I will bind your wrists to the chair."

She stared at him in disbelief.

"The bonds will allow you to enjoy what will happen," he explained.

"How?"

"Trust me. Idle hands are a distraction, lest you are confident you know what to do with them."

He began tying one of her wrists to an arm of the chair. Unable to speak, Miss Katherine could only watch as he bound one wrist, then the other. Done, he pulled out his handkerchief.

"And the deprivation of sight will enable you to focus upon the sense of pleasure."

Her voice quivered. "Deprivation…"

"What is your safety word?" he tasked her as he covered her eyes with the linen.

"J-Jean."

He secured the handkerchief at the back of her head. "And you will not hesitate to use it."

Straightening, he looked to Miss Terrell. She sauntered over and knelt before Miss Katherine. His pulse quickened, recalling how Miss Terrell had once applied her sumptuous mouth to Miss Greta.

"Worry not, Miss Katherine," said Miss Terrell. "I shall be gentle."

"P-Please," the viscountess pleaded, her body tense as a drawn bow.

"She will merely begin by caressing your legs," he said.

Miss Terrell reached beneath the hem of the skirts. Miss Katherine stiffened further. From the movement of the skirts, he could see that Miss Terrell caressed the length of Miss Katherine's calves.

Picking up *Fanny Hill* from where it rested upon her lap, he read from the excerpt Miss Katherine had recited.

As he read, he kept an eye upon Miss Terrell to see that the willing blackamoor did not rush her touch. Miss Terrell seemed to take into consideration Miss Katherine's reluctance and kept her hands no farther than the knees.

"Such soft and shapely legs you have, m'lady," Miss Terrell said.

Charles selected another passage from the novel. "'Her sturdy stallion had now unbuttoned, and produced naked, stiff and erect, that wonderful machine, which I had never seen before, and which, for the interest my own seat of pleasure began to take furiously in it, I stared at with all the eyes I had: however, my senses were too much flurried, too much concentered in that now burning spot of mine, to observe anything more than in general the make and turn of that instrument; from which the instinct of nature, yet more than all I had heard of it, now strongly informed me, I was to expect that supreme pleasure which she had placed in the meeting of those parts so admirably fitted for each other.'"

"Oh!" Miss Katherine gasped.

He looked to see that Miss Terrell had gone past a knee. The gown about Miss Katherine's thigh rustled with Miss Terrell's movements.

"How smooth and charming are the thighs," Miss Terrell murmured.

He imagined the deft and dark hands of Miss Terrell against the dove-white skin of Miss Katherine, whose complexion was as pale as an Oriental concubine's. The heat in his body rose, and he turned to the less provoking account of a fictional woman.

"'Long, however, the young spark did not remain before giving it two or three shakes, by way of brandishing it, he threw himself upon her, and his back being now towards me, I could only take his being ingulphed for granted, by the directions he moved in, and the impossibility of missing so staring a mark; and now the bed shook, the curtains rattled so that I could scarce hear the sighs and murmurs, the heaves and pantings that accompanied the action, from the beginning to the end; the sound and sight of which thrilled to the very soul of me, and made every vein of my body circulate liquid fires: the emotion grew so violent that it almost intercepted my respiration.'"

From the corners of his eyes, he could see that Miss Terrell had reached Miss Katherine's pelvis. Miss Katherine began to whimper.

"I only mean to touch the silky down gracing your temple of pleasure," Miss Terrell reassured.

"'Whilst they were in the heat of the action, guided by nature only, I stole my hand up my petticoats, and with fingers on fire, seized and yet more inflamed that center of all my senses: my heart palpitated, as if it would force its way through my bosom: I breathed with pain; I twisted my thighs, squeezed and compressed the lips of that virgin slit, and following mechanically the example of Phoebe's manual operation on it, as far as I could find admission, brought on at last the critical ecstasy, the melting flow, into which nature, spent with excess of pleasure, dissolves and dies away.'"

Miss Katherine groaned long and low. Miss Terrell must have gone past the patch of down. Miss Katherine twisted against her bonds.

"Shhhh," Miss Terrell gently hushed. "We have all of us a wanton spirit. Do not fear to allow it wings from time to time."

Once again, Charles found himself surprised by the quality of her speech, then remembered she had been a mistress of a gentleman, perhaps several. Her upbringing must have included an education.

Miss Katherine's breath grew erratic, sometimes

panting, sometimes sighing.

"Oh, what a charming creature thou art!" Miss Terrell remarked. "What a happy man his lordship must be to have made a woman of you."

Impressed by her memory and content to give the reins to her, he lowered the book to watch the two women.

"Oh, that I were a man for your sake!" Miss Terrell quoted.

His cock pulsed. At the Red Chrysanthemum, he had once beheld two women fucking. One had strapped a dildo to her pelvis and thrust into her mate as well as any man. It was one of the more memorable visions.

"Come share in my ecstasy," Miss Terrell coaxed. "Grant your body the reward it deserves."

Miss Terrell took Miss Katherine by the legs and pulled her farther down the chair. She pushed the skirts to the waist, spread the thighs, and nestled her face between them. Miss Katherine exclaimed as Miss Terrell licked her.

Charles had to look away to calm the surge of tension in his groin, but he could not resist for long. Turning back, he saw Miss Terrell move her tongue at the other woman's bud with the deftness of a finger. Miss Katherine squirmed and gasped. With whitened knuckles, she grasped the arms of the chair as Miss Terrell lapped at her with increased intensity.

The blood pounded in his head. He imagined taking a position behind Miss Terrell, throwing up her skirts, and indulging his own lust while she continued to pleasure Miss Katherine with that bold and naughty tongue.

"Oh! Oh!" Miss Katherine cried.

Her body jerked against the bonds, her feet scuffed the floor, and she mumbled several whimpers as tremors went through her body. With a sigh, she began to descend from her climax, and Miss Terrell slowed her tongue in unison. When Miss Terrell withdrew, Miss Katherine slumped in the chair, her head rolled to one side.

"She has a delightful quim," Miss Terrell said. A hand

of hers trailed down to cup her mound through her skirts.

He wondered how many women Miss Terrell had lain with. He liked women who could engage with their own sex. For a man, little could compare to the sight of two women pleasuring one another. When first he had learned that Greta, as Mistress Scarlet, had taken to women, he had been excited. But Greta did not truly appreciate the fair sex as Miss Terrell appeared to do. Far from being titillated by them, Greta sought women to punish them for the pain Master Damien had caused her when he had left her for another.

With her other hand, Miss Terrell caressed her bosom.

"Take care, Miss Terrell," he warned her.

Reluctantly, she dropped both hands to her sides.

"Untie Miss Katherine," he instructed.

She did as told. Miss Katherine sat upright and could not look Miss Terrell in the eye. Approaching Miss Katherine, he knelt before her.

"There is nothing more beautiful than a woman in rapture," he said. "You have done well, Miss Katherine. And for that, I forgive your error in spending without my permission."

"Oh," she gasped in dismay. "Your pardon."

"I think Lord Wendlesson would be proud."

Crimson colored her cheeks, but she appeared pleased.

"What think you for Mr. Cleland?" he asked.

"He has a talent with prose," she answered.

"We shall read from him again then."

There was a knock at the door, and a maid on the other side informed them that the viscount had arrived to take her ladyship home.

Charles extended a hand to Miss Katherine and assisted her to her feet. Miss Terrell assisted her with her articles.

He bowed over Miss Katherine's hand. "Till tomorrow night, Miss Katherine."

"Till tomorrow," she replied with eyes averted.

As he watched her depart, he took in a relieved breath.

He had not expected that Miss Katherine would submit herself as she had done, but, now that she had suffered the joy of *orgasmos*, the outlook was far more promising. The greater challenge this evening, then, lay in what to do with Miss Terrell.

# CHAPTER FOURTEEN

Master Gallant narrowed his eyes at Terrell. "I would take it kindly if you did not meddle in my affairs."

"Did I not benefit your instruction of Miss Katherine?" she returned, still standing beside the chair Miss Katherine had vacated. "Was I not an asset to you?"

He did not answer, which meant to her that he concurred.

"I should be happy to assist you tomorrow evening," she said with a pretty curl of her lips. Blessed with even, white teeth, she could make men pause to marvel at her smile.

His countenance darkened. "I am not interested in your assistance, Miss Terrell."

"No?" She dropped her gaze to his crotch. "Your cock would indicate otherwise."

He only stared at her, and she found she could not read his thoughts. She almost always knew what men thought. With her, they usually had but one matter on their mind. But she felt strangely tentative with Master Gallant. She had spent the last several years of her life flaunting her charms before his sex. She no longer feared rejection, even after receiving a bruised cheek from one man who did not appreciate her advances, for nothing could be worse than the life she once led as a slave in Barbados.

But with Master Gallant, she felt unsure of herself. Not relishing this uncomfortable sensation, she forced herself to find confidence.

She stepped toward him. "Did you approve of how I fondled myself?"

"My approval means nothing to you."

"You underestimate your opinion. I am quite curious to know what you thought as I pleasured myself."

She stood close enough to discern the movement of his chest as he breathed. As she gazed up at him, his eyes looked more grey than blue in the dim lighting of the room.

"I would do it again, if you would permit me," she said. "Master Gallant."

"Why should I reward your waywardness?"

"Then punish me. You have yet to address my earlier insubordination."

He crossed his arms, she suspected to keep her from coming too close. "I fully intend to take disciplinary actions. Leaving you tied to the rafters for half an hour was clearly insufficient. Shall we try an hour? Or should I have you exercise your arms further?"

She frowned. These were not the sorts of punishment she wanted, though she would gladly suffer them if she thought they would assure her access to him.

"Are you afraid to attempt a more wanton punishment?" she challenged.

"You wish your punishment to bear a lascivious quality."

"Indeed."

He grinned without curling the corners of his mouth. She studied his lips and found them to be of an agreeable fullness. She wanted to trace them with her tongue and taste him in her mouth.

Spotting the book, he went to it and picked it up. "You wish for a salacious punishment. Then you will read, starting with page one, till I tell you to stop."

Her dismay was as great as what Miss Katherine had evinced. His proposal was worse than the prospect of being tied up for an hour and left in solitude. She could not perform his directive.

She squared her shoulders. "No."

He raised his brows. "No?"

Her bottom lip quivered till she closed her mouth. She said nothing, pretending she did not see the book he held before her. Her chest constricted, and she felt an ugly awkwardness.

"Perhaps you forget that the submissive one takes orders from the dominant one," he said. "There is no option to decline."

"I would you render a different punishment."

"I have no wish to."

She saw that he was determined. As was she. For even if she wanted to do as he bid, she could not for the simple fact that she could not read.

"Then I will have to defy you once again," she said, "and you would owe me two punishments."

He stared at her in disbelief before glowering at her. "This is your game, then?"

"Perhaps you would find me more amenable if you agreed to take me as your submissive. For a mere sennight. I will not ask for more."

*But you will*, she could not resist thinking.

Unconvinced, he asked a question they both knew the answer to. "And Sir Arthur would agree to this?"

"Sir Arthur need not know."

"Artifice and deception are not my preferred activities. And you would be wise not to underestimate Sir Arthur."

"Leave Sir Arthur to me. I can keep him occupied well enough."

Seeing that he remained skeptical, she covered the small distance between them till her skirts brushed his legs. She softly grasped the lapels of his waistcoat. His nearness lit flames in her, and she hoped her presence might have a similar effect in him.

"What is it you fear, Master Gallant? Is it Sir Arthur? Or is it...me?"

He took her hands off of him and lowered them to her sides. "Sir Arthur and I must deal with one another outside the Red Chrysanthemum."

"He is a friend of yours?"

Her question seemed to displease him.

"Sir Arthur chairs a Parliamentary committee on Foreign Affairs. I work for the Secretary of State for Foreign Affairs."

He had not yet released her hands. His grip upon her made desire course more strongly through her, lending her courage. She fit her body to his, her bosom touching his chest. "I suppose I ought be pleased to know it is not me you fear."

He immediately dropped her hands and stepped away. "Perhaps it is I *you* should fear."

Watching him retrieve the silk he had used to bind Miss Katherine to the chair, her heart leaped in anticipation. At last!

"Come here," he commanded, moving to the foot of the bed.

She went to him with much eagerness. He held the book before her once more.

"Your last chance, Miss Terrell. Will you read?"

She shook her head. He tossed the book onto the bed, grabbed her left wrist and spun her around. Pinioning her wrists behind her, he tied them together with the silk. She yelped in surprise when he picked her up and pitched her onto the bed. He used the other silk to bind her ankles and, bending her legs behind her, secured her ankles to her wrists. She felt like an animal trussed for the spit and ready for roasting. Only an animal would not have its limbs bound behind it. Her heart hammered as she wondered what he would do next.

Picking up the chair with one hand, he set it nearer the

bed. He reached for the book and sat down. He flipped through several pages till he found one he liked. It was not quite what she had hoped for, but she liked the naughty prose of Mr. Cleland. She wriggled against her bonds, relishing her helplessness. And yet, she felt oddly safe.

"'The first that stood up, to open the ball, were a cornet of horse, and that sweetest of olive-beauties, the soft and amorous Louisa'," he read. "'He led her to the couch (nothing loth), on which he gave her the fall, and extended her at length with an air of roughness and vigour, relishing high of amorous eagerness and impatience. The girl, spreading herself to the best advantage, with her head upon the pillow, was so concentered in that she was about, that our presence was the least of her care and concern. Her petticoats, thrown up with her shift, discovered to the company the finest turned legs and thighs that could be imagined, and in broad display, that gave us a full view of that delicious cleft of flesh, into which the pleasing hair, grown mount over it, parted and presented a most inviting entrance, between two close hedges, delicately soft and pouting. Her gallant was now ready, having disencumbered himself from his clothes, overloaded with lace, and presently, his shirt removed, shewed us his forces at high plight, bandied and ready for action. But giving us no time to consider the dimensions, he threw himself instantly over his charming antagonist who received him as he pushed at once dead at mark, like a heroine, without flinching; for surely never was a girl constitutionally truer to the taste of joy, or sincerer in the expressions of its sensations, than she was: we could observe pleasure lighten in her eyes, as he introduced his plenipotentiary instrument into her; till, at length, having indulged her to its utmost reach, its irritations grew so violent, and gave her the spurs so furiously, that collected within herself, and lost to everything but the enjoyment of her favourite feelings, she retarded his thrusts with a just concert of spring heaves, keeping time so exactly with the most pathetic sighs, that one might have numbered the strokes in agitation by their distinct murmurs, whilst her active limbs kept wreathing and intertwisting with his, in convulsive folds: then the turtle-billing kisses, and the poignant painless lovebites, which they both exchanged, in a rage of delight, all conspiring towards the melting period.'"

He stopped to look at her. The scene he had painted with the words had warmed her. A new wetness began to flow between her legs. She could not discern if the reading aroused him similarly, but why would he bother with it if he would not be affected by it?

"Will you not by *my* gallant, Master *Gallant*?" she asked.

Unamused, he replied, "I did not give you leave to speak."

He returned to reading. "'Harriet was then led to the vacant couch by her gallant, blushing as she looked at me, and with eyes made to justify any thing, tenderly bespeaking of me the most favourable construction of the step she was thus irresistibly drawn into.

"'Her lover, for such he was, sat her down at the foot of the couch, and passing his arm round her neck, preluded with a kiss fervently applied to her lips, that visibly gave her life and spirit to go through with the scene; and as he kissed, he gently inclined her head, till it fell back on a pillow disposed to receive it, and leaning himself down all the way with her, at once countenanced and endeared her fall to her. There, as if he had guessed our wishes, or meant to gratify at once his pleasure and his pride, in being the master, by the title of present possession, of beauties delicate beyond imagination, he discovered her breast to his own touch, and our common view; but oh! what delicious manual of love devotion; how inimitable fine moulded! small, round, firm, and excellently white; then the grain of their skin, so soothing, so flattering to the touch! and of beauty. When he had feasted his eyes with the nipples that crowned them, the sweetest buds touch and perusal, feasted his lips with kisses of the highest relish, imprinted on those all delicious twin-orbs, he proceeded downwards.'"

By now the licentious passage had enflamed her whole body. Terrell grew weary of lying on the bed, bound and unable to touch herself, to address the pining in her loins. Why did he not touch her by now? Surely he did not plan to read much more?

"Permission to speak, Master," she said.

He eyed her carefully before answering, "Granted."

"You read exceptionally well, but will it not be more enjoyable to perform the scenes you read?"

"The author has stirred your eros, Miss Terrell?"

"Very much," she acknowledge in a husky contralto.

He said nothing at first, then returned to the book. "'Her legs still kept the ground; and now, with the tenderest attention not to shock or alarm her too suddenly, he, by degrees, rather stole than rolled up her petticoats; at which, as if a signal had been given, Louisa and Emily took hold of her legs, in pure wantonness, and, in ease to her, kept them stretched wide abroad. Then lay exposed, or, to speak more properly, displayed the greatest parade in nature of female charms. The whole company, who, except myself, had often seen them, seemed as much dazzled, surprised and delighted, as any one could be who had now beheld them for the first time. Beauties so excessive could not but enjoy the privileges of eternal novelty. Her thighs were so exquisitely fashioned, that either more in, or more out of flesh than they were, they would have declined from that point of perfection they presented. But what infinitely enriched and adorned them, was the sweet intersection formed, where they met, at the bottom of the smoothest, roundest, whitest belly, by that central furrow which nature had sunk there, between the soft relievo of two pouting ridges, and which, in this girl, was in perfect symmetry of delicacy and miniature with the rest of her frame. No! nothing in nature could be of a beautifuller cut; then, the dark umbrage of the downy spring moss that over-arched it, bestowed, on the luxury of the landscape, a touching warmth, a tender finishing, beyond the expression of words, or even the paint of thought.'"

She could hardly believe it. Was it truly possible that he intended to do nothing but read? Tethered and unable to move off the bed, she could not employ her body to seduce him. She was truly helpless, deprived the use of her greatest weapon.

"Permission to speak, Master," she requested with mounting desperation.

"Denied," he said before returning to read. "'Her truly enamoured gallant, who had stood absorbed and engrossed by the pleasure of the sight long enough to afford us time to feast ours (no fear of glutting!) addressed himself at length to the materials of enjoyment, and lifting the linen veil that hung between us and his master member of the revels, exhibited one whose eminent size proclaimed the owner a true woman's hero.'"

She barely heard the words. She wanted to scream. Perhaps she would.

"I know you capable of more than words," she said.

He gave her a sharp look. "Do not test me, Miss Terrell, or I will have a word with Sir Arthur."

She swallowed the rest of her statement. She could not afford to vex Sir Arthur. She needed the money. Would Gallant truly tell on her?

More astonishingly, did he truly not wish to fuck her?

He continued to read. "'Standing then between Harriet's legs, which were supported by her two companions at their widest extension, with one hand he gently disclosed the lips of that luscious mouth of nature, whilst with the other, he stooped his mighty machine to its lure, from the height of his stiff stand-up towards his belly; the lips, kept open by his fingers, received its broad shelving head of coral hue: and when he had nestled it in, he hovered there a little, and the girls then delivered over to his hips the agreeable office of supporting her thighs; and now, as if he meant to spin out his pleasure, and give it the more play for its life, he passed up his instrument so slow that we lost sight of it inch by inch, till at length it was wholly taken into the soft laboratory of love, and the mossy mounts of each fairly met together."'

She moaned in desire, frustration and despair.

"'It came on at length: the baronet led the ectasy, which she critically joined in, as she felt the melting symptoms from him, in the nick of which, gluing more ardently than ever his lips to hers, he shewed all the signs of that agony of bliss being strong upon him, in which he gave her the finishing titillation;,we saw plainly that she answered it down with all effusion of spirit and matter she was mistress of, whilst a general soft shudder ran through all her limbs, which she gave a stretch out, and lay motionless, breathless, dying with dear delight; and in the height of its expression, showing, through the nearly closed lids of her eyes, just the edges of their black, the rest being rolled strongly upwards in their ectasy; then her sweet mouth appeared languish-ingly open, with the tip of her tongue leaning negligently towards the lower range of her white teeth, whilst natural ruby color of her lips glowed with heightened life. Was not this a subject to dwell upon? And accordingly her lover still kept on her, with an abiding delectation, till compressed, squeezed and distilled to the last drop, he took leave with one fervent kiss, expressing satisfied desires, but unextinguished love."'

Gallant snapped the book shut. Terrell was softly panting, for she had struggled throughout his reading to free herself from the silk ties, but she could only roll and toss upon the bed, unable to relieve the awkward position the bonds had forced upon her body. The salacious descriptions, enflaming her imagination, served only to torture her body. Lust, curling and writhing inside of her, needed release, or some acknowledgement at least.

Rising to his feet, Gallant approached the bed and

untied the silk from her. She groaned in relief to have the freedom of her limbs in front of her.

"You are free to go, Miss Terrell," he said, his tone still stern.

Flabbergasted, she did not move. That was all he intended to do with her? He had her bound upon the bed, vulnerable and available to do as he wished, and all he planned was to read from that bloody book? Others of his sex would have paid—*did* pay—a good guinea to have their way with her.

"Good night," he bid her as he opened the door.

In disbelief, she watched him depart. What manner of man was he? *Was* he man? He could not be if he could refuse himself such ready and waiting pleasure as she offered. Did he not desire her enough because she was a blackamoor?

Pressing her lips together, she went after him.

"Master Gallant!"

He was descending the stairs and did not stop.

"We are done, Miss Terrell," he said without looking back at her.

She followed him, matching his quick pace. "I was mistaken."

This caused him to pause. She caught up and stepped in front of him.

"I accept your apology," he said, "and pray you will henceforth pay me no further heed."

She responded with a toss of her head. "You'll have no apology from me, lest you beat it out of me."

His eyes widened.

"I was mistaken," she continued, "when I thought you did not fear me, but I think you do. I think you do fear me, Master Gallant. Perhaps you fear that once you have tasted of dark flesh, you will only want for more. Or perhaps you fear, with me, you will be tempted to unleash your darkest, most wicked nature."

A muscle rippled along his jaw. "Miss Terrell! Do you

think Madame Devereux would approve of your mischief if she knew of it?"

"She does well by me. She will not cast me out."

"What of Sir Arthur? He undoubtedly pays a pretty price for your favors."

"I am woman enough for two men."

He drew himself closer to her and lowered his voice. "And what makes you think I would desire cunnie that has been used by another?"

If she were a young woman of polite society, she would have slapped him across the face for his insolence. Her hand itched to do just that. But she was not a gentlewoman. She was a whore. That was what he intended to say. His words stung because she knew, no matter how she improved herself, even if she gave up the Red Chrysanthemum and devoted herself to the manner and behaviors of superior society, as she had once attempted to do with all her might, she would never belong. But mostly, the words stung because they came from him.

Her reaction seemed to rattle him, for he straightened and looked ill at ease.

"Forgive me," he said. "I spoke harshly, but you understand—"

"Miss Terrell!"

They both whipped around to see Sir Arthur now stood in the hallway with them.

"Your pardon," he said upon seeing Gallant. He looked to Terrell, then back at Gallant. "Do I intrude?"

"Not at all, Sir Arthur," said Gallant. "Miss Terrell had been assisting a patron of mine, and I was merely informing Miss Terrell that her services will no longer be needed."

With a bow, Gallant took his leave.

"Assistance?" Sir Arthur echoed once they were alone. "I do not recall approving any extraneous activities."

"You made no prohibitions, Sir Arthur," Terrell

replied. "And if you had seen the poor wretch, frightened as she was, you would not have denied her. You seem to me a man of great generosity. You would have done all in your power to aid her."

Sir Arthur appeared partly mollified. "Nevertheless, I will require you to seek my permission from now on."

He looked down the hall as if expecting Gallant to reappear. She recaptured his attention by approaching him. She played with his cravat as if to straighten it.

"Did you forget something, Sir Arthur?"

He looked down at her, hunger flashing in his cold grey eyes. "I wished to collect upon the 'encore' you promised me."

# CHAPTER FIFTEEN

*Charles strained against the iron shackles pulling his wrists to the bedposts. He knew not how his bed came to have shackles, nor where his clothes had gone. He was naked but for the rumpled bed linen covering his waist and the length of one leg. The moon, still at its zenith, shone brightly in the sky, but it felt as if an eternity had passed. The moonlight bathed a path from the window to the bed. He did not remember having left the curtains open and yanked once more against the shackles.*

*"You'll be wanting this."*

*His gaze darted to the door. Where had she come from? How had she gotten in? The woman emerged from the shadows, revealing herself to be more naked than he. She had not a shred of clothing, and though he could not make out her form perfectly, the blood rushed to his cock, responding to the swell of her hips, her supple thighs and rounded breasts.*

*He needed the key she held. Knowing this, her lips curled into a half-smile. She advanced toward the bed, the movement of her hips and thighs hypnotic. Standing at the foot of the bed, she allowed him to drink in her nakedness. With her darkness, she might have blended into the night if not for the moonlight.*

*"The key is yours if you can earn it."*

*"How?" he asked.*

*Her gaze fell to where his cock tented the bedclothes. "Ravage me."*

*"Gladly," he found himself saying, to his own surprise. His cock throbbed. "But I cannot while shackled to the bed."*

*"I think you can."*

*Dropping the key, she crawled onto the bed, her movements like that of a preying panther. He tensed. Despite his prior acknowledgement, he was not prepared to fuck. Not yet. Not while he was helpless. He would not be the one ravaging so much as she.*

*Her smile broadened as if she were aware of his thoughts. She hovered above him on hands and knees, her breasts swaying. She lowered herself to kiss him. He turned his head away.*

*No. He had merely tried to turn his head away and found he could not move. Her mouth captured his, her lips full and succulent. His head swam, his body warming despite his inability to do anything but submit to her. With her lips still locked to his, she reached for the bedclothes and pulled the sheet down, exposing his rigid member. She wrapped a hand about him. His protests were muffled by the kissing, but his pelvis reacted differently and yearned toward her.*

*Releasing his mouth, she positioned her hips above his, straddling him as she rested upon her haunches. The hairs of her mound tickled his cock. She ground herself at his cods.*

*"Wait," he protested.*

*But she ignored him. In one quick movement, she raised herself and sheathed his cock. He roared as her wet heat threatened to engulf his whole body. He tried to buck her off of him, but the effort only angered her. She slapped him hard across the face.*

*Stunned, he paused. She took the opportunity to pump herself up and down his length. He groaned. He could not resist the pleasure building inside of him. Soon he found himself thrusting in rhythm to her motions, wanting to drive himself deeper and deeper into her. If his hands were not shackled to the bedposts, he would hold her about the waist so that he could ram his cock deep enough for her to feel him in her throat.*

*She emitted cries of delight as she took him, riding his cock as slow or as fast as she wanted, using him for her pleasure. A small part of him resisted the ravishing, but his body surrendered. It was no match against her, and his cock erupted against his will.*

*No defeat had ever felt so divine.*

*He knew not if she had spent. When he opened his eyes, he only noted her victorious smile. His gaze then went past her…*

*With a start, he realized Miss Greta stood upon the threshold, a frown gracing her countenance as she stared at the scene before her. He tried to explain the situation, but she had whirled upon her heels and left, taking with her the key.*

Charles woke with a gasp. Staring into the darkness, he blinked until he saw that he was still in his own chambers, alone. The curtains were drawn, and only a thin sliver of dawn shown between them. The bedclothes near his groin were wet and a viscous fluid clung to his cock. He shook his head as if to discard the remnants of the dream. After wiping himself, he threw back the linen and got out of bed. At the basin atop the sideboard, he splashed a plentiful amount of water onto his face.

Drying himself, he went to open the curtains. He looked out at the empty square below. A busy day of meetings with prospective supporters awaited him, and he was glad for it. He was eager to begin campaigning rigorously, especially now that he did not expect to see Miss Greta for some time, if ever.

He considered sending another request to the Brentwoods. If he could attain their support, he would not need to rely upon Sir Arthur, though he had assured Sir Canning that he would do nothing further to discourage Sir Arthur from backing his candidacy.

"The man can do much for your career," Sir Canning had said, "and he is partial to doing so because of your shared interest in China."

"But we differ in approach," Charles had replied. "Sir Arthur would impose trade upon China by brute force."

"The Company would not take such drastic measures without the approbation of Crown or Parliament. But I do wonder what can compel China, if not force? The Dutch have been exceedingly conciliatory in their approach. I understand they do not hesitate to bow to the ground before the emperor, yet the treatment they receive is no different than ours."

"I confess Sir Arthur's character concerns me as well. I do not recall the rumors as it was years before I had ever met the man, but—"

"There is always gossip with Members of Parliament," Canning had dismissed.

Charles had tried to recall the details. "It concerned his wife."

"And thus has no bearing upon political concerns, and it is that which matters. His personal affairs are irrelevant."

Charles had granted his employer the truth of this last statement. He hoped that he had not aroused Sir Arthur's suspicions last night. The man was unlikely to have heard the exchange between Miss Terrell and himself, but Sir Arthur did not look pleased that they even occupied the same place.

Recalling his words to Miss Terrell last night, Charles winced. Her eyes had betrayed some pain. But it needed saying, though his statement was less true than her accusations. Her words still rang in his ears.

*You fear that once you have tasted of dark flesh, you will only want for more. You fear, with me, you will be tempted to unleash your darkest, most wicked nature.*

He needed to stop her. She was far too persistent. She needed a set-down or a healthy dose of fear. The woman was obstinate and foolhardy. Or steadfast and intrepid. Reading the passages from *Fanny Hill* had been no easy task. Of course he would have liked to enact the debauchery described. But Miss Terrell was the last person he would permit himself to engage with. He ought not even dream of such a thing.

# CHAPTER SIXTEEN

"**I**f you behave, I will refrain from tying you to the chair once more," Terrell said.

"Impudent trollop," Sir Arthur replied but complied by taking the chair he had sat in yesterday.

"Have I not always made it worth your while?"

He smiled as far as his thin lips would allow. "Will I be favored with the same encore?"

"If you behave," she answered with a coy smile. It never ceased to amaze her how enamored his sex could be of her cock-sucking. She had taken him into her mouth last night in the very same room they occupied now. When she had drawn his member into her throat, he had gasped as if confronted with the vision of death. Eyes wide, he had watched in awe as she swallowed him. Then, after she had suckled him in earnest, he had bucked his hips ravenously at her. His seed had tasted quite brackish, but she had triumphed at making him spend with such ease.

"And what does my minx have in store for me today?" Sir Arthur asked, watching as she shifted the angle of the sofa so that he could view its length fully.

"A surprise."

Sir Arthur surveyed her from head to toe. "Do you not have other attire?"

She glanced down at the corset and petticoats she had

worn yesterday. "I changed my shift."

"When I keep a mistress, she is dressed in the finest fashions."

"Indeed?" Terrell responded with interest. She sat at his feet and crossed her arms over his lap. "And what qualities recommend themselves as your mistress?"

"She must be faithful. I will not be made a cuckold."

His eyes had darkened, and his lips closed into a stern line, but she chose to challenge him. "A wife makes a cuckold. A mistress is not a wife."

"If a woman accepts my coin, I expect she will be constant."

He spoke with such emphasis that she wondered if he meant to warn her.

"What else?" she asked.

"She must be pretty, of course."

"With your affluence, you could afford a harem of pretty wenches."

"I could, but I am not a greedy man. One wench is sufficient for me."

"But you would not complain of two?"

He raised his brows as a knock sounded at the door. She rose to allow entry to Miss Isabella, a member of the Red Chrysanthemum. A Spanish beauty, Isabella had long, straight tresses, dark striking brows and an olive complexion. Over thirty years in age, she had a full figure with rounded hips undisguised by the vertical drape of her gown. Terrell and Miss Isabella had been asked by Master Gallant to attend Mistress Scarlet during the display in which Terrell had found him so compelling.

"May I present Miss Isabella," Terrell introduced.

Sir Arthur appeared intrigued. Miss Isabella stood before him and curtsied.

"I've another performance I think you'll enjoy," said Terrell.

She stood behind Miss Isabella and began to unpin her frock. Sir Arthur leaned back in his chair, placed the walking stick aside, and joined his hands in a steeple. Miss Isabella stepped from her gown, which pooled upon the ground. Terrell untied the petticoat while Miss Isabella unpinned her own hair, a shade lighter than Terrell's and possessed of a silken gleam. Standing behind Miss Isabella, Terrell caressed the woman's bosom through her stays and shift, then trailed her hands down the midsection to rest upon the belly before gripping the hips. Sir Arthur grunted.

With Miss Isabella undressed to her shift, stays and stockings, Terrell pulled her onto the sofa. The two women sat facing each other and kissed, soft lips against soft lips. Terrell enjoyed the delicate qualities of her own sex, and this was not her first encounter with Miss Isabella. The two had fondled each other in their corner of the stage when Master Gallant had turned his full attention to Mistress Scarlet, the main presentation. Ardor fanned through her loins as Terrell recalled how Master Gallant had instructed her to tie Mistress Scarlet to the table and invited the audience to touch and inspect the redhead.

Terrell still marveled that Mistress Scarlet had acquiesced to the submissive behavior. In all the time Terrell had known the woman, Mistress Scarlet had always carried herself as a dominant and shown no interest in the other sex. How Master Gallant had managed to command the imperial Mistress' submission intrigued Terrell.

She kissed Miss Isabella with greater fervor as she replayed the scene between Master Gallant and Mistress Scarlet, whom he had bent over a table. He had inserted a pair of silver balls into her cunnie earlier. They seemed to agitate her, for her brow had furrowed often once they were inside. What were they? Terrell had meant to ask Mistress Scarlet, but the woman had disappeared without word. Even Madame did not know where or why. Terrell suspected the sudden departure of Mistress Scarlet related to Master Gallant somehow, but she could not understand why Mistress Scarlet would leave a man who could elicit such pleasure.

"Beg to spend, Mistress Scarlet," Master Gallant had instructed.

Terrell remembered the woman had appeared to resist, as if she did not wish to spend, but it was plain that her body desired to, was tortured by its denial. Had Mistress Scarlet possessed too much pride to beg? And how had she managed to forbear his beautiful thrusting and his fingers at her clit? Terrell would have given much to have Master Gallant's cock in *her*, and had even offered to beg on behalf of Mistress Scarlet, that the latter might know relief and the divine ecstasy that awaited her.

In the end, Mistress Scarlet had surrendered. It was folly not to. Her pleas to Master Gallant were barely above a whisper, but Terrell had seen the movement of the lips and knew the words that she would have longed to say to Master Gallant. He had obliged then, grinding Mistress Scarlet into the table as he plunged himself into her, sending her into that rapturous paroxysm.

A gentle applause from the audience had followed. Too distracted by her own unmet cravings, Terrell had not applauded, but she had meant to. Beyond doubt, the man deserved approbation. Terrell had never before seen such an elegant display of dominance.

Brought to the present by Miss Isabella, who planted kisses upon her neck and décolletage, Terrell unlaced the stays before her and pulled down the shift to expose two heavy orbs. From the sides of her eyes, she saw Sir Arthur sit at attention. She fondled the breasts, finding them quite lovely to behold and to touch. They were malleable, and Terrell pushed them up high to take a nipple into her mouth. Leaning back to allow Terrell greater access, Miss Isabella gasped and groaned as Terrell swirled her tongue about the pointed bud.

As a young adolescent blossoming into womanhood, Terrell had discovered the marvel of spending by attending to that small bud of flesh between her thighs. Her breasts grown, she had often touched herself there as well, relishing how her nipples seemed to feed the sensations swirling below her navel. She had been more than curious about the opposite sex. One strapping Negro in particular had caught her attention. Despite the exhaustion of toiling in the fields, they had managed to find energy enough to grope and fondle each other beneath the bearded figs.

The thought that her kind might desire to engage in similar fashion with a man *not* of her kind did not immediately enter into mind. She had felt the leer of white men as young as ten years of age, had seen their kind put unwanted hands upon many a Negress. But it was not until she had befriended Miss Ruth that a new world opened to her.

Hearing sounds coming from one of the equipment sheds one day, she had peered through a dusty window and was astounded to see a Negress upon her knees, sucking the cock of none other than the owner's son! After much grunting and a few bucks of the hips, he had replaced his fall and left.

Terrell looked upon the Negress, who rose to her feet and wiped her mouth as if nothing were amiss. Miss Ruth did not work in the fields but in the Great House. Dressed in white muslin, petticoats, and new slippers, she appeared to Terrell as a princess.

Miss Ruth saw Terrell through the window before the latter had a chance to move. She laughed.

When she had come out, Terrell had not moved from her spot. She wanted to understand what it was Miss Ruth had done and why. The Negress had seemed to *enjoy* the act. Terrell had only seen women cringe or on the verge of tears when touched by a white man. Miss Ruth crossed her arms and leaned against the corner of the shed. Terrell thought Miss Ruth, ten years her senior, the prettiest blackamoor she had ever seen.

"Why such a dumb look upon you, girl?" Miss Ruth smirked.

Terrell took several seconds to find her tongue but finally asked, "Ain't you afeared?"

"Afeared of what?"

"What you done, be that—be that allowed?"

Miss Ruth laughed. "When the master demands it, you best satisfy."

"It don't trouble you none?"

"Trouble me? Look at me, and look at you, girl."

Miss Terrell looked down at her bare feet and the dirt stains upon her old, tattered garments.

"You're pretty enough, though," Miss Ruth said. "You behave yourself, you might earn your way out of the fields and into the Great House, as I have done."

After that, Ruth had taken an interest in Terrell and assumed the mantle of a mentor. Terrell learned how to appreciate the other sex, men of the white variety, because of what they could provide: better shelter, clothing and food. Life in the Great House was infinitely better than slaving in the fields.

After suckling Miss Isabella's teats, Terrell returned to kissing her mouth. Lying back, Terrell pulled Isabella down atop her. She knew that the vision of two women lying together, bosom to bosom, pelvis to pelvis, could not fail to titillate the man.

Sir Arthur stroked himself as he watched the women caress each other, writhing body to writhing body, tongues intertwining, moans muffled between the soft smacking of lips. Miss Isabella cupped her neck and playfully tugged upon Terrell's bottom lip, but Terrell, aroused from her earlier reverie of Master Gallant, wanted more. Threading her fingers into Miss Isabella's hair, she brought Isabella's mouth down harder upon her own. They ground their hips together as if one of them might be in possession of a cock.

Not content to remain the lone audience member, Sir Arthur rose from his chair and approached the sofa. Terrell groped Miss Isabella behind the thighs and about the buttocks. Sir Arthur unbuttoned his fall and positioned himself behind Miss Isabella. He threw her shift up over her waist, and Terrell found herself caressing bare flesh. She pried apart the buttocks. Miss Isabella arched herself to further provide him access to her cunnie and moaned when he sank his length into her.

Terrell found Miss Isabella's pleasure bud. Her fingers brushed against cock whenever Sir Arthur pulled out. As the angle of penetration was difficult, his member would occasionally pop out. Terrell would glide his cock back into its proper place. Soon, he began thrusting in earnest. She caught his stare a number of times, the look upon his countenance leaving no doubt as to whom he would rather be inside of.

With a cock in her cunnie and Terrell fondling her clit, Isabella began riding the wave of ecstasy. Her body trembled between them. Sir Arthur pumped his hips into Miss Isabella before finding his own release. He grunted several times before disengaging from Isabella with a shudder and stumbling back into his chair.

Knowing that Terrell had not spent, Miss Isabella reached to pull up her skirts to provide some much needed attention to her neglected cunnie. But Terrell shook her head.

She was saving herself for Master Gallant.

# CHAPTER SEVENTEEN

"**D**o you suppose Master Gallant awaits the return of Mistress Scarlet?" Terrell asked Sarah as the latter prepared for another evening with Captain Gracechurch.

Little George, sitting upon his mother's bed, giggled as Terrell hid behind a handkerchief, then emerged with widened eyes and her mouth agape.

"Madame does not think Mistress Scarlet will return," Sarah replied as she undressed from her gown and petticoats.

"Mistress Scarlet did not seem much inclined to talk of Master Gallant," Terrell recalled. "I wonder what manner of relationship they had, she being a dominant as well as he—ah!"

George had grabbed a fistful of her hair.

Sarah shrugged. "Perhaps they took turns."

Terrell dwelled upon the statement with interest as she tried to extract her hair from the little boy's surprisingly strong grip. Mistress Scarlet had been one of the most dominating women at the Red Chrysanthemum. It had been quite astonishing to see her submitting to another, but it was hard to believe that the woman would shed her mantle as Mistress Scarlet completely. Did Master Gallant enjoy women who could occupy both the submissive as well as the dominant role?

George yanked harder, letting go when Terrell tickled him.

"I have something better for you to handle," she told him and retrieved a little wooden horse, brightly painted with an assortment of hues, from beneath her cot.

Sarah gasped. "Terrell, it's beautiful. But...how did you come by it?"

"I took a stroll about St. James's this morning, and an old man was there peddling the figurines. I watched him paint one, and it was no easy feat as his aged hands shook considerably."

George promptly put the horse in his mouth.

"None of that, Georgie," his mother admonished. "You are too old to be putting such things in your mouth"

George removed the toy and banged it upon the wall.

"Georgie!"

Terrell laughed. "Leave him be."

"But it surely cost you a pretty penny and you are not in the habit of making extravagant purchases."

"It pleased me to buy it," she said, seeing that Sarah still had doubts. "The old man reminded me of a Negro who fashioned very similar toys and sold them on the streets of Bridgetown. He was quite fortunate to have had such skills. Most slaves, when they are too old to serve a useful purpose, are banished from the plantations to fend for themselves."

Terrell did not mention that one plantation owner simply threw his aged slaves off a cliff.

She sat behind Sarah upon the bed to assist with the stays. George knocked the horse against the wall several more times till the head came off.

"Oh, dear!" Sarah exclaimed, going over and taking the parts. "I worried of this! I pray it can be mended."

"If it cannot, I am certain the old man will be there tomorrow."

"No, no. I know how parsimonious you are with your

funds."

"You and Georgie bring me such joy, the expense is nothing."

Sarah sat down again, and Terrell continued unlacing the ribbons. She had vowed, when she had been cast off by Sir Fairchild, that she would not take money for granted ever again. She would not be without funds when old age claimed her. She would not be one of the sad and desperate blackamoors, many of them granted their manumission in the final years of their lives, begging on the streets for scraps of food. Nothing could be worse than the bondage imposed upon her people, but starvation came close.

"Georgie is a strong little fellow," she commented to Sarah. "Was his father quite muscular?"

Sarah lowered her eyes. "I had little interaction with him. I think, from the few times he did join my bed, that he was more brawny than I expected. I saw him clothed most of the time."

"Sir Arthur is similar, much stronger than his outward appearance suggests," Terrell noted as she undid Sarah's ribbons.

"I would not pay Master Gallant too much attention while Sir Arthur seeks your favors," Sarah cautioned.

"You know Sir Arthur?"

"I am a little acquainted with him, and remember well a garden party we had both attended. I had ventured far into the gardens and was admiring the irises when I heard a young man and a woman in the gazebo behind me. They had taken no notice of me because a row of small trees separated us. The man introduced himself and remarked upon the various flora. A moment later, I heard another man come upon them, Sir Arthur. The woman cried out, and I heard the young man say, 'Pray, Sir! I think you hurt her!' Sir Arthur replied, 'You need not interfere. She is my wife.' I looked through the hedges to see Sir Arthur dragging his wife away by her wrist.

"We were all joined at the tables for tea later, and the woman who was Sir Arthur's wife spoke not a word the entire time. Sir Arthur glared a great deal at the young man from the gazebo. I thought Sir Arthur would very much like to have killed the man. I noticed quite the dark bruise upon the wife's wrist."

"Perhaps Sir Arthur feared his wife intended to make of him a cuckold."

"Perhaps. I did see his wife on one other occasion. We happened to pass each other in a posting inn, for I was returning to London while she was headed to Bath. Her pomade and powder failed to conceal the bruises upon her cheek and her neck. I attempted to introduce myself once again, but she had no obvious desire to converse. She looked quite the forlorn creature. I could not help but feel sorry for her. I would take great care with Sir Arthur. He seems the temperamental sort."

"He would not be the first such man I have had at the Red Chrysanthemum. Is he indeed wealthy? He appears so, but I know that many a gentleman can style themselves in affluence and few would suspect that they carried great amounts of debt."

"I believe Sir Arthur need never worry of debt. His fortunes from the East India Company are vast."

Terrell let out a contented breath, pleased by the confirmation.

Sarah seemed to know her thoughts. "Nonetheless, I would accept his coin with caution. When I learned his wife passed away, I could not help but wonder—"

"He is a widower? Has he ever taken a mistress?"

"I know not. My time in that society, as you know, was cut short."

Sarah allowed her shift to fall from her shoulders to her waist. Terrell looked in awe at the beautiful expanse of skin exposed to her. Her ladyship possessed a most beautiful back with nary a blemish. Despite having born a child, she had resumed her youthful figure, and her back had the perfect amount of flesh about two elegant shoulder blades. Terrell wanted to run her hand upon such smooth loveliness. She had once possessed such perfection. What she now had she hid from everyone, except Sarah.

George, wanting attention, emitted a squeal. Sarah picked him up and wiggled her nose at his belly. The little child laughed in glee.

"I shall not mourn the life I once had as long as I have him," Sarah said as she embraced George to her.

Terrell looked upon them, marveling that the love for a child could provide such fulfillment. "As I cannot have such a treasure of mine own, I am content to crave the society you left behind."

"And you think Sir Arthur would provide you passage?"

"If he would take a blackamoor for a mistress."

Sarah made no comment. Perhaps she did not think Sir Arthur would. Or perhaps she did not agree with Terrell's stratagem. A Negress, however, had few options. If she wished to attain the better comforts of life and secure enough funds to provide for herself in later years when youth and beauty would no longer serve, Sir Arthur was her most promising prospect at the moment.

"Do you expect Sir Arthur tonight?" Sarah asked, setting George back down and replacing her old shift with a fresh one.

"He has come and gone, a happy patron," Terrell replied, recalling his improved affability and the gleam in his eyes as he bid her and Miss Isabella adieu. He had promised to call upon her tomorrow at the same hour.

"Mrs. Hartshorn is to watch George, but I am certain he would prefer you if you are free."

"I would, m'lady, but I expect Master Gallant tonight."

"What is it you intend with Master Gallant?"

"I have not yet decided."

As she helped lace Sarah's better stays, stays that made the bosom swell high above the décolletage, she thought once more of Mistress Scarlet. Till Master Gallant's return, Mistress Scarlet had been one of the more senior members, but his early years at the Red Chrysanthemum must have overlapped with hers. No one else, save Madame herself, knew of any history between the two.

"You said he rebuffed you twice?"

"I know there to be men who would never touch black flesh, but I do not think Master Gallant indifferent."

Sarah raised her brows. "You are certain of this?"

Looking down in thought, Terrell replayed her various encounters with him. She had never doubted herself before, but she had to admit to being baffled by Master Gallant. Why was he so devilishly hard to seduce? If she were to prostrate herself, naked, upon the bed, she could not be certain that he would not turn away and walk out the door. But she had seen the tenting at his crotch when she had serviced Miss Katherine. And, though she could not elucidate the evidence of his desire, she had *sensed* it.

Admittedly, her pride had taken quite the blow when he had chosen to do nothing more than read to her last night. Sir Arthur had benefited from her unleashed arousal, but her frustration had continued long into the night, leading her to toss about her bed. She did not understand why she desired Master Gallant with such desperation, why she could not oust him from her mind and simply turn her attentions elsewhere. His aura remained pregnant in her body, and she believed she would know no relief till he had claimed her.

But how could she accomplish this? Perhaps she had not been bold enough. Because he had made her doubt herself. Well, she refused to be intimidated by him, by any man.

At last, she looked up at Sarah and replied, "I am certain, and I mean to make that certainty known to him."

# CHAPTER EIGHTEEN

**"I** should be pleased to support you," said Mr. Dempsey to Charles. "I supported your father in each of his elections, and my father supported your grandfather in his. It was disappointing that neither did win. But have you approached Sir Arthur? He owns half of Porter's Hill and talks much of razing the older buildings to develop a new square. His plans seem rather grandiose and the cost staggering, but he projects the returns to exceed our investment tenfold or more."

The two men sat in the drawing room of the elderly gentleman. They were joined by Mrs. Dempsey and Miss Bridget Dempsey, who sat beside her mother knitting a purse. Throughout dinner, Mrs. Dempsey had smiled often at Charles and attempted to encourage discourse between him and the daughter. Charles obliged as much as he could, and they traversed the usual benign and trite subject matters of weather, the coming Season, what shows Drury Lane might reprise, etc.

Miss Dempsey reminded him of Greta as they both had reddish hair. A few years younger, Miss Dempsey had a mix of flaxen in her shinier curls and more curves in her form. Given her station in life, Miss Dempsey was a much more suitable match for him, were he in the market for a wife. The daughter of a humble apothecary, Greta had little to recommend herself on the surface, but Charles saw intelligence and spirit. While Miss Dempsey exhibited all the proper manners, spoke French to perfection, and danced elegantly in the quadrille, he discerned no passion in her. Born into comfort and undoubtedly doted upon as the only daughter, she showed little interest in anything beyond what might be featured in *The Lady's Magazine.*

Charles knew his mother to be eager to see him settled. Many a promising maiden had come his way. But if he married, he would have to forsake the Red Chrysanthemum. He was not prepared to do so.

"Sir Arthur owns less than half," Charles corrected.

"Nearly half," Mr. Dempsey replied. "Given the support you have already, Sir Arthur can assure you victory. I do not doubt that he would compel his tenants to vote according to his wishes. I will endeavor my best with the tenants in my burgage, but I do not think I can guarantee their presence at the polls as well as he."

"I understand Sir Arthur's support would ease my path, but I intend to seek votes wherever I can have them."

"But why make your life more difficult, young man?"

"I do not wish to take any circumstance for granted, but it is possible to win without Sir Arthur."

"I suppose it is mathematically possible, but in truth, not probable."

"The Brentwoods—Mrs. Brentwood, in particular— have swayed many an election."

"And have you their endorsement?"

Charles thought of Viscount Wendlesson, whose wife he was to meet in a few hours. "I hope to."

Sensing a lull in the discourse, Mrs. Dempsey said, "I hope you gentlemen will now consider a topic in which we ladies might also engage."

A recommendation to which Mr. Dempsey responded as an opportunity to obtain for himself a glass of port, leaving Charles to oblige Mrs. Dempsey and Miss Dempsey. Both ladies expressed a great desire for the

Season to start. The city was rather dull this time of year. Mr. Dempsey participated in the conversation only to remark upon the superior hunting to be had in the country, but Mrs. Dempsey abhorred traveling. She and Miss Dempsey went through their expectations of which young women might have their come-out, whose banns might be announced before the end of the Season, and if so-and-so might bring charges of criminal conversation against his wife.

Charles did his best to follow along but was much relieved when the evening drew to a close and he could be upon his horse headed to the Inn of the Red Chrysanthemum. Along the way, he passed by Barlow's apothecary. Seeing the light of a candle inside, he stopped and dismounted from his horse. He opened the door to find Mr. Barlow sweeping the floor.

"You work late into the night," Charles commented.

"Ah, good evening, sir," Mr. Barlow greeted. "I had a cat come into the shop. Damned creature knocked over all my bottles of laudanum. Greta used to put a bowl of milk out for the thing, and it still comes round though she is gone."

Charles paused before asking, "Your daughter continues in good health?"

"Yes."

"Good. Please send her my regard."

Mr. Barlow looked down, and his eyes shifted awkwardly about. "I, er, I had, good sir, as you had inquired of her previously. I thought I might convince her to return."

Sensing the man had more to say, Charles prompted, "And?"

"I received her letter this morning. She means to stay in Liverpool as long as possible, but if, well…I will continue to press her as her grandmother misses her dearly."

Charles looked down in brief contemplation. He had no expectations, but it was clear to him that Greta, if she could not even be persuaded by her father, meant to avoid *him* at all cost. As Mr. Barlow appeared in some anguish—the man had detected Charles' interest in his daughter and no doubt had deemed the match in great favor—Charles gave the man a reassuring smile.

"I would not distress yourself overmuch," he said. "Their sex can be quite stubborn."

The man's shoulders sagged. Perhaps he took Charles' response as an indication that his interest in Miss Barlow only extended so far.

"Yes," Mr. Barlow sighed, but then he brightened. "But fickle, too."

Charles nodded, but he did not think Greta the fickle sort. In response to Damien, she had turned to Mistress Scarlet, and there she had stayed for nearly two years. When she came upon whom she believed her destiny, she gave all of herself. Clearly, she did not believe Charles her destiny.

After bidding Mr. Barlow a good evening, Charles stepped into the cool night air, mounted his steed, and proceeded to the Red Chrysanthemum. He had little time to dwell on the heaviness in his heart, however, for coming upon the inn, he saw a carriage. The light of a lantern revealed the Wendlesson crest.

He was surprised to find Miss Katherine had arrived early—but soon discovered the reason.

"His lordship and his wife await upstairs in your appointed room," Tippy told him as she took his hat and gloves.

"His lordship?" he echoed, unsure if the presence of the viscount portended good or bad.

Tippy nodded before receiving his cloak. "I informed them that you had not arrived and I had no instructions for the evening as of yet."

"Well, as they are here, we may dispense with any preparations. Thank you, Tippy."

She bobbed a curtsy, and he headed for the stairs,

stopping only to retrieve *Fanny Hill* from the inn's small library. In the room he had occupied with Miss Katherine and Miss Terrell the prior evening, he found the viscount and Miss Katherine, who sat with her eyes downcast, her hands in her lap.

"Lord Wendlesson, Miss Katherine," Charles greeted. To his lordship, he asked, "Will we have the pleasure of your company this evening?"

Wendlesson cleared his throat. "I considered your advice, that I should take part in my wife's education, as it were. It would seem she made much progress last evening, and I commend you on obtaining the assistance of Miss Terrell. It has proved a wise action."

Charles started and wondered if *that* was what compelled more than his recommendation to his lordship.

"You owe no credit to me," Charles said. "The presence of Miss Terrell was a unique circumstance not prompted by any decision on my part."

Wendlesson raised his brows. "You did not ask her to assist you?"

"I believe, as she had no further commitments that night, she offered her support to your wife."

"Well, in either case, I am glad she proved of use and would like to call upon her services once more. Tonight."

Charles frowned. After his dream last night, he had no wish to see Miss Terrell. He would atone for his unkind statement at some later time.

"She may not be available."

"Send for her and let us find out."

"She is spoken for."

"By whom? Sir Arthur?"

"Yes. We ought to consult with Madame Devereux if we are to occupy Miss Terrell's time any further."

"Fine, fine. I am certain I can persuade Madame while you procure Miss Terrell."

The viscount left before Charles could think of any other objection. He turned to Miss Katherine.

"Is it your desire as well to have Miss Terrell present?" he inquired. "This is *your* education, and I will do what is in *that* interest."

Miss Katherine nodded. "He was quite pleased when I described the…what happened."

He approached and knelt beside her. "Were *you* pleased?"

A familiar flush crept up her cheeks. She nodded. "Especially now that my husband is pleased."

"The reverse is true, too. Your husband is a good man, and what pleases *you*, pleases him."

"The presence of another female did afford me some comfort yesterday. I-I am still in much, er, fear of what is to come. A female, a member of my own sex, has a more gentle touch."

Charles nodded. He rose to his feet. Miss Terrell had an agenda. Her motivations need not lie in tandem with that of Miss Katherine, but he would not tarnish Miss Katherine's confidence in the blackamoor without cause.

"If Madame Devereux does not permit Miss Terrell's participation, and you desire the companionship of another female, there are others I can appeal to," he said.

"If possible, I should prefer Miss Terrell as she is already—already acquainted with me."

"Then I shall determine if she is disposed and willing. But we will commence our lesson upon my return, with or without Miss Terrell."

She nodded.

He left the room and went downstairs to inquire where Miss Terrell might be.

"She might be with Sir Arthur," he said to Tippy.

The maid shook her head. "He come round early, as he done yesterday. Miss Terrell is likely in her room watching Miss Sarah's son."

"And where is her room?"

"Up in the attic."

"The attic?"

Being an inn, there were rooms aplenty in the Red Chrysanthemum. Rarely were they all engaged. He shook his head at Joan's parsimony. He headed back upstairs, all the way to the attic this time. He knocked upon the door.

"Master Gallant," Miss Terrell greeted with a wide smile. He could not help but marvel at her even, white teeth. Were blackamoors commonly blessed with such perfect smiles?

"I was just about to seek you out and ask if I might be of assistance?" she continued as she allowed him passage into the room.

Wanting a private word with her, he entered. The space hardly qualified as a room, for he could not stand upright. There were two beds, a small chest of drawers and a table, upon which a lone candle provided the only light.

"This is where you sleep?" he asked.

"With Lady Sarah and her son."

"Lady Sarah?"

"She was once married to a baronet. To me, she is Lady Sarah, a much truer lady than many a privileged member of the *ton*."

"Where are they now?"

"Lady Sarah is with a patron and her son with Mrs. Hartshorn. I am, therefore, free this evening and at your disposal, Master Gallant."

"I will have a word with you first," he said, "but let us step out where we can stand without bending."

He would have to talk to Joan about the accommodations for Miss Terrell and Lady Sarah. They could have better.

Miss Terrell followed him to the stairs, upon which they could stand without bumping their heads into the ceiling.

"About your assistance, Miss Terrell," he said when they had descended the stairs midway.

She was a few steps ahead of him, and when she turned, she stared straight into his crotch. Though taking another step would bring him closer to her, he opted for that over the unnerving level of her eyes.

"Your presence did comfort Miss Katherine," he said. "For that reason alone, I am willing to accept your assistance for another night."

She closed the final step between them. "I am happy to be of assistance."

She began playing with the bottom-most button of his waistcoat, but he grasped her by the wrist and replaced her hand by her side.

"That is precisely what I will not allow. There is only one charge that will take place this evening: furthering the introduction of Miss Katherine into the ways of the Red Chrysanthemum. No other objective will interfere in this singular purpose. Do you understand?"

"Did I not dedicate myself appropriately last night? Was your purpose not aided by my efforts?"

He had to admit she had done well by Miss Katherine. Nonetheless, he replied, "I wonder that I can trust you. Miss Katherine is the priority."

"I understand, Master Gallant. If I should detract from the task at hand, I pray you punish me. As hard as you like."

"There is much more of *Fanny Hill* I could read to you," he retorted.

Her smile fell into a frown. He could not resist a sense of triumph, fleeting though it was, when he was with this woman. Recalling how he had made her frown their last moment together yesterday, he said, "I mean to apologize for my statement yester night."

She looked down, confirming that his words yesterday had, indeed, not been well received.

"It was spoken in haste," he continued, "in an effort to make it known that I do not desire your seduction or your attentions. Nevertheless, it was unkind of me, and I'm sorry."

She looked pensive, and he wondered if his prior words

had stung her more than he thought.

"No one's ever said sorry to me before," she murmured. She squared her shoulders and lifted her chin. "But you needn't worry of such things, Master Gallant. My cunnie is not made worse for wear. I promise you'll like it all the same."

Turning on her heels, she went lightly down the stairs, saying over her shoulder. "Come. Let us not keep Miss Katherine waiting."

He did not follow immediately. He saw that his statement last night had hurt her, but he had not expected such ready forgiveness. And how quickly her bold confidence had rallied! And her impudence returned!

"The Viscount Wendlesson awaits as well," he said when he caught up to her.

She paused and smiled. "The more the merrier."

He was not surprised that the addition of another did not daunt her.

"Your lordship," she said with a curtsy upon entering the room.

"Miss Terrell," replied the viscount, his eyes gleaming with eagerness.

Charles felt his groin tighten. It troubled him that Miss Terrell was the reason Wendlesson had changed his mind concerning his participation, but if the end was improved by the means, perhaps he ought not entertain his misgivings.

"What had Joan to say?" Charles asked.

"She was hesitant at first. Seems Sir Arthur is the sort given to jealousy. Ha! Why he comes here then and does not take up with an opera dancer instead is odd, but he always struck me as an eccentric. But I persuaded Madame that Miss Terrell was not sharing her charms with any other man. Rather, she is merely comforting a member of her own sex."

Charles waited for the mention of money.

"And a few extra guineas sealed the deal," Wendlesson

finished.

Thinking of the small room that served as Miss Terrell's board, Charles said, "And the compensation for Miss Terrell?"

"Ah, yes, well, I have a few shillings upon me."

"You are too kind, my lord," Miss Terrell said with another curtsy.

Wendlesson clapped his hands. "Shall we begin then?"

Charles took in a deep breath. Lord Wendlesson was clearly pleased. Miss Katherine had made progress and seemed to brighten upon seeing Miss Terrell. But for himself, had he just allowed a fox into the henhouse?

# CHAPTER NINETEEN

The evening was proceeding better than planned. Terrell had expected to meet with resistance from Master Gallant when she offered her services to him for another night. Instead, he had sought *her* out, apparently at the request of Lord Wendlesson, but that did not signify to Terrell. She welcomed another chance to be with Master Gallant, no matter how it was brought about.

*I'm sorry*, he had said. His sincerity pulled at her heartstrings with a ferocity that surprised her. She found herself wanting to assist him with Miss Katherine for his sake. She had never before met a man like Master Gallant, and she wished to prove that she could be a worthwhile submissive for him.

"What now, Master Gallant?" the viscount asked.

His lordship was tall and broad in form. He had not the refined physiognomy of Master Gallant, but Terrell did not find him homely. The few times their paths had crossed here at the Red Chrysanthemum, he had never done more than simply acknowledge her. She had noticed he preferred more petite women, with slender hips and an innocent countenance, but tonight she sensed a difference in him.

"I had thought to set the tone with a little reading,"

Master Gallant replied, producing a familiar book.

She had learned enough of her letters to recognize that the title was indeed the same as the one from yesterday. She hoped he would not ask her to read.

"But first, Miss Katherine and Miss Terrell will assume their proper positions as submissives," Gallant continued.

The women exchanged glances before kneeling and placing their hands behind them. Wendlesson looked to Gallant with approval.

"Miss Katherine," Gallant addressed the viscountess. "Please relay to his lordship what you learned yesterday."

"I learned that a s-submissive does not speak lest she is commanded or permitted to," Miss Katherine replied.

"Very good. And?"

"And she is to obey her master."

"Without question."

"Without question."

"And if she does not?"

"She will be…punished."

"And will she be grateful for the disciplining?"

"Yes."

Gallant looked to Wendlesson. "Your wife is a very apt pupil."

"Indeed she is," said Wendlesson, eying Miss Katherine with approval.

Miss Katherine dared to smile.

"But why are they clothed?" he asked. "Submissives ought not be permitted the luxury of clothing lest they have earned the privilege."

Both women stiffened. Not wanting to appear insubordinate so early in the evening, Terrell said nothing. Eager to inveigle herself into Master Gallant's graces, she had failed to consider this aspect of being a submissive. With most of her patrons, she dictated the terms, even if she might not bear the formal role of a Mistress. On the occasions when she had assumed the role of submissive to a patron, she had set her limits before engaging in any *business*. Her limits included no undressing lest she consented to it.

"We are still in the education phase, Lord Wendlesson," Gallant said. "It is not necessary to impose upon them all the customary rules at once."

"What of Miss Terrell? She does not require an education."

Terrell felt her pulse quicken. She had not removed her chemise for a man in years.

"Let us treat them as equivalents for the time being," Gallant suggested, "till we are certain of the gain from doing differently. We have agreed upon safety words. For Miss Katherine, the safety word is 'Jean', inspired by her favorite composer. For Miss Terrell, the word shall be 'obedience.'"

They all looked at him, save Terrell, who kept her gaze lowered to bury her smirk. The Master did not like her previous safety word.

"The ideal safety word consists of but one syllable," Charles acknowledged, "but I will make an exception for Miss Terrell, as she has protested the need to have one at all."

"Indeed?" said Wendlesson, intrigued.

"Let us commence."

Gallant opened the book and held it before Terrell. She groaned silently. She had hoped to prove to Master Gallant that she could be a dutiful submissive. Now she could not.

"You may begin at the top of the page, Miss Terrell," he instructed.

"Miss Katherine is undoubtedly superior at reading, Master Gallant," Terrell replied, keeping her eyes downcast.

"She will have her turn."

He waited with book in hand. She glanced at the page with the small type. She recognized a few words from sight, but to string them together in a sentence would be no easy task. She could hear the awkward, stilted manner in which she would read. She could see the look of disappointment, disgust or pity upon their faces. Many a man or woman could not read, but they were of the lower classes. Slaves certainly did not read, but she had not been a slave in some time. She had been a courtesan to gentlemen, peers even, and to members of the *ton*. And she had every intention of returning to that society.

"Did Master not have his fill of reading last night?"

She kept her eyes averted, but she sensed him frown and doubted he had forgotten how he had disciplined her last night with much reading. She would suffer it again if she had to.

"I believe she defies you, Master Gallant," Wendlesson remarked.

# CHAPTER TWENTY

"**Y**es," Charles agreed, displeased, "but I will not permit her punishment to consume what precious little time we have."

"Why not?"

"She will receive her due when I am ready to give it."

"But she could serve as an example of the consequences of disobedience."

"I would we place greater emphasis on the rewards of obedience to start with." He turned to the viscountess. "The top of the page, Miss Katherine."

It seemed Miss Terrell breathed a breath of relief when Miss Katherine accepted the book from him. He did not understand the obstinacy of the former, lest she was deliberately attempting to provoke him into punishing her. Had she not boasted she could be the perfect submissive? He shook his head, recalling how Miss Greta had once promised him perfection, then broke that promise within days.

"'Presently, when they had exchanged a few kisses, and questions in broken English on one side, he began to unbutton, and, in fine, stript unto his shirt.

'As if this had been the signal agreed on for pulling off all their clothes, a scheme which the heat of the season perfectly favored, Polly began to draw her pins, and as she had no stays to unlace, she was in a trice, with her gallant's officious assistance, undressed to all but her shift.

'When he saw this, his breeches were immediately loosened, waist and knee bands, and slipped over his ankles, clean off; his shirt collar was unbuttoned too: then, first giving Polly an encouraging kiss, he stole, as it were, the shift off the girl, who being, I suppose, broke and familiarized to this humour, blushed indeed, but less than I did at the apparition of her, now standing stark naked, just as she came out of the hands of pure nature, with her black hair loose and a-float down her dazzling white neck and shoulders, whilst the deepened carnation of her cheeks went off gradually into the hue of glazed snow: for such were the blended tints polish of her skin."'

Miss Katherine had slowed her reading pace, and a flush had crept into her cheeks. Her husband grunted and rubbed the bulge at his crotch. Miss Terrell's breath had grown uneven.

"'This girl could not be above eighteen: her face regular and sweet featured, her shape exquisite; nor could I help envying her two ripe enchanting breasts, finely plumped out in flesh, but withal so round, so firm, that they sustained themselves, in scorn of any stay: then their nipples, pointing different ways, marked their pleasing separation; beneath them lay the delicious tract of the belly, which terminated in a parting of rift scarce discerning, that modesty seemed to retire downward, and seek shelter between two plump fleshy thighs: the curling hair that overspread its delightful front, clothed it with the richest sable fur in the universe: in short, she was evidently a subject for the painters to court her, sitting to them for a pattern female beauty, in all the true pride and pomp of nakedness."'

"Well done, Miss Katherine," he said. During her narration, he had gone to the sideboard and retrieved the red silk scarves he had used yester evening, along with two cords of rope. He went to the chair and drew it toward her. "Miss Katherine, pray have a seat."

Thinking he might repeat the event of the prior night, Miss Katherine sat in the chair and gripped its arms.

He went to stand before Miss Terrell. "On your feet."

She obeyed without question this time.

"You will sit."

She looked about the room for another chair.

"Upon the bed," he clarified.

He saw that this pleased her. She went straightway and sat, not on the edge, but boldly in the center with both legs upon the bedclothes. He looked at the headboard, styled in the rococo fashion. Scarf in hand, he wrapped it over her eyes and tied it behind her head.

"Does the deprivation of sight distress you, Miss Terrell?" he asked.

"No, Master."

"Do you recall your safety word?"

"I shall not require it."

In truth, no woman had ever needed the use of her safety word with him. He was far too attuned to their responses, their limits, and knew when to withdraw. But Miss Terrell did not know this. For her to make an assertion discounting the need for a safety word was mere foolish bravado. A small part of him was tempted to prove her wrong.

He stood on one side of the bed. "Lay down, closer toward me."

When she did as told, he wound one of the ropes through the intricate filigree atop the headboard. He pulled her left hand overhead and tied the rope about the wrist, then bound the other end of the rope to the right wrist.

"How do you fare, Miss Terrell?"

"Quite well, Master Gallant."

"You are not afraid?"

"No, Master Gallant. I trust in you."

"Trust is critical," Charles said, for the benefit of the viscount. "If you did not trust me, you would be frightened."

"Yes, Master."

"Fear can titillate," said Wendlesson.

"Not if it overwhelms trust," Charles replied.

Charles looked to Miss Katherine to see that she was at ease, but she did inhale sharply when he went to the sideboard and returned with a long braided crop. He slid the side of the crop gently up Miss Terrell's bare arm. Her lips parted and she sighed softly. He tried to remain impervious to the sight of her bound to the bed. This was for instruction purposes only.

Or so he told himself.

"Do you know what I have in hand, Miss Terrell?" he inquired.

"A crop, I hazard. Master."

"Do you wish your blindfold removed?"

"No, Master."

"Why not?"

"I prefer not to have the distraction of sight, that my body may fully contemplate what you are to do to me."

Good. It was the answer he wished for.

"And your restraints? Do you feel helpless?"

"Helpless yet safe, Master Gallant."

Satisfied, he drew the tip of the crop across her chest and down the cleavage of her breasts. Though a modest fire crackled in the hearth, the room had grown warm. He trailed the crop past her abdomen and down a leg to her foot and over the toes. He tapped the crop lightly to the arch in her foot. She gasped, no doubt knowing how sensitive the bottoms of the feet could be. He brushed the side of the crop along the inside of the leg, and she purred. Using the crop, he pushed her skirts up to her thighs. He glanced over at Miss Katherine, who watched intently but without apparent apprehension.

"Do you recall your safety word, Miss Terrell?"

"No, Master Gallant."

He snapped the crop at the inside of her thigh. She

yelped.

"Try, Miss Terrell."

"Umm, submission."

He struck her again. She yelped louder.

"Obedience."

"Much better."

For a moment, he had worried she might have intentionally forgotten in an attempt to force his hand and bring about her punishment. He had no desire to frighten Miss Katherine. He understood how she might have perceived the Red Chrysanthemum if she had not been properly introduced to its practices. Though he had been warned of the activities that took place at the inn, the sights and sounds had still managed to shock him his first time here.

"You are lenient with her," the viscount said. "I vow she would never dare forget her safety word if you had a heavier hand."

His lordship eyed Miss Terrell with obvious hungry. Charles felt an odd possessiveness stir inside him. He wanted to warn the man against showing too much interest in anyone but his wife.

"My actions were sufficient," Charles replied. He returned his attention to Miss Terrell, his gaze traversing the peaks and valleys of her body. His hand tightened about the crop as he imagined her squirming and writhing beneath his blows.

"Will my lord read next?" he asked.

"Me?"

"I would Miss Katherine be free to observe Miss Terrell."

"Very well."

Wendlesson received the book from his wife with little enthusiasm and commenced reading. "'The young Italian (still in his shirt) stood gazing and transported at the sight of beauties that might have fired a dying hermit; his eager eyes devoured her, as she shifted attitudes at his discretion:

neither were his hands excluded their share of the high feast, but wandered, on the hunt of pleasure, over every part and inch of her body, so qualified to afford the most exquisite sense of it.

'In the mean time, one could not help observing the swell of his shirt before, that bolstered out, and pointed out the condition of things behind the curtain: but he soon removed it, by slipping his shirt over his head; and now, as to nakedness, they had nothing to reproach one another.'"

Charles noticed Miss Terrell to press her thighs together. "Are you aroused, Miss Terrell?"

"Mmmm," she purred. "The author paints a vivid scene."

She rolled her hips a little and lifted her left knee. The skirts fell toward her hips, exposing her flank nicely.

"Do you wish to touch yourself, as you had done last night?"

"I wish to be touched, Master."

He touched her with the crop.

"Pray continue, your lordship," he said to Wendlesson. As the viscount read, he rapped the crop against her exposed thigh.

"'Then his grand movement, which seemed to rise out of a thicket of curling hair, that spread from the root all over his thighs and belly up to the navel, stood stiff and upright, but of a size to frighten me, by sympathy for the small tender part which was the object of its fury, and which now lay exposed to my fairest view; for he had, immediately on stoppings off his shirt, gently pushed her down on the couch, which stood conveniently to break her willing fall. Her thighs were spread out to their utmost extension, and discovered between them the mark of the sex, the red-centered cleft of flesh, whose lips vermillioning inwards, expressed a small ruby line in sweet miniature, such as Guide's touch or colouring: could never attain to the life or delicacy of.'"

Charles pulled the crop back and snapped the side of it

to her thigh. She let out a gasping cry.

"Thank you, Master."

"You're welcome, Miss Terrell." Seeing a mystified expression upon Miss Katherine, he asked Miss Terrell, "Did that please you?"

"Yes, Master."

"Did the strike of the crop not smart?"

"It did, Master Gallant."

"Yet you welcome it."

"Indeed. I felt my body at attention, Master."

"It did not diminish your arousal?"

"Not at all. His lordship reads well."

Charles turned to Wendlesson. "Will you oblige?"

The viscount, who had been staring at Miss Terrell as if he had forgotten the presence of his wife, nodded and continued.

"'Phoebe, at this, gave me a gentle jog, to prepare me for a whisper question: "Whether I thought my little maiden-head was much less?" But my attention was too much engrossed, too much inwrapped with all I saw, to be able to give her any answer.

'By this time the young gentleman had changed her posture from lying breadth to length-wise on the coach: but her thighs were still spread, and the mark lay fair for him, who now kneeling between them, displayed to us a side view of that fierce erect machine of his, which threatened no less than splitting the tender victim, who lay smiling at the uplifted stroke, nor seemed to decline it. He looked upon his weapon himself with some pleasure, and guiding it with his hand to the inviting slit, drew aside the lips, and lodged it (after some thrusts, which Polly seemed even to assist) about half way; but there it stuck, I suppose from its growing thickness: he draws it again, and just wetting it with spittle, re-enters, and with ease sheathed it now up to the hilt, at which Polly gave a deep sigh, which was quite another tone than one of pain; he thrusts, she heaves, at first gently, and in a regular cadence; but presently the transport began to be too violent to observe any order or measure; their motions were too rapid, their kisses too fierce and fervent for nature to support such fury long: both seemed to me out of themselves: their eyes darted fires: "Oh! oh! I can't bear it. It is too much. I die. I am going," were Polly's expressions of ecstasy: his joys were more silent: but soon broken murmurs, sighs heart-fetched, and at length a dispatching thrust, as if he would have forced himself up her body, and then the motionless languor of all his limbs, all shewed that the die-away moment was come upon him; which she gave signs of joining with by the wild throwing of her hands about, closing her eyes, and giving a deep sob, in which she seemed to expire in an agony of bliss.'"

Charles alternated between caressing Miss Terrell's limbs with the crop and striking them. She emitted all manner of lovely sounds, from sighs to moans. He considered pushing the crop farther up her skirts. How might she react if he rubbed the crop along her mound, if the tip should find the pleasure bud beneath? But such thoughts made the blood pound in his head, and he wanted no titillation. Nor would he allow himself to touch her intimately.

He turned to Miss Katherine. "Are you prepared to join Miss Terrell? Remember that you need but utter your safety word if you wish to discontinue."

She nodded and rose to her feet. He had her lay on the other side of the bed, which was just large enough to fit the two women. He handed the crop to Wendlesson and wrapped the second scarf about her eyes, which were not devoid of concern.

"Remember your safety word," he reassured her. "I will explain all that will happen. I will bind your wrists to the bed, as I did with Miss Terrell, and no more."

She allowed him to wind the rope about her wrists and secure them to the headboard.

"A fine sight," said Wendlesson, who stood at the foot

of the bed.

Charles looked upon the scene of the two women with their lovely arms pulled to the bed, the scarves making their mouths the most prominent feature in their physiognomies. His gaze fell upon Miss Terrell's lips, and he noted how their suppleness made them protrude. His cock pulsed.

Crop in hand, Wendlesson approached his wife.

"As Miss Katherine is unacquainted with the crop," Charles stayed him, "let us begin first with an ostrich plume."

He went to the sideboard and found one for the viscount.

"His lordship will caress you with the plume," he informed Miss Katherine.

Though disappointed, Wendlesson put down the crop, accepted the plume and touched it to her neck. She giggled. He drew it across her collar and up her arms.

"Do you savor its rich softness, Miss Katherine?" Charles asked.

"Yes..." she said after another giggle.

"Yes, Master," Wendlesson corrected.

"Yes, Master."

The plume brushed her cheek, and she giggled again when it tickled her neck.

"Now the crop?" Wendlesson inquired.

"Now your hand," Charles said, looking over at Miss Terrell, waiting patiently and silently. "Caress the parts touched by the plume."

Complying, Wendlesson stroked her neck, her collar, her cheeks, and her arms. She sighed.

"Now the same with your lips."

Wendlesson leaned over his wife and kissed the length of her arm. He planted kisses atop her chest and décolletage.

Charles stared at Miss Terrell's lips. "Now take the mouth."

Wendlesson kissed his wife, softly at first, then with growing ardor. Miss Terrell made no movement, though her chest heaved as her ears were necessarily filled with the smacking of lips and the muffled murmurs from Miss Katherine. Charles went to the bed and untied Miss Terrell. He pulled the scarf from her eyes and beckoned for her to get off the bed. Wendlesson's kisses had moved from Miss Katherine's lips to her bosom. Charles gestured for Miss Terrell to take a seat in the chair, which still faced the bed. He stood beside the chair.

"Bare her legs," he instructed Wendlesson. "And remember the plume."

The viscount pushed up her skirts and stroked her legs with the feather. Miss Katherine had slim legs like those of Miss Greta, with thighs slightly wider than the lower half of the leg. Only the women of southern Asia could claim more slender legs. Miss Terrell, in contrast, had defined curves to her legs, especially about the calves and upper thighs. If he were not cognizant that the time belonged to Miss Katherine, he might have played the crop upon Miss Terrell longer. There was more of her to explore.

"Now employ your hands upon those charming limbs."

Miss Terrell watched with interest, but he knew her to glance his way often. Wendlesson reached a hand to the tops of Miss Katherine's thighs. He cupped her mound and begun to rub her. She emitted a lush groan. Miss Terrell closed her eyes for a moment, imagining or wishing she might be touched in similar fashion. For the briefest of seconds, Charles considered fondling her as she watched the erotic scene before her. It might relieve the pressure at his crotch to touch her. But he shook the thought from his head. This was her punishment.

Wendlesson pleasured his wife till she was visibly agitated and panting for more. She writhed softly upon the bed. Charles had not tied the ropes tightly, but he need not have with Miss Katherine. Befitting her nature, her body moved in a shy and demure manner. He had no qualms binding Miss Terrell more forcefully. Though not much larger than Miss Katherine, Miss Terrell seemed, nonetheless, to be made of stronger mettle.

"Now you may try the crop," Charles said, "and begin with a light touch."

Wendlesson took the crop and slid it along a leg. From the corners of his eyes, Charles could see Miss Terrell squirm in the chair, her cheeks flushed. She opened and closed her thighs, then stared at his crotch. He could not prevent the blood from stiffening his cock.

"May I pleasure you, Master?" she asked.

"No," he replied sternly and as persuasively as he could.

"Will you touch me?"

"No."

"Then, may I touch myself?"

"No. You will sit and bear witness and do nothing more."

She pursed her lips in displeasure.

Wendlesson had graduated from tapping the crop against Miss Katherine to an occasional light slap, which drew little yelps from her.

"Caress her in between the blows," Charles reminded him.

Wendlesson did as instructed, keeping Miss Katherine aroused with one hand while striking her with the other.

"You allowed me to pleasure myself yesterday," Miss Terrell said.

"That was yesterday," Charles replied.

"But you enjoyed the sight, did you not, of such a wanton act?"

Ignoring her question, he said, "Today you are being punished, Miss Terrell."

"You intend I should sit here for the remainder of the evening?"

He repeated himself, "And do nothing more."

She stared at him like a petulant child being denied

biscuits before supper, then tossed her head. "Very well. I can do without caressing myself."

Unsure what she meant, he crossed his arms before him and focused on Wendlesson and Miss Katherine. The two seemed to have forgotten others were present. The former fondled her vigorously.

"May I—may I spend, Master?" Miss Katherine huffed.

At that, Wendlesson unbuttoned his fall. His cock had been hard for some time, and he eagerly spread her thighs and positioned himself between them. He speared himself into her. Miss Terrell grunted. Charles tried to remain impartial to the scene before him and the presence of Miss Terrell beside him. As Wendlesson thrust into Miss Katherine, Miss Terrell continued to grunt and whimper as if participating in the exertion.

"May I?" Miss Katherine asked.

Lost in his efforts, Wendlesson made no reply. Miss Terrell had shut her eyes and grasped the arms of the chair. Curious, Charles turned his gaze upon her. Her breath had shortened.

"Please," Miss Katherine pleaded.

Charles stared at Miss Terrell, who sat still in the chair but whose brow furrowed in concentration.

"Please!"

"Granted!" Charles shouted when he heard no word from Wendlesson.

A few moments later, Miss Katherine emitted a cry. Miss Terrell followed with a shudder that went through the whole of her body. With a long exhale, she sank into the chair as if…spent. Charles could hear Wendlesson grunting and panting as he continued to seek his conclusion. The bed creaked beneath his thrusting. Gradually, Miss Terrell opened her eyes. She looked up at Charles and her lips curved into a satisfied smile. Charles continued to stare in disbelief. Had she, indeed, spent or was it an act? It would appear she had experienced some small paroxysm, but how the devil had she managed that?

"Please, it-it is uncomfortable," Miss Katherine said.

Wendlesson was pounding into her, his brow beaded with perspiration, the veins in his neck protruding.

"Please. Please!"

Charles expected the man to spend at any moment, but he continued to shove himself desperately into Miss Katherine.

"Please! Jean!"

When Wendlesson did not cease, Charles strode over and barked, "Lord Wendlesson!"

The viscount snapped to attention and slowed his movements. Charles removed the blindfold from Miss Katherine.

"It was b-beginning to hurt," she explained.

"I'm sorry," Wendlesson huffed. "I did not hear."

He disengaged from her. His shaft, short but with a wide girth, was still hard.

Charles untied her from the bed. "You performed remarkably. Would you not agree, my lord?"

"Yes, yes."

"You must be pleased with her progress."

Wendlesson nodded. "Yes."

Charles assisted her from the bed. "Miss Terrell will accompany you to the dressing room and assist you with your toilette."

She nodded, then looked with concern to her husband, who sat upon the bed, stroking his erection.

"Is there more—should I—?" she asked of Charles.

"Your lesson for the evening is concluded," he replied and handed her over to Miss Terrell.

After the women had left, Wendlesson said gruffly, "You sent them away, but I have yet to spend."

"The pleasure of the submissive takes precedence."

"That may be your priority. It need not be mine."

"It is for her sake that I agreed to these lessons, not yours."

Wendlesson glared at him.

"You will find her more apt to accept *your* terms if there is benefit for *her*," Charles tried.

"Very well. Then send for Miss Terrell. I will spend before I leave."

Charles stiffened. "Can you not attend yourself?"

"It would take far too long," Wendlesson snapped. "When I was younger, it was not a difficulty, but in past years, I crave something more. I crave their screams of pain. That will send me over the edge."

"And that alone will bring you to spend?" asked Charles, stunned.

Wendlesson nodded. "What you witnessed was little different than what transpired on our wedding night, only she was in much greater pain, and I doubted she spent. It is not enough for me to be in her cunnie, you understand? And if I am ever to have an heir…"

"I see."

Silence fell between them. Charles heard and saw the anguish in his lordship's situation, but he could not rush Miss Katherine.

"Your wife is a promising student," Charles said at last. "If you give her time, I believe you will have your wish."

"For tonight I will take Miss Terrell."

"Her function tonight was to assist your wife, not see to your pleasure."

"I don't give a damn what her function was. I need tending to."

"Then find another means of doing so. I doubt Madame extended her approval to include—"

"She need not know."

Charles shook his head. "I will not be party to any such deception."

"*Your* involvement is hardly necessary."

Charles felt his jaw harden. "Miss Terrell is spoken for."

"Not by you, though one would think you Miss Terrell's keeper. One might even think you *jealous*."

"Jealous?" Charles echoed, affronted, even as he realized the accusation was not entirely false.

"Though you may consider yourself above desiring her, you are not immune—"

"I have no interest in Miss Terrell."

"No?"

"Her qualities do not compel me as much as they do you. If I had any interest in taking a submissive here at the Red Chrysanthemum, I assure you, it would not be Miss Terrell, even were she the last woman remaining."

"I, too, am not enamored of her dark coloring, but among her kind, she is tolerable. And she has the requisite parts to satisfy me at present. If you'll not send for her, I will."

"You would do this while your wife awaits?"

Wendlesson rose to his feet. His nostrils flared. "Do not presume to preach fidelity to me, Gallant."

Charles kept his stance, half expecting to come to blows with the man. But Wendlesson no longer looked at him and, instead, gazed past him toward the door. Charles hoped it was Miss Katherine the viscount saw. His lordship might then be compelled to take his leave.

But it was Miss Terrell.

# CHAPTER TWENTY-ONE

Though her heart throbbed—it seemed with more discomfort than any crop might impose upon her body—Terrell recalled herself. It would not do for the gentlemen to realize she had overheard the final moments of their dialogue. She did not want the awkwardness that would follow, the tense attempts on their part to apologize, which would only fuel her anger or, worse, bring tears to her eyes. Suppressing the ache in her chest, she forced a smile and leaned against the doorframe, using her curves to provoke. She eyed Wendlesson's erection.

"Gentlemen, do I sense tension?" she asked with as much gaiety as she could muster. "Perhaps I can put you at ease."

Both men appeared relieved, no doubt thinking that she had just come upon them.

"Where is Miss Katherine?" Gallant asked.

"Tippy is assisting her," Terrell replied, closing the door behind her. "I returned to see if I might be of further service?"

She glanced at his crotch to give him an indication of what she meant.

"Yes," Wendlesson answered. "As you can see, I could use your services."

"You are not obligated," Gallant interjected. "In fact, Madame would not approve your risking the ire of your steady patron."

"Madame need not know."

Her response made him frown.

"I would provide enough compensation to ease her disapproval," Wendlesson added. "Let us not tarry."

"Sir Arthur has already agreed to a rich price for Miss Terrell's exclusive favors."

"Why are you here, Gallant?"

"I could service the both of you," Terrell replied.

Gallant strode over to where his coat hung on a coatrack. "I have fulfilled my duty for the evening and will be party to nothing more."

"But—"

"I bid you both good evening."

He closed the door behind him, leaving her alone with Wendlesson. She had little time for disappointment to fill her, for Wendlesson had gripped her by the neck.

"Come, wench."

"First, we must agree to this compensation you spoke of," she answered. "A guinea."

"A guinea! You think your cunnie made of gold?"

"My cunnie is better than gold."

"Very well! I agree only because I do not wish to keep my wife waiting."

She would have preferred the company of Master Gallant to the guinea, but it was decent compensation. How many women, black or white, could command a guinea for their cunnie?

Wendlesson pushed her down to her knees and presented his veined cock. She took it into her mouth. He grunted in satisfaction and promptly began to fuck her face. Several times he popped his cock out to slap his hand across her cheek. He was a strong man, and the blows nearly sent her sprawling to the ground. But she recovered each time and gulped his cock as hard as she could.

"My God," he gasped.

She had seen him with a submissive before and knew what he liked.

"The crop, Master Wendlesson," she said.

Nodding, he went to retrieve the implement while she threw up her skirts and presented him her arse. He landed the crop upon a buttock. She cried out. He rained the crop down upon her backside till she was certain pink welts covered her. Her screams filled the room.

Tossing aside the crop, he placed his cock at her folds and shoved himself in. She continued to cry out as if in pain, though her cunnie, still wet from before, allowed him easy passage despite the girth of his cock. She imagined it was Master Gallant pounding into her.

But she was the last person at the Red Chrysanthemum he would desire. Nay, he had said he would *not* take her were she the last woman remaining. Was she mistaken about his arousal? She had thought his refusal to be prompted by his loyalty to Madame or his reluctance to cross Sir Arthur, but she had also thought she could overcome these impediments and thaw his forbearance. If he would but surrender to her once, he would understand that the ecstasy she promised him was no falsehood, that a Negress need not be inferior pleasure.

Lord Wendlesson's cock stretched her, and she wondered if he would have availed himself of a sheep if that was all that was present. Perhaps not. She, at least, had the titillating form of her sex. She had breasts and hips and waist and lips. The only significant variances between her and a proper Englishwoman lay in the structure of her bones, the texture of her hair and the color of her skin.

The last made all the difference.

Among their kind, she knew that she could not compare to a flaxen-haired maid with alabaster skin. Had she not ceased long ago to care how white men perceived her? All that mattered was that they provided her a living and not return her to a life of bondage. Why did she now mourn the darkness of her skin? Why, now, did self-pity threaten to crumble years of stoicism? Could a few simple words by Master Gallant truly throw her world topsy-turvy?

# CHAPTER TWENTY-TWO

At the bottom of the stairs, Charles paused. He did not expect to hear the footsteps of Miss Terrell behind him. If he were a betting man, he would wager she was still up in the room, her cunnie stuffed with Wendlesson's thick cock. He knew not why he felt vexed at the moment. It was none of his damned affair what Miss Terrell and Lord Wendlesson were about. He would have advised Miss Terrell against servicing the viscount, but as his lordship had distinguished, *he* was not her keeper. He ought not trouble himself if she wished to risk Sir Arthur or Madame Devereux's displeasure.

But he could not help some responsibility in her business with Wendlesson. He ought never had permitted her intrusion into the instruction of Miss Katherine, though the viscountess might not have progressed as quickly without Miss Terrell. But what if Wendlesson demanded to have Miss Terrell again on the morrow? Charles did not think the benefits of her participation outweighed the potential hazards anymore.

"My articles, and have my horse ready," Charles said to a footman.

He was done with the Red Chrysanthemum for the night. Looking forward to falling into his own bed at home, he hoped no dreams of an erotic or disturbing nature would plague him in his sleep.

After receiving his hat and gloves, he was only too eager to depart. The longer he stayed, the more his mind might wander to the room upstairs. In passing a parlor, however, he glimpsed Miss Katherine, ready in her cloak, hat and gloves. She had seen him as well.

"Master Gallant, does my husband follow you?" she asked.

"Shortly," Charles replied, hoping that he spoke true. He entered the parlor and sat down. She took the settee opposite him.

"What think you of the evening?" he asked gently.

She immediately blushed. "What think you, Master Gallant?"

He allowed her evasive response. "I think you and the viscount ought be proud. In truth, I marvel at how you have overcome your timidity."

She looked down at the hands in her lap. "It did please me to have Edmund here tonight. And your demonstration first upon Miss Terrell did put me at ease."

Charles smiled, but it was a tight smile. He said nothing of his desire to terminate the services of Miss Terrell.

"Do you think his lordship is satisfied with tonight's instruction?" she inquired.

"If he does not fully appreciate your progress tonight, he will." He paused, wondering how much he should intrude into marital affairs. "Regardless, you are to be commended. That *you* are satisfied is paramount."

She smiled. "I would never have thought…yet I think the blindfold was of infinite use."

"Good."

"I owe my improvement to your exceptional direction."

"I did very little, Miss Katherine. You remembered to ask permission to spend. You remembered to use the safety word when you required. You surrendered your body to pleasure. You did all these things."

She looked at him with bright eyes. "I only wish I did not have to utter my safety word. I could not be like Miss Terrell. She must be quite brave to refuse the need for one."

"Miss Terrell is…unique. You must not make her your comparison. I do not know her well enough to say if her words are true or boastful hyperbole."

A brief silence fell between them before she asked, "I wonder what delays my husband?"

He had begun to put on his gloves and was glad for the occupation. This was why he did not engage with husbands and wives.

"We each of us have our trials to overcome," he said before his lack of a response might draw suspicion.

Puzzled, she knit her brows.

Though reluctant to divulge the personal matters of another, he decided, for her sake, it was better she knew.

"Some men find it harder to spend," he said simply.

"Ah, yes, I wish—I tried—I would I were not scared. Is he much displeased then?"

"I cannot serve as his interpreter or his messenger, but when you feel the time is right, when you think him in a good disposition, you might wish to broach the subject. You see what he is partial to. That you would attempt to satisfy him in this regard speaks greatly to your dedication as his wife and to *your* courage."

They both turned at the sound of heavy footsteps. The viscount appeared on the threshold.

"There you are," Wendlesson said to his wife. His eyes narrowed upon seeing Charles.

"I was merely praising Miss Katherine for her efforts this evening," Charles said, rising to his feet. "If you have more to add, I leave that to your discretion."

Lord Wendlesson colored, but Charles gave him little time to respond. With a curt bow to the two of them, he exited the room. To his relief, he did not cross paths with Miss Terrell.

No dreams troubled his sleep that night, but he slept fitfully all the same and awoke with the dawn. He had no set obligations for the day and decided to pay a visit to his mother and father at Ashlington House. The distance to Porter's Hill afforded him ample time to think on what more he could do for his election. There were still many voters to canvass and many others to influence.

Eventually his mind came to rest upon the Red Chrysanthemum and Miss Terrell. Miss Katherine had surprised him with her improvement. Perhaps she would not need Miss Terrell tonight. His lordship, however, might prove harder to persuade. Charles was loath to bring the matter to Joan. The trouble was his own doing for permitting Miss Terrell to intrude in the first place. He shook his head. The blackamoor was an impressively determined chit.

Recalling his words to Wendlesson last night, he took in a relieved breath once more. For a moment last night, he had thought she had heard everything. In truth, he had spoken as much to convince himself as the viscount. He had not disputed Wendlesson's statement regarding her coloring because he had no wish to prolong the conversation or provide any indication to the man that he was not, as suspected, immune to her charms. Her blackness did not disturb him, and he found Wendlesson's comment, *she is tolerable*, to be a dreadful understatement. She had not the classic beauty he or Wendlesson would have sought in her sex, but she was more *provocative* than any woman he knew. She did not hide her vanity behind a coquettish fan but boldly asserted the self-knowledge of her advantages. The most accomplished flirt would take days to accomplish what Miss Terrell did in seconds.

Granted, the Red Chrysanthemum gave her leave to behave in a manner even she might refrain from in more refined settings, but even at the Inn, Charles knew no one like her. She surprised and unnerved, and if he were brutally honest with himself, she frightened him no trivial amount. *That* was perhaps the reason he would take any other submissive above her. He had no doubts that he could control another submissive, man or woman, but Miss Terrell was a panther he wondered he could tame.

At Ashlington House, he was received first by Mrs. Gallant, who greeted him with the glow of a mother's affection, receiving him as if she had not seen him in a month instead of a sennight. Though greying and more wrinkled about the eyes, she still retained her beauty. Charles had her eyes and long, full lashes, as well as the soft golden locks of her youth.

"I would have come a sooner, but Sir Canning was in town early," he said after he had kissed her with equal affection but greater reserve.

"I know you to be busy," she replied, patting his hand as she drew him to take a seat in the drawing room. "Your father awoke early and is taking a nap."

"No need to rouse him. I will stay till he wakes."

"How fared your meeting with Mr. Dempsey? You met with him yesterday, did you not?"

"He assured me his support."

"But how wonderful!"

Mrs. Gallant instructed a maid to bring tea and refreshment.

"I had breakfast before I came," Charles informed his mother.

"And what manner of repast was it? You will have a proper meal here."

He knew better than to protest further. His mother was as stubborn a woman as could be had with her sex.

"Was Miss Dempsey in attendance when you visited with Mr. Dempsey?"

"I had not mentioned I called at their house, but, yes, both Miss Dempsey and Mrs. Dempsey were at home."

"Miss Dempsey is rather pretty, is she not? I wondered some young bachelor had not offered for her the very year she had her come-out."

"Perhaps one did."

"She would have been wise to turn him down then. If his devotion be steadfast, another year would prove it, but she would be better off waiting."

"Miss Dempsey will not want for suitors."

"Indeed? And does she find favor in your eyes?"

He'd known the question to be forthcoming and smiled. "She is pretty, and her manners pleasant enough, but you, of all people, must comprehend what I seek in a mate."

Mrs. Gallant pursed her lips. "And how are you to find any such mate if you are gone? To China, no less! And for such a long time." She shook her head. "I still do not understand why you felt such a need to travel half the world away."

He raised his brows. "Do you not, my dear?"

"Well, I understand why your father had to, but you did not."

"Father spoke of it as a most wondrous place."

"Macartney was less than impressed, if I recall, save for the Great Wall."

"Which I desired to see, and it is every bit as grand as described, but I would have been hard-pressed to travel had I been married. China is no place to bring a wife."

Mrs. Gallant had to concede that to be the case. "And have you a prospect for a wife?"

The maid entered with tea, and Charles was glad for the distraction. He had wanted to see his parents, though not to discuss his marital situation. But Mrs. Gallant would not let the subject go easily.

"Well?" she demanded.

"Alas, I must disappoint you."

She frowned. "I hope you will not be like your brother. I have all but forsaken hope that he will ever marry, though I should not be surprised if he brings home some native woman from an island somewhere."

Michael, Charles' senior by four years, was a naval

captain.

"You are my better hope, dear Charles."

He drank his tea. The beverage reminded him of China, the East India Company, and Sir Arthur.

"I would not necessarily lay the odds in my favor," he said.

"But you are a fine prospect, worthy of even Miss Dempsey. When you are an MP, it will be even more so."

"Till she discovers my wicked and wanton predilections in the bedchamber."

"Oh, *that*." Mrs. Gallant waved a dismissive hand. "Have you not had your fill?"

His cup stopped midway to his mouth. "Have you?"

"My situation differs. Your father and I are birds of a feather."

"And I would my situation to liken yours. I would have a wife who shares my penchants."

"And is there someone at the Red Chrysanthemum to whom you are partial?"

He thought of Greta. "There was, but she left and is unknown to return."

Mrs. Gallant, being his mother, caught the wistfulness in his tone. She put her hand over his. "If she cannot appreciate all your admirable qualities, she is not worthy."

"She is worthy, my dear, but the heart is not always persuaded by qualities."

"Is there another young woman whom you might consider?"

He shook his head. "No."

Mrs. Gallant sighed. "Your father and I were fortunate to have found each other at the Red Chrysanthemum. I believe it a rare happenstance. The Red Chrysanthemum is not a place to seek and find love."

"At present, it is a seat in Parliament I seek."

"And which you shall obtain."

This was spoken by Mr. William Gallant, who had come into the room. The senior Gallant, now seventy years of age, had married later in life to a woman ten years his junior, but, perhaps because he had taken his time in choosing a wife and because he had attained the sort of wisdom only time and experience could proffer, the affection and devotion between the two were stronger than any Charles had witnessed or heard of in other husbands and wives. It was the sort of marriage he wanted for himself.

"I had received a letter from Mr. Dempsey that he is inclined to back your candidacy," finished the senior Gallant.

"And Charles confirms it is done," Mrs. Gallant said, rising to assist her husband.

"Well done. And have you heard from the Brentwoods?"

"They have not extended a meeting as of yet," Charles replied, thinking of Lord Wendlesson's offer and that the viscount may not renew it after the events of the prior evening.

"Their endorsement is less important if you have the support of Sir Arthur. I have written several friends who are acquainted with him, and they hope to persuade him, though they say he is not easy to please. Had I taken more of an interest in India instead of China, I might have made more of a fortune for myself. I could have returned to England a Nabob, like Sir Arthur's father. The senior Arthur was near penniless. Now they are among the wealthiest families in the land."

"We do well enough, father. And my interests lie in matters of policy more than riches."

"Alas, you are a son too much after my own heart."

"In far too many ways," said Mrs. Gallant. "Perhaps we ought not have introduced him to the Red Chrysanthemum."

"*That* was your doing, my dear."

"She could not prevent it," Charles reminded them. "She knew not I followed her."

After returning from Cambridge, Charles had stayed with his parents in town. One night he had returned late from meeting a friend at a gaming hall and saw his mother, dressed in dark clothing as if to blend into the night, emerge from the Gallant house. Where she could have been headed at such an hour, he could not fathom, lest she had herself a paramour. His mother and father shared every confidence. There could be no reason for her to steal away into the night lest it be for a clandestine tryst. She had walked with purpose for several blocks to a corner where a sedan awaited her. Charles had followed her all the way to the Red Chrysanthemum, his mind churning in disbelief that his mother, who seemed devoted to her husband, would make of her beloved a cuckold.

He had attempted to follow her into the building, but the imposing footman at the door would not permit him entry. He had waited for his mother in grave disappointment and some anger at her betrayal and grief that she found it necessary to seek the affections of another man.

"I remember well the night my own son accused me of criminal congress!" said Mrs. Gallant. To her husband, she said, "It was *your* idea to meet at the Red Chrysanthemum as if we were strangers."

William Gallant grinned. "Ah, yes, it was good sport, was it not? I thought you rather enjoyed the charade."

"Till our son confronted me!"

"My dear," Charles said to his mother, "the truth was a thousand times better than the prospect of adultery to me."

"But you did not immediately believe me when I explained that I had met with your father." She turned to her husband. "You were gone when he demanded I prove myself, leaving me to explain the whole situation to him."

"Yes, yes, I remember," said Charles' father.

"A mother should never have to undergo such an awkward situation!"

Charles took her hand. "It was fortunate it was you. I would not have believed a woman could take pleasure in the activities at the Red Chrysanthemum. Just as I thought you an adulteress, I would have thought father an ogre, forcing his poor wife to submit to his cruel wickedness. I was ready to think my father an abominable brute."

Mrs. Gallant shook her head. "I never thought my gentle Charles would take to the Red Chrysanthemum with such interest. Your brother, if he had known, would not have surprised me. I had thought you would easily find a sweet young woman to marry and settle into an ordinary life and provide me at least two grandchildren by now."

She let out a heavy sigh.

"My love," said William, "we cannot place expectations upon him that we would not have tolerated for ourselves."

"Do you not wish to see your grandchild?"

Knowing she worried that perhaps his father might not survive long enough, Charles pressed her hand. "I will make a concentrated effort at matrimony after the election," he assured her.

She brightened. "Perhaps, if your father is in good health, we could come to town at the start of the Season. I could call upon Mrs. Dempsey and thank her for their support of you."

"Do you think Mr. Dempsey to have any influence upon Sir Arthur?" asked the senior Gallant.

Charles said nothing. He did not know which subject he wished to converse less upon, marriage or Sir Arthur.

"I doubt it," Charles answered. "Sir Arthur makes his own decisions."

"He is very much interested in expanding trade in China."

"Of course. The trade is lucrative for the Company and could be made more so if they did not need to send all the revenues they collect in India to support their commerce with China."

"The emperor still demands silver?"

"Yes. The Chinese are no more impressed with our goods and products today than they were when you and Macartney visited."

"Nevertheless, your recent travels to China must provide Sir Arthur valuable insight."

"I do not think Sir Arthur and I would agree to much."

"Do not underestimate what you may have in common."

Charles said nothing. The only thing the two men might have in common was the reaction of their cocks when Miss Terrell was near.

# CHAPTER TWENTY-THREE

Terrell observed the outline of his hardened cock against his trousers.

"I will have your cunnie tonight, Miss Terrell," Sir Arthur said. "Not Miss Isabella's. Yours."

She had anticipated this and was prepared to honor his demand. She wore her customary attire. Some men required more provocation, but Sir Arthur's arousal needed no coaxing.

"And you will have it, Sir," she said, "but let us build the anticipation, that you may spend with force."

"I have not all evening," he replied. "I am to have dinner with two of the Company Directors on an important matter. I anticipate long hours of discussion."

"How much time have you here?"

"Twenty minutes."

She feigned a pout to hide how much she welcomed the news. "I am to have so little of your time?"

"My apologies," he said, though she could tell he was not at all sorry.

"Fear not. I can do much in twenty minutes."

He smiled. "I had a feeling you could."

"You may have my cunnie, Sir Arthur, if you can catch me first."

He raised his brows. The room was not large, and he doubtlessly thought her easy prey. But she was young and limber. When he moved toward her, she easily put the settee between them.

"You wish to play games, Miss Terrell?" he asked.

He seemed mildly amused but also a little exasperated. It was difficult to interpret the man for he often appeared displeased.

"Games can heighten excitement, Sir Arthur. Think of how much grander your victory will be when you have expended some effort in its attainment."

"You are a clever little blackamoor."

He set down his cane, and his eyes narrowed to anticipate her move.

She tossed her hair back. "I await, Sir Arthur."

He moved to his right, but she was ready for him. He returned to the center and made an attempt to lunge for her over the settee. She escaped him easily and stood behind the chair she had once tied him to.

"Teasing doxy," he grunted.

He feinted left but then leaped to the right. Her agility enabled her to recover in time, and she ran back to the settee. He stumbled over a footstool in his haste to reach her and cursed.

"Come, we use valuable time," she taunted.

He circled round the settee, but they only succeeded in exchanging positions. After several minutes, they were both breathing harder. His eyes blazed with frustration. She had an eye to the clock above the mantle and knew she would allow him to catch her soon enough, but *he* did not know this. With a roar, he grabbed one end of the settee and shoved it aside so that it could no longer serve as a barrier. In that time, she had retreated toward the bed. He advanced. She climbed over the bed with the ease of a squirrel moving among the trees. He had not her quickness, and she stood safely on the opposite side, holding onto a bedpost.

"Damned slattern, I did not pay to be taunted," he huffed.

She discerned his patience to be at an end. They now had but ten minutes. She made a curt move to the right. He tried to dodge over the bed. She moved to the left. He scrambled up and dashed around the end of the bed. She returned to the right, though there was nowhere to go but the head of the bed and the wall, and tried to scramble over the bed. He caught her, shoving her against the headboard. The side of her head struck the wood, and she was momentarily dazed. He yanked her head back by her hair.

"I wonder that you'll play games with me after this, Miss Terrell," he growled from behind.

She felt him fumble with his fall. Her skirts were thrown over her waist, and seconds later, after poking her and missing his intended target a few times, he plunged himself into her. She allowed him to pommel his cock into her. Aroused by the primitive chase, she was moist, and his lack of attention to her pleasure did not perturb her. But his rough yanking of her hair was a little alarming. In his fury, he might not know if he snapped her neck. He drove his hips at her, seeking his own fulfillment.

She decided it was better that he spend soon. She flexed her cunnie along his member. He grunted. With a final howl, like that of a dying animal, he began to shudder against her. She could feel his seed spread within her.

When he pulled out of her, she felt a surge of relief. He was not a large man, but he was still stronger than she. The superior might of his sex did not often frighten her, but she wondered that she could trust him to contain the use of his strength. There was a hint of uninhibited violence in his motions.

Free of his hold, she turned around to face him. He was panting and had to lean against the bedpost for support.

"And we have two minutes to spare," she said. "You

may not have enjoyed the sport, but I think you will agree that you spent with greater glory as a result of it."

He said nothing. Straightening, he replaced his fall. When he had composed himself and smoothed back his hair, he took up his cane and approached her.

"Clever Negress," he said with a playful pinch of her chin. "Perhaps I will reconsider your little games. Till tomorrow, Miss Terrell."

He adjusted his cravat and took his leave. She watched him depart and was reminded that she needed to proceed with more caution with the man. She sat upon the bed a while, feeling his seed trickle from her. She was a little sore there for he had not waited or sought for her cunnie to lubricate itself. Her cunnie had taken two cocks in less than four and twenty hours time, yet neither had been that of Master Gallant.

His words from last night continued to burn her ears. *I have no interest in Miss Terrell...her qualities do not compel me...it would not be Miss Terrell were she the last woman remaining.* Had he not the courage to speak the truth to her face? she had wondered in anger as sleep eluded her the better part of the night. Was it simply her blackness that deterred him? Had she misunderstood his arousal? Had he responded to her only because he was the sort of man who found titillation in the degradation of being with a blackamoor?

Her heart heavy, she had clung to her pillow in between tossing and turning in bed. She had tried to sustain her dander toward him because the other emotion tugging at her heart, sorrow, was not one she stomached well. She did not understand her sensitivity or the intensity of her feelings. Perhaps she had erred in seeking his attentions. She ought to have contented herself with the Worthingtons and Arthurs of the world. They had more of what she desired in terms of wealth. Did she honestly think she could entice a man with more worthy qualities? But what could be more worthy than wealth?

Well, it was his loss if he would not have her! She could

have presented him such rapture. He was a fool not to even sample what other men paid good coin for!

Yet, why did she feel as if the loss was hers? Why did that awful sensation continue to wring her heart? Why did she still desire him after he had said what he had?

The questions had haunted her for hours with a few bursts of rage relieving the frustration, the helplessness, the wretchedness, till sleep provided a more lasting respite.

"Sir Arthur was in a merry way," Madame Devereux told her when they crossed paths in the hall after Terrell finally emerged from the room.

"That man has a merry way?" Terrell could not resist.

"None of your imp, miss," Devereux cautioned, though she herself seemed in a good disposition. "He did tell me that you exceeded all expectation."

"I am gratified to hear it."

Devereux nodded. "I think you will make of him a frequent patron. She has proved rather disappointing. I thought her extremely pretty, but I think her skills do not compare to yours."

Terrell doubted Sophia was pleased to hear such a thing.

"With a man like Sir Arthur, your efforts will be well rewarded."

Madame patted her cheek and went on her way. Terrell could not dismiss the uneasy feeling that came with thinking of Sir Arthur, but she dismissed the senseless sensations. All that mattered was his coin.

She went upstairs to her room and found it vacant. Yesterday, she had retrieved the book that Master Gallant had left. Picking up the novel, she sat and turned its pages. Here was proof once again that she could never fit in the society she sought or possess the right qualities to attract Gallant. How she wished she could read! The story, the images that could be conjured by these plain letters, was extraordinary. Sitting upon her bed, she reached her hand up her skirts and fondled herself to the memory of the various passages Miss Katherine and Master Gallant had read aloud. After several minutes, she achieved her climax.

Yet she could not shake the emptiness within her. She had woken in the morning with no more clarity than she had when she fell asleep. Should she assist in Miss Katherine's instruction tonight? Master Gallant would undoubtedly dispense with her services, but would he be persuaded by Wendlesson? The viscount would favor her presence. Nevertheless, despite being a guinea richer, she would rather not have to attend to his lordship's satisfaction a second time. The seeds of betrayal, planted while Wendlesson pounded into her, had fully sprouted the following day. How would Miss Katherine receive the knowledge that her new friend had lifted her skirts beneath her husband? Terrell doubted Wendlesson had confided his deed to his wife. Miss Katherine would be devastated if she knew.

The Wendlessons were not the first married couple Terrell had had congress with, but the others had possessed experience, with both parties seeking the threesome. The Wendlessons were newly wed and Miss Katherine a neophyte and clearly in love with her husband. Her ladyship had granted Terrell entry into her instruction, had sought her assistance, and relied upon her company. *She*, in turn, had repaid her by fucking her husband for a guinea.

Lying back upon the bed, Terrell let out a deep sigh. She had merely acted as she always had at the Red Chrysanthemum. She availed herself of every opportunity because she could not trust to luck or benevolence. The world was cruel and merciless. As a slave, she had been granted little quarter. Could she spare quarter for anyone else? Those at the bottom of society had litte choice if they wanted to survive. They could not afford more virtuous qualities. If she had acted in the vein of a selfish creature, it was out of necessity and she ought not feel shamefaced.

But she did.

"I must make amends," she muttered to herself. Her guilty conscience would not find relief till she had improved the situation for Miss Katherine. She had to participate in at least one more lesson. She was certain she could guide Wendlesson's arousal toward Katherine, and if she succeeded, he would no longer require anyone but his wife.

But what if Master Gallant would not permit it? A part of her, in stubborn defiance, wanted not to care. She could inveigle her way into the lesson. But then she would have to face Gallant once more. Perhaps, now that she better understood what he truly thought of her, she would see the aversion she must have overlooked in him before. And that would pain her. As much as she liked to think that no man could affect her in that way, it would not be the case with Gallant.

The revelation surprised and troubled her. She was a fool to give a damn what his opinions were if he disdained her, yet still she could not help being drawn to him. How could she have misjudged him so?

No. It could not be. His cock did not lie. And she could not have imagined the look of lust in his eyes. If he did not desire her seduction, as he had professed, he could have made far worse statements to repel her. Though she did not fully comprehend the incongruence in what he had told Wendlesson with his actions and responses to her, she perked with hope. She was done with despair. She wanted a return to her prior confidence. She would know once and for all how Gallant truly found her. If her qualities did not compel him, then what sort of qualities did? Those of Mistress Scarlet? Did he prefer a more domineering woman? She could be such a woman for him.

Resolved, Terrell went downstairs to the dressing room but did not find Miss Katherine. She went to inquire of the doorman, Mr. Baxter, if the viscountess had arrived.

"Miss Katherine is not to come tonight," Mr. Baxter informed her. "This note came from her, and I am to present it to Master Gallant."

"Not to come?" Terrell echoed. "But why?"

"The note provides the explanation."

"And?"

Mr. Baxter hesitated but he opened the note. "It says the Countess is ill, and that she must remain by her ladyship's bedside tonight."

Terrell took the note. "I will give it to Master Gallant, as I mean to ask after Miss Katherine with him."

She did not elucidate further but went in search of Jones, a tall and imposing blackamoor. Madame employed him to assure the order of the Red Chrysanthemum.

"Miss Terrell," he greeted with obvious pleasure.

Madame would allow no consorting amongst her employees or Terrell might have entertained his attentions from time to time. He was nearly as strapping as some of the slaves whose bodies had been made brawny through hard labor.

"I've a task for you," she said, amazed at how quickly her mind conjured a plan, fixing the details as she spoke. Thinking on her intentions made her heart race. She had a surprise for Master Gallant.

# CHAPTER TWENTY-FOUR

Charles was rarely tardy. It was not a matter of concern to a dominant. A submissive had to wait as long as needed. But he had Lord Wendlesson to contend with and a small window of time to work with Miss Katherine. He had rushed to the Red Chrysanthemum after returning home to first shed his dust-covered clothes and change into fresh attire. He had stayed long at Ashlington House, for there was much to discuss in the way of the election. His mother had written to a cousin of hers who was acquainted with the Marchioness of Hertford, whose London home was a sort of center for Tory electioneering. Together, they called upon their neighbor, Mr. Stephenson, who had also pledged his support for Charles.

Then, while riding back to his townhouse in London, he had come across a carriage that had lost a wheel. One of the occupants, an elderly lady, did not fare well out in the elements. He had offered his horse to take her to the nearest posting inn. The events resulted in his arriving twenty minutes late to his appointment at the Red Chrysanthemum.

"Did Miss Katherine arrive with Lord Wendlesson?" he asked of Mr. Baxter as he gave the man his hat and gloves.

"Miss Katherine?" Mr. Baxter inquired. "Ah, if you find Miss Terrell, she means to speak with you regarding

Miss Katherine."

Charles frowned. No doubt the viscount had sent for the minx already. He would have preferred to do without Miss Terrell, but he was too fatigued from his travels to reach a strategy for what to do with her.

After handing Baxter his cloak, he took the stairs three steps at a time. He reached the third floor as quickly as he could. He heard no voice from inside the room and wondered if the Wendlessons had tired of waiting. He opened the door.

Upon entering, the world was rendered pitch-black.

A bag or sack had been thrown over his head and tightened about his neck. He tried to tear away the casing blinding him, but he was knocked to the ground. A hefty knee kept him down, and his hands were pinioned behind him, his wrists bound with a familiar rope. He struggled, but his assailant moved with surprising quickness and strength, yanking him to his feet by one hand.

Charles did not think Lord Wendlesson possessed the muscle to manhandle him as if he were no more than a child. Thrown into a chair, his arms were lifted and pulled behind its back. More rope wrapped his torso to the chair, his ankles were bound to the wooden legs, and even his thighs were secured to the seat of the chair.

But if not Viscount Wendlesson, then who would assail him in such fashion? Was this some manner of jest? Had he offended his lordship? Charles heard the heavy footsteps of his assailant retreat toward the threshold. The door closed. Hearing nothing but the crackle of moderate flames from the fireplace, he wondered if he had been left alone. The air inside the hood had grown warm with his breath. He could not discern what fabric encased him, but he hoped to be relieved from its confines soon.

He was not alone. His body tensed at the sound of footsteps advancing toward him. The tread was softer, lighter than that of his assailant. He tried his bonds, but they held. She stood near him. He could sense her presence, discernible, too, by the fragrance she wore. He could not place the perfume with any man or woman he had come across at the Red Chrysanthemum. Could this be a scheme of Joan's, part of his indenture to her?

"Who goes there?" he asked, though he did not expect a reply.

He strained against the ropes and heard a sharp cracking sound against the side of the chair. A crop. Did she mean to warn him against struggling? To answer his own question, he did his best to loosen the bonds and received the slap of the crop upon his upper arm. Despite the layer of his coat and shirt, he felt the sting. She had struck him hard as a message. He ceased any visible efforts to escape his bindings. He was fairly certain she stood in front of him and could not see him testing the bonds behind him.

Something touched his cheek. The crop again. Would she strike his face? But the crop only caressed his cheek, its end brushing against his chin, then down his neck. It traveled from his collar to his chest, then his midsection, past waist and pelvis, and along the inside of one thigh. After reaching the knee, it reversed course back along the thigh till it grazed his cods. The crop tapped his thigh playfully before, without warning, it slapped him— painfully close to his cock. He knew not if the woman missed her target intentionally or not.

"Mistress," he appealed. "I am engaged for the evening. I am expected by Viscount Wendlesson and Miss Katherine."

This time it was her hand that slapped him—across the face. It was a firm slap and not from a weakling. She did not mean to let him go.

"Madame would not be pleased if I fail to make the appointment this evening."

She slapped him again. *What the devil—*

"If you intend to keep me indisposed," he said, his cheek smarting and the warmth inside his hood making speech uncomfortable, "I only ask that you send word to the Wendlesson, that they may not be kept waiting."

Instead of leaving, she rained the crop down upon him. On his thighs. His arms. His chest. But he was more vexed than hurt. He did not want to keep the viscount and viscountess waiting, though they should have been in the room first. He considered the possibility that his female assailant might be Miss Katherine, but the woman moved with too much confidence, her blows too strong. Like him, the Wendlessons must have been delayed. He doubted they currently occupied the same room.

To be sure, he asked, "Are we alone?"

No answer. Perhaps the woman did not wish her voice to betray her identity.

"Strike my left thigh if yes, the right if no," he suggested.

The crop fell against his left thigh.

"Do the Wendlessons know I am indisposed?"

The crop fell against his right thigh.

"Will you not send word to them?"

The right thigh.

"Why not?" he demanded, then rephrased the question to one she could answer. "You intend they should wait?"

The right thigh. Had she struck the wrong leg?

"Will they have to wait for me long?"

She struck his right inner thigh, close to his cods. He tried to understand how this was possible, provided she told the truth, but was soon distracted when she pushed his forehead back, forcing his chin up. Something smothered his mouth. Her mouth. Her nearness made the perfume flood his nose. She kissed him ravenously through the linen, found his bottom lip, and bit and pulled. His head swam and the blood coursed, unwanted, down his lower body.

"Surely Joan—Does Madame Devereux condone this?" he asked when she released his lips.

To no surprise, she slapped his right thigh.

"Then this is solely your doing?"

She slapped his left thigh. He thought of Mistress Brownwen. She did not patronize the Red Chrysanthemum with any frequency nowadays, but she would have the interest to see a man at her mercy. He would not have expected her to have the nerve to assault him without his permission, however.

"What do you intend with me?" he asked.

A hand grasped him between the thighs. He grunted as the padded part of the palm rubbed against his cock.

"May I be relieved of the hood?" he tried.

The right thigh. There was one other likely possibility, he contemplated to himself.

"Free only the mouth, that I may feel your kiss upon my lips."

She seemed to consider his request, then rolled the bottom of the linen up to his nose. He breathed in the relief of cooler air. He sensed she stood straddled with legs on either side of him, but he could not feel nor hear the rustle of skirts. She ran a thumb across his lips, then covered his mouth with her own, gently kissing this time.

He felt plump, soft lips, a tongue that enticed his into a hot, wet dance. She held his head still with her hands as the kiss deepened. Her mouth became more demanding, her tongue plunging deeper. Tension coiled in his pelvis.

When at last she released his mouth for breath, he said, "I think we may dispense with the hood and the leg tapping, Miss Terrell."

He sensed her stiffen, but then the hood was torn from his head. Miss Terrell stood over his lap, her curls falling past her shoulders. She wore a corset with a high back and a low scooped front, an article from the mid-18th century when a nipple might peek from a woman's décolletage. The garment forced her breasts to swell upward. They gleamed before him. She wore no shift, nor, as his gaze went lower, any petticoats. Instead, she had on a…loincloth. No, it was merely a scarf tied round the hips and knotted in front to cover the most intimate parts of the pelvis. The crop was tucked into the scarf at her hip. Her legs were completely bare. Upon noting the lush thighs, he tried to stay his cock from hardening.

"Where are the Wendlessons?" he demanded.

"They are unable to come tonight," she replied as she played with tendrils of his hair. "The countess was unwell, and Miss Katherine attends her at bedside."

He jerked his head from her hand. "Why did you not tell me this before?"

"You did not ask."

She began unbuttoning his coat.

"Untie me," he directed, wishing he could stop her hands, which went to his cravat next.

"Why? You are free of engagements this evening."

The devilish minx.

"You knew the Wendlessons would be absent," he said.

"I came upon the note from them."

"Came upon or intercepted?"

"Does it matter?"

He shook his head in disbelief. "Untie me now."

"Tonight I am *Mistress* Terrell, and you would do well to cooperate."

*What in damnation…*

His cravat undone, she began to unbutton his waistcoat. He strained against his bonds and earned the back of her hand against his cheek. Though he did not often curse before the fair sex, he emitted a resounding oath.

"This is an outrage," he said. "If Madame did not approve—"

She slapped him across the other cheek. Hard.

But her gall stunned more than the blow. Who did this chit think she was? What submissive in her right mind would dare treat a dominant in such fashion?

He gave her a stern stare. "Take care, Miss Terrell. You do not wish for me to take matters to Joan."

She finished unbuttoning his waistcoat. "You will think differently when I am done. You will wish an encore of tonight."

In an instant, he recalled his dream from the other night. His cock perked in response, and he forced himself to think only on his indignation.

"It is against the rules to coerce a member against his or her will. It will result in prompt expulsion from the Red Chrysanthemum."

Brushing aside his waistcoat, she undid his braces and slowly pulled his shirt from his trousers. The placement of her hand so near to his crotch made him stiffen.

"If, in five minutes time," she said, "you truly and fully have no desire to be fucked, I will release you."

*Bloody hell.* He knew not he could last five minutes. What was it she intended? Whatever it was, he wanted no part.

Or did he?

"I warn you, Miss Terrell."

Ignoring him, she straddled his thighs and pushed his shirt all the way up his chest. The weight of her derriere on his legs set his whole body aflame. He stared with widened eyes at the swell of her hips, more dramatic than those of most women her size, and that part covered yet underscored by the knot of the scarf.

Lowering her head, she licked at a nipple.

"Miss Terrell!"

She closed her succulent lips about the bud and sucked. The sensation tickled and electrified.

"Desist!" he commanded.

But she only sucked harder. This was intolerable. Yet what could he do? He wanted to consider all that he might say to intimidate, cajole or entice the impudent doxy to stop, but forming complete thoughts was no easy feat when his nipples were on fire.

"You wish for me to take you as my submissive," he managed, "but this behavior hardly aids your case."

"I think it does," she murmured against him before biting his nipple.

He grunted through gritted teeth. She swirled her tongue around his other nipple. He felt the sensation in the tip of his penis. He had to do something. But his threats had had little effect on her. He refused to bribe her. He would not reward such unacceptable conduct.

"Miss Terrell! You place your membership here in jeopardy," he tried once more.

She intensified her licking and sucking. "You are worth the risk, Master Gallant."

He gasped at the sensations assaulting his body. "Your conduct is utterly reckless!"

She covered his midsection with kisses. Heat churned in his groin. He closed his eyes, wishing for a way to transport himself from his body that he might not succumb to her delicious caresses. Those lips of hers…

"If Madame should discover your devilry—are you willing to imperil your arrangement with Sir Arthur?"

She grasped him by the chin. "Do not fear me, my pet. Take pleasure in your submission. I give it to you gratis."

He resorted to bribery. "I would sooner pay you to leave me be."

"It is not coin but cock I wish from you."

His ears burned. The brazen jade. He was torn, furious at his helplessness yet oddly *aroused* as well. Was his vanity to blame? He had declined overtures before but never came across a member of the Red Chrysanthemum who desired him with such intensity that she would resort to such drastic measures. He watched as her hands dropped to his trousers and began to undo his fall.

"Miss Terrell, you will stop this foolishness!"

His temples throbbed, feeling his last defenses were about to be breached. She drew back his fall. To his relief, his cock was only partially hard. He prayed it would go no further, but, deep down, he knew the odds were against him.

She slid off his thighs and, kneeling upon the ground, positioned herself between them. With his ankles and calves tied to the legs of the chair, he could not close his knees. He tried to block the effect of seeing Miss Terrell between his legs, but she had only to touch his cock, which lengthened toward her in an instant. She stroked his shaft softly with her fingers. He stymied any reaction—the desire to moan, grunt or sigh—and stilled his body as if nothing were happening. But his cock hardened with every second.

"I think I begin to convince you, Master Gallant."

"Do not credit yourself so quickly. It is merely a reflex. The touch of a vile beast might elicit the same response."

She stopped, and her countenance grew grave.

"And is a blackamoor comparable to a vile beast?"

"No," he protested, baffled by her statement. "I merely meant the desire to spend is a weakness in my sex. A woman might be foul, old, and homely. She may be covered in warts and reek of odors too ghastly to name, but a man will find a way to spend if her cunnie is forced upon him."

The look in her eyes only hardened. Surely she knew he did not mean to accuse her of being foul, old, and homely. She seemed to recall herself and closed her hand about his shaft, and it took all of him not to groan. The sensation of her fingers wrapped about him was exquisite.

He was damned.

# CHAPTER TWENTY-FIVE

$\mathbf{A}$ vile beast? Foul, old, and homely? Did he suggest she was no more desirable to him than these?

Tempering her indignation, she stroked his shaft delicately. He betrayed no emotion. But she had heard the desperation in his voice, and she would turn his resistance into craving before night's end. He would beg for her to fuck him. He would beg a *blackamoor* to fuck him.

"What are your intentions?" he asked hoarsely.

In response, she licked at the tip of his cock. He inhaled sharply. She pressed her tongue at the underside of his shaft and dragged up its length. She closed her mouth over the top and sucked. She drew back and allowed his cock to pop out of her hot, wet orifice.

"Miss Terrell…"

His member tasted as fine as she had imagined it would. She took him into her mouth once more, deeper. A low groan escaped his lips. Gradually, she withdrew completely and, for a moment, refrained from touching him, that he might mourn the absence of her mouth. She stared at his lovely Thomas, admiring its shape and how it stood at proud attention. She licked over his pisshole, then lapped at the underside of the crown.

Looking up, she found him staring at her, his jaw clenched, eyes widened. She felt a heady surge. He was not the first man she had bound. She once had a patron who insisted on being rendered helpless, asked to be beaten, and begged her to torment his cock without allowing him to spend. Master Gallant did not appear so inclined. The touch of anger had not left his eyes. She began to doubt herself. Perhaps she had been mistaken, and he and Mistress Scarlet did not exchange roles. Though she would never have thought the staunch Mistress would submit to any man, she had witnessed the woman's surrender to Master Gallant. It had amazed her then that anyone could conquer Mistress Scarlet.

And now she held captive the man who had slain the dragon that none before him could. Her pulse raced, and her hand nearly trembled. She had rendered this mighty man powerless. To see such a man of strength and forbearance at her mercy both frightened and excited. He was hers. Hers to toy with. Heat flared in her loins at the sudden rush of power. It was not often she held dominion over a white man. His kind had controlled her life since birth. Even though she had had her freedom these past few years, she yet depended upon them, relied upon them for her livelihood. In that, she was not wholly free.

Realizing she had done and said nothing for some time, she suppressed the conflict and unease raging inside her. She could not let him witness her uncertainty. She had gone down a path and would take it to its end. It was too late to turn back.

"Do you require a safety word, Master Gallant?"

"Impudent chit," he replied.

"I would recommend a word with but one syllable, preferably something simple and boring."

But he paid little heed to her prattle. "What do you hope to accomplish with all this?"

"Your pleasure. Does it gall you to realize you can be aroused by a blackamoor?"

Again, he appeared confounded. "You wish to prove something with all this mischief, Miss Terrell?"

She paused. *Yes*, she was inclined to answer. She wanted to prove him false, that her qualities did compel him, at least in the venereal sense, and that a Negress could be desired by a man like him. She wanted him to recant his statement, that far from being the last member of the Red Chrysanthemum he would wish to be with, she might be the first. All manner of men have desired her. Men of standing. Men of wealth. Why not Charles Gallant?

*Because he was better than all those men who had desired her.* Because he was *good* and *decent*, and good decent gentlemen did not desire blackamoors like her. A peculiar pain reared itself once more. He thought himself better than her. Well, if she could not prove herself to be worthy of his regard, she would prove that she could make him spend as well as—better than—anyone he would consider over her.

Lowering her head, she engulfed his cock with her mouth. He stiffened against the chair, groaning despite himself. She swirled her tongue against his shaft and sucked till her cheeks caved.

"Miss Terrell!"

She released him from her mouth but replaced the grasp with her hand, smoothing her salivation over its length. He shivered when she grazed the sensitive underside. She slid her hand down to cup his cods.

"If you proceed," he warned, "you may consider this your last night at the Red Chrysanthemum."

Defiantly, she squeezed her hand about his sack. He emitted a loud grunt and would have bent over were he not tethered to the chair.

"Do not make me punish you, Mister Gallant. I vow I can be as severe a mistress as Mistress Scarlet."

He looked puzzled by her statement but was distracted once more when she took his cock into her mouth. She allowed it passage to her throat. *My God, he tastes fine.* She felt him pulse inside her mouth and relished the fullness of him. Relaxing her throat, she slid more of him into her. She wanted all of him, wanted to swallow him as deeply as she could.

"Miss Terrell!"

But his cry emerged as a haggard gasp this time. She took him into her throat until her nose tickled the hairs at his pelvis.

"Damnation," he whispered.

It had taken her much practice not to choke when she took cockmeat deep into her throat. She had trained herself using dildos long and wide. Ruth had explained that the accomplishment would drive his sex mad with arousal, and this had indeed proved true. Master Gallant was no different.

She released him and immediately wanted to take him back into her mouth. Not only did he feel marvelous, the motion distracted her from the trembling inside of her. Her heart was beating madly, and she felt herself on fire from head to toe. Through the torrent of emotions and thoughts warring inside of her rose one that did not confuse: desire.

"Do you wish me to stop?" she asked.

Their gazes locked, and the seconds passed like hours. All the considerations that had passed through her moments ago no longer mattered. She wanted only to pleasure him, to give him that divine ecstasy and thereby claim him. For a brief moment, he would be hers and only hers.

"No."

She blinked. "No? You wish me *not* to stop?"

His breath was haggard but his speech firm. "Do not stop."

Relief and joy washed over. Taking a deep breath, she eased her mouth onto the crown. Grasping his shaft with both hands, she licked and sucked vigorously at the head of his erection.

"My God," he gasped.

Showing him no mercy, she encased him once more to the hilt. She would make him spend as he had never spent before. With her mouth, she pulled at his cock, sucking as hard as she could, as if she could detach his member with the force of her mouth. Her lips caressed his length as she moved her head up and down his shaft.

From his fierce grunting, she could tell victory would soon be hers. She cupped his sack and squeezed. He roared at the pain. She alternated between swallowing his cock and pressing his cods together till he thrashed in the chair. Worried he might fall over, she abandoned the scrotum and concentrated upon pleasuring his cock. She sensed the subtle thrusting of his hips. If he were not bound in place, she was certain he would be pushing his cock deeper into her.

His surrender was imminent. She fit two fingers beneath his cods and anus. She pressed and rubbed the small but sensitive area.

It was his undoing. His roar filled her ears. His hips bucked against the restraints. Hot liquid shot down her throat. She had to release some of him to prevent herself from gagging. She tasted him upon her tongue, savored the convulsing of his cock, and milked as much of his mettle as she could. There was a faint and familiar saltiness to his seed, and a tang that did not seem to exist elsewhere. She drank her fill, then licked him clean.

He shuddered several times before his shoulders relaxed. He looked at her without expression, his eyes glazed, pupils dilated. Triumphant, she licked at his cock. He grunted, his member being overly sensitive.

Desire, hot and heavy, burned through her veins. Though his climax gratified her as much as her own might, she needed to release the pressure inside her. It was madness how much she desired this man, even after all that he had said. And despite his declarations, he had spent at the hands of a blackamoor. She could have exalted in her victory and made known his hypocrisy to him, but, at present, she only wanted to spear herself upon his cock. It would need to harden again first.

Sitting down upon the floor before him, she spread her bent legs. The ends of the scarf covered her intimate parts. She caressed the insides of her thighs.

"Your cock makes for a fine meal, Master Gallant," she said and licked her top, then bottom lip, "the taste of your mettle sweeter than any confection."

He breathed deeply still and stared at her in silence.

"I would swallow your cockmeat whenever you demanded," she added as her hands slid toward her cunnie. Leaning back on her left arm, she slipped her right hand beneath the scarf to fondle the button of pleasure there. "Would you like for me to dine upon your cock a second time?"

He said nothing. She stroked herself with her forefinger, then raised the digit to her mouth. Pretending the finger to be a cock, she closed her lips about it and sucked while fixing her gaze upon him. Though softened, his cock shifted. She swirled the finger inside her mouth and sucked harder. His eyes fixed upon the digit she pulled and pushed between her lips. Having coated it well, she returned to caressing the bud beneath the scarf. She flexed her cunnie, causing the pleasure to ripple through her nether regions.

Still caressing herself, she lay fully upon the ground. She lifted her hips, and he would have stared directly at her cunnie but for the covering of the scarf. For several minutes, she gyrated and writhed upon the floor, her desperation to be filled growing. She panted and moaned. Her hips went up and down. She rubbed herself harder and faster. With her free hand, she touched herself all over, the breast, waist, and belly, imagining it was his hand that caressed her body. Knowing that she performed for *him* made the whole enactment more erotic for her.

She glanced through lowered lashes to see that he had not looked away. With his mouth dropped open and his eyes molten, his expression differed little from that of Sir Arthur when he had born witness to the sight of her frigging herself. Satisfied, she closed her eyes. The tension in her body could coil no further, and she allowed it to release in spasms through her limbs. With loud gasps, she convulsed upon the ground.

When the climax of her pleasure finally began to ebb, and all tremors had dissipated from her body, she removed her hand from beneath the soaking scarf and looked over at Gallant. There was a hard set to his jaw, and he did not look pleased.

But between his thighs, his cock protruded tall and hard.

# CHAPTER TWENTY-SIX

*D*amnation.

Charles felt uncomfortably hot, and it was not all due to his exertions against his bonds. His cock was stiff once more and tense, as if he had not spent—gloriously—but moments before. What manner of witchcraft did the Negress before him employ? He knew the answer entailed no sorcery at all, but only her nubile body and an uncanny ability to employ its qualities in the most mesmerizing movements. He moved his gaze from the sodden scarf between her thighs—he had both wished to see it removed and prayed for it to remain—to her eyes, bright with desire still. The blood pulsed to the tip of his cock.

He stared at her supple lips, lips that had wrapped his shaft in the most exquisite pleasure. Where had she learned to swallow cock in such magnificent fashion? How many cocks must she have taken into that bewitching mouth of hers? His cock had never been sucked so deeply, so vigorously. He had fought the desire to spend, though he had known, within seconds of being inside her mouth, that resistance was futile. And did he not immediately regret his surrender. The climax that had erupted from him could have launched his body to the rafters.

But he ought to be furious with her. Furious that she

had ignored all his warnings, his pleas. Furious that she had succeeded in proving his weakness. Furious that she had dared restrain and force herself upon him. She had lied. She had said she could be the most perfect submissive. Instead, she had done the very opposite and treated him as the submissive one. He had no trouble assuming the role provided he had agreed to it. Far from being consulted, he had been manhandled and pushed unwillingly into the position. The audacity of Miss Terrell was beyond any he had ever witnessed.

But none of that mattered to his cock. The damned member would betray him once again. It wanted to be buried inside her mouth, his hand fisted in her hair, pushing her face to his pelvis till his hairs tickled her nose.

Miss Terrell rose to her feet, not in the slightest tired. "May I partake of the main repast?"

She straddled him and locked her hands behind his neck, her cunnie hovering perilously close to his erection.

He wanted to say no. Or yes. He wanted to say yes, but pride would not permit him to grant her a second victory.

Placing her lips beside his ear, she whispered, "I will take your silence as a 'yes.'"

He did not dispute her. She sank herself onto his length. There was no protesting now. Her hot, sopping cunnie sheathing his cock had wiped out all thought. She gasped, her mouth widely agape. Perhaps she had not intended to take him into her so fully or swiftly, but the heavy moisture in her cunnie allowed his cock to glide easily into her. He felt her flesh caress him, and he had to close his eyes to keep from bursting inside of her.

Neither of them spoke. Neither of them moved. He did not want to give her the satisfaction of spending twice, but being inside her cunnie was every bit as marvelous as being inside her mouth. Her cunnie had to have seen heavy use, but it was extraordinarily tight, as if she might have been a virgin still.

*Bloody hell*, he cursed when her cunnie rippled along his

cock. He opened his eyes to find her smiling at him. The minx knew just how to provoke him, provoke his body. She wriggled, then ground herself on him.

"Oh...*yes,*" she murmured.

And this, too, provoked him. He recalled her words: *I would swallow your cockmeat whenever you demanded.* How many men would have leaped, stumbling over themselves, at such a proclamation? They would deem him an undeserving fool if he refused such an offer. Indeed, he was tempted to determine if she spoke true. After all that she had said and done, he was not inclined to trust her. Perhaps he ought to accept her declaration and punish her by demanding her mouth to exhaustion. The thought made his cods boil.

She pressed herself up till only the crown of his cock remained inside her. She flexed her cunnie, making him groan, then fell atop him. His cock rammed into her. He grunted, amazed at the pleasure engulfing his shaft. Threading her fingers through his hair, she yanked his head upward and covered his mouth with hers. He thought he could, at the least, resist the raping of his mouth. But the soft texture of her lips proved too much. He parted his lips to allow her tongue passage and thought he tasted his own seed upon her.

She kissed him with vigor, her tongue exploring every crevice of his orifice, sucking his lips till they tingled. His head swam. He needed desperately to thrust into her. That he could not because he was bound to the chair only magnified his desperation.

Pushing aside the linen about his throat, she licked and kissed him there. When she began to suck his neck, he cursed. *God help him.* What man of flesh and blood would not succumb? He wondered that he could resist responding to her ministrations if his life depended upon it. She tightened her grip in his hair, and he welcomed the pain. He would have preferred another slap in the face to what she did next.

She pushed herself up his shaft, her cunnie pulling along his member. When she slid back down, her cunnie pushed against him. It was beyond glorious. He wished his hips free, that he might meet her thrusts and drive his cock deeper into her. As he was bound, however, all the exertion was hers. He had but to sit and enjoy the hot, wet cunnie embracing him as it went up and down his shaft. He was going to spend. The only unknown was when.

"You must not," he grumbled. "A condom…"

He had to force the words, for his cock wanted none of it. It wanted to remain pulsing in her wet heat, skin to cunnie.

"Fear not," she murmured between soft bites of his neck. "I am barren."

He heard her words as if from the end of a tunnel. He tried to grasp their meaning.

"You cannot be certain," he said.

"I am."

He wanted to believe her, but she was doubtlessly too young to claim herself barren. She quickened her motions, her legs showing no signs of tiring, though she had begun to pant in earnest and perspiration glistened upon her brow, her nose, and bosom. He made one last effort at protesting, but the primal part of him wanted to stake his claim of her and spill his seed inside of her. He wanted also to see her spend upon his cock. That alone gave him the forbearance to withhold his release.

She pumped herself along his length, using his shoulders as leverage, but as she neared her climax, or because she tired, her motions became more erratic, compelling his cock into different angles.

He had never tried so hard not to spend. Because he did not want to hand her another easy victory. Because he did not want to face the possible consequences of spilling his seed inside of her. But reasoning could not win the day. Not when she felt so divine upon his cock. Not when the sounds of her groaning and grunting filled his ears.

Not when her ass slapped against his legs. Not when she cried out and erupted into spasms, her cunnie grasping his member, her body shaking atop his with such violence that he thought she might fall from his lap.

And that was when he could contain himself no longer. With a roar, his release poured from him with a force that threatened to knock him to the ground were he not bound to a chair. His body jerked against the rope, and she had to hold onto him to keep her balance. He met her liquid heat with his own, relief and pleasure rippling through him from head to toe. He pumped himself into her womanhood, desiring to unload more than he had into her. His cock throbbed as if in anger.

She had won. His forbearance could not prevail over the charms of her body. When the intensity had subsided, he slumped into his bonds, spent. He did not think he had ever been fucked like that before.

Their foreheads touched. She breathed heavily still but spoke for the both of them. "*My God.*"

She crushed her lips to his. His fury momentarily cast aside, he did not pull away. At last, she disengaged herself and stood, stumbling a little for her legs were shaky. She went to the sideboard and poured herself a glass of port. Still dazed, he watched as she returned to him, riveted to the movement of her hips and the enchantment of her navel above the now crooked scarf.

She presented the glass to his lips and he drank, though he wondered that she did not untie him as of yet. With a hand on his shoulder, she finished off the last of the port in the glass, then bent to speak into his ear in a low and sultry tone.

"Stay awhile, Master Gallant. I shall return."

She squeezed his shoulder and walked past him.

*Where the devil is she going?* But he could not turn his head far enough to see. He only heard the door open and close. Left alone, he growled in frustration. His indignation returned. She had succeeded in ravishing him. What more did she intend? To make him suffer? Did she wish to avenge the time he had left her strung to the rafters for thirty minutes?

He strained against his bindings, but they held. He looked about for any implement that might cut or loosen the ropes but found nothing. Even if he could hop his way over to the sideboard, he would not be able to open the drawers. He had no choice but to wait for her.

He would have to inform Joan. Miss Terrell had gone too far. Joan would have to dismiss her from the Red Chrysanthemum, per her own rules. Sir Arthur would not be pleased, but he did not require the Red Chrysanthemum to partake of Miss Terrell's charms. Though Charles did not want to be responsible for Miss Terrell's loss of room and board, she was a clever young woman. And pretty. And seductive. While she enjoyed the favor of Sir Arthur, she would not require the Red Chrysanthemum either.

Charles looked down at his traitorous cock, which lay to the side. She had not replaced his fall. The Red Chrysanthemum abounded with comely members of the softer sex, but they did not all inspire his cock as Miss Terrell did. Was it the novelty of being with a Negress? While in China, he had been curious to lay with an Oriental. Their small, light bodies differed from those of the women in England. But he had never taken much notice of blackamoors before.

He shook his head at himself, at how easily he had surrendered to her. She held much more influence over him than he was comfortable with. While his cock had enjoyed her mouth and her cunnie, he had ceased to mind his bindings and incapacity. But now that he could once again think—with the appropriate head—he did not appreciate the submissive position he had been placed in. *He* was the dominant. Not Miss Terrell. He needed to make that known to her. He needed to reclaim his authority.

After what must have been twenty minutes, Miss

Terrell returned. She had exchanged her scarf and corset for a shirt, a man's shirt, that might have served as her nightgown. He could see the tops of her bosom over the drawstrings of the décolletage. Beneath the hem, her feet and calves were bare. Despite the plain garment, she still compelled.

"How delightful," she said playfully. "You've not moved."

Where the bloody hell would he have gone?

"Would you care for another glass of port?"

"Am I to be relieved of these bonds, Miss Terrell?" he asked.

"Not yet. And I am still Mistress Terrell."

"Then I will decline the port, Mistress Terrell," he said. He did not want to drink from her hands again as if he were a babe.

"Suit yourself."

She stood behind him and rested an arm on each of his shoulders. She held a book before him. *Fanny Hill.*

"First, I will have you read, Master Gallant, from the top of the page."

Despite her claim to being the Mistress, he noticed she had addressed him as the dominant several times. This, then, was her revenge. She had made him wait, pinioned and helpless, as he had made her wait. Now she made him read, as he had asked her to read.

"'Next we took from the side of the room a long broad bench,'" he began, deciding that his compliance might encourage her to release him sooner, "'made easy to lie at length on by a soft cushion in a callico-cover.'"

She leaned her head beside his to look fully upon the book. "'Do you begin from the top of the page?'"

"Yes," he answered, wondering why she asked the question. Her fragrance tickled his nose and he wanted to sneeze.

"Proceed. But slower."

He did as told. "'And everything being now ready, he

took his coat and waistcoat off; and at his motion and desire, I unbuttoned his breeches, and rolling up his shirt rather above his waist, tucked it on securely there; when directing naturally my eyes to that humoursone master-movement, in whose favor all these dispositions were making, it seemed almost shrunk into his body, scarce showing its tip above the sprout of hairy curls that clothed those parts, as you may have-seen a wren peeping its head out of the grass.

"'Stooping them to untie his garters, he gave them to me for the use of tying him down to the legs of the bench: a circumstance no farther necessary than, as I suppose, it made part of the humour of the thing, since he prescribed it to himself, amongst the rest of the ceremonial.

"'I led him then to the bench, and according to my cue, played at forcing him to lie down: which, after-some little show of reluctance, for form-sake, he submitted to; he was straightway extended flat upon his: belly, on the bench, with a pillow under his face; and as he thus tamely lay, I tied him slightly hand and feet, to the legs of it; which done, his shirt remaining-trussed up over the small of his back, I drew his breeches quite down to his knees; and now he lay, in all the fairest, broadest display of that part of the back-view; in which a pair of chubby, smooth-cheeked and passing white posteriors rose cushioning upwards from two stout, fleshful thighs, and ending their cleft, or separation by an union at the small of the back, presented a bold mark, that swelled, as it were, to meet the scourge.'"

She purred at the image and looked down at his cock, which, while not erect, showed visible signs of awakening. Cleland's prose had warmed his blood. He would have thought his cock to lay dormant the remainder of the night, given his fatigue and after having spent twice.

"You fancy the scene do you, Master Gallant?"

He ignored the question and continued to read. "'Seizing now one of the rods, I stood over him, and according to his direction, gave him in one breath, ten lashes with much good-will, and the utmost nerve and vigor of arm that I could put to them, so as to make those fleshy orbs quiver again under them; whilst he himself seemed no more concerned, or to mind them, than a lobster would a flea-bite. In the meantime, I view intently the effect of them, which to me at last appeared surprisingly cruel: every lash had skimmed the surface of those white cliffs, which they deeply..."'

Having reached the end of the page, he waited.

"Do you require a respite?" she asked.

"Not at all, Mistress," he replied. He had a newfound suspicion.

She hesitated, then turned the page.

He finished the sentence. "'...reddened, and lapping round the side of the furthermost from me, cut specially, into the dimple of it, such livid weals, as the blood either spun out from, or stood in large drops on; and, from some of the cuts, I picked out even the splinters of the rod that had stuck in the skin.'"

He skipped the next sentence. "'I was however already so moved at the piteous sight, that I from my heart repented the undertaking, and would willing had given over, thinking he had full enough; but, he encouraging and beseeching me earnestly to proceed, I gave him ten more lashes.'"

He skipped to the next paragraph, but she said nothing.

"'Resuming then the rod and the exercise of it, I had fairly worn out three bundles, when, after an increase of struggles and motion, and a deep sigh or two, I saw him lie still and motionless; and now he desired me to desist, which I instantly did; and proceeding to untie him, I could not but be amazed at his passive fortitude, on viewing the skin of his butchered, mangled posteriors, late so white, smooth and polished, now all one side of them a confused cut-work of weals, livid flesh, gashes and gore, insomuch that when he stood up, he could scarce walk; in short, he was in sweet-briars.""

When next he skipped a paragraph, she stiffened at the lack of transition but said nothing, confirming his suspicions. She had not acted out of deliberate defiance, risking punishment, when she had refused to read for him before. She was not being contrary. She simply did not know how to read.

"'He had then little to do, but to unloose the strings of my petticoats, and lift them, together with my shift, navel-high, where he just tucked them up loosely, and might be slipt up higher at pleasure. Then viewing me round with great seeming delight, he laid me at length on my face upon the bench, and when I expected he would tie me, as I had done him, and held out my hands, not without fear and a little trembling, he told me he would by no means terrify me unnecessarily with such a confinement; for that though he meant to put my constancy to a trial, the standing it was to be completely voluntary on my side, and therefore I might be at full liberty to get up whenever I found the pain too much for me."

"You may turn the page, Mistress."

"Of course!" she snapped. "I merely pause to praise how well you read."

She turned the page for him.

"'All my back parts, naked half way up, were now fully at his mercy: and first, he stood at a convenient distance, delighting himself with a gloating survey of the attitude I lay in, and of all the secret stores I thus exposed to him in fair display. Then, springing eagerly towards me, he covered all those naked parts with a fond profusion of kisses; and now, taking hold of the rod, rather wantoned with me, in gentle inflictions on those tender trembling masses of my flesh behind, than in any way hurt them, till by degrees, he began to tingle them with smarter lashes, so as to provoke a red colour into them, which I knew, as well by the flagrant glow I felt there, as by his telling me, they now emulated the native roses of my other cheeks.

When he had thus amused himself with admiring, and toying with them, he went on to strike harder, and more hard, so that I needed all my patience not to cry out, or complain at least. At last, he twigged me so smartly as to fetch blood in more than one lash: at sight of which he flung down the rod, flew to me, kissed away the starting drops, and sucking the wounds, eased a good deal of my pain. But now raising me on my knees, and making me kneel with them straddling wide, that tender part of me, naturally the province of pleasure, not of pain, came in for its share of suffering: for now, eyeing it wistfully, he directed the rod so that the sharp ends of the twigs lighted there, so sensibly, that I could not help wincing, and writhing my limbs with smart; so that my contortions of body must necessarily throw it into infinite variety of postures and points of view, fit to feast the luxury of the eye.'"

This time he stopped for, in his mind, he saw not Fanny but Miss Terrell displayed in similar fashion, her backside as properly abused. She reached for the corner of the page to turn it, though he had not reached the end, then reconsidered.

"Your reading has excited my appetite," she said, tossing aside the book. "I hunger again for cockmeat."

Her words made his cock jerk. She did not fail to notice and went to stand before him. She smiled at his erection. "I see you be wanting more as well."

"First, I bid you untie me, Mistress," he said, "to improve the circulation in my…extremities."

She hesitated but bent down and undid the ropes about his legs. He stretched the limbs. She undid the bonds about his arms, and relief rushed into them. Standing, he shook the numbness from his arms.

His anger returned with the freedom. Now it was his turn for a little revenge.

# CHAPTER TWENTY-SEVEN

He was not the vengeful sort. Charles disliked resentment. But Miss Terrell needed to be taught a lesson. She could not indulge her mischief with impunity.

"Would you like me to imitate Miss Fanny Hill?" she asked. She glanced at the crop she had left behind. "I believe my crop could do for a rod."

She stepped toward him and reached a hand to his hardened cock, but he grasped her swift by the back of the neck. He wound his hand up into her hair and pulled her head back. She gasped, arching her back.

"You'll not dare your impudence with me again," he snarled. He had not had his arse whipped since his first year at the Red Chrysanthemum.

"I see you are ready to exchange roles," she said between short breaths. "I take it my performance as a mistress meets with your approval. Does it excite you to submit first?"

*What the bloody hell was she on about?*

Ignoring her question, he said, "I am done with you, Miss Terrell, but first, you will be punished for your deed."

He could see a mix of emotions in her eyes, bright

despite the dark color of her irises. Punishment was what she had claimed she wanted, but she would rue her wishes when he was done. He dragged her toward the bed by her hair. She stumbled to keep up and nearly fell to the ground when he stooped to pick up the cords of rope. She grabbed at his arm to keep him from pulling too hard upon her hair. If he moved roughly, he was too incensed to care.

"But—" she began. "I thought you—"

"I did warn you, Miss Terrell. You should not have ignored me."

He tossed her, face first, at the bed. Her body curved over the side. Releasing her hair, he yanked her left hand behind her and wrapped the rope about the wrist.

"I did not think you sincere," she protested, her voice filled with concern. She struggled against him, but he kept her pinned to the bed. "I thought you to be playacting, as I was."

"You thought wrong. A grave mistake I vow you will not repeat when I am done with you."

He bound another cord of rope about her other wrist.

"I gave you the opportunity of a safety word," she accused hotly.

He paused. She was right. In the moment, he had not paid heed, partly because was too overcome with his own indignation and because he had been too astounded at what she was attempting. Grabbing her by the hair once more, he turned her head and looked into her eyes as much as he could with the awkward angle.

"Would you have ceased if I had uttered one?"

Her lashes lowered, and, after a pause, she murmured, "Perhaps not at first."

At least the minx was being honest. He released her

head and went to tie the left rope to the farther bedpost at the foot of the bed.

"What does it matter what I *might* have done?" she challenged. "You wanted my cunnie."

He went to secure the end of the other rope to the bedpost near the head of the bed.

"I merely gave you what you desired," she continued, "though you would not admit to it, leastways not with words."

She stared straight at his still hardened cock. He quickly replaced his fall.

"And was my mouth, my cunnie, not every bit as glorious as you imagined they would be?"

Her words chafed because they were true. Nevertheless, a proper dominant would have ensured he had a safety word and not run roughshod over his protests. The chit thought herself high and mighty, but he would give her a proper set-down. He surveyed her, one arm pulled toward the foot of the bed, the other to the head of the bed, her delicious rump rounding the side of the bed.

"You thought my cunnie unworthy of your consideration," she continued, "but now you know mine is as agreeable as that of any white woman."

"Be silent!"

Her talk was making his head throb. And his cock, too. He strode over to the sideboard. This room did not offer the array of implements that the room on the second floor did, but he found a wooden paddle. He preferred it to the crop. He wanted something that would jolt his arm when he used it.

Walking back toward the bed, he stared at her derriere. He could see the shape of the two half-spheres through her thin shift. Though he had exerted little of himself, he began to breathe heavily. He unbuttoned his sleeves and rolled them to his elbows. With his free hand, he pulled up her shift and bared her arse.

He lost his breath.

The buttocks were so beautifully formed, the flesh smooth and unblemished. Alexandros of Antioch could not have sculpted such perfection. Charles remembered well how the orbs had felt beneath his hand, which itched for a reprise. But a hand would not be punishment enough for this one.

He examined the paddle. He would have gone for a thicker one had it been available. Perhaps one with holes to allow for a faster, harder blow. She had craned her neck around to see what he held. The corners of her mouth curled a little, and he wondered that the paddle would be sufficient. He clasped both hands on the handle and smacked it against her arse.

The crack of wood to flesh, followed by her cry, rang in his ears.

The proper dominant in him could not resist reminding her of her safety word, though, like her, he wondered that he would desist. This was not about discipline but about justice and retribution.

"I presume you do not require a safety word," he said while he allowed the sting of the blow to filter through her flesh.

"Is that the best you can do?" she returned.

Her impudence astounded him, but he gave her a second whack that made her legs buckle. Her arse took on a pinkish tinge. The sight of it made the blood pump faster through his veins. This woman had toyed with him, taken advantage of his circumstances, ignored his protests, and, finally, forced herself upon him against his will. He brought the paddle down on her backside several times. When he was done, she would not sit for days.

Her cries had turned into wails. She clutched at the rope stretching her arms. Her arse glowed red. *God help him.* His cock was as hard as flint. He no longer wanted to paddle her. He wanted to sink his cock into her. What man, when presented with such lush, round cheeks, would not want to feel them slapping against him?

Warm from his exertions and his arousal, he wiped the perspiration from his brow. His heart pounded and his cock strained against his trousers, but he would not indulge its cravings. Why was it when he punished her, he felt as if he were the one being punished?

She had succeeded in proving her point. Even this, what ought to have been her penance, might be considered a triumph for her. She had wanted the worst of what he might do to her. Well, she would have it. Without mercy. He spanked her with the paddle as hard as he could. Her breath caught in her throat, and she seemed not to know whether to inhale or exhale. Her legs had begun to quiver. Her derriere had to smart something fierce by now. He struck her again. She buried her face into the bedclothes and mumbled a curse.

"A perfect submissive would thank her master," he said.

"Forgive me. Thank you, Master."

"You could never be the perfect submissive, Miss Terrell. You are far too willful and wayward."

"Then teach me."

An emotion he could not immediately place surged in him. "I have a student at present, and she is far less unruly."

"I can be taught, Master Gallant. Was my behavior not improved last night?"

"And you have undone all goodwill with your deplorable actions tonight."

He could not see her face, but he knew her to be thinking. He allowed her the time to consider his statement and for repentance to blossom.

"Deplorable?" she said at last. "By all means, accuse the lowly blackamoor. The wicked Negress caused your lasciviousness."

He blinked, hardly able to believe her words. Where was the contrition? She dared accuse him of inequity, of eschewing blame for something *she* had done? The chit was outrageous.

"You forced yourself upon me," he said evenly.

"You ceased to protest."

"I should never have been placed in such a position to begin with."

"I merely brought to surface desires you buried beneath prejudice and conceit."

Her response stunned him. His dream flashed through his mind. Even if, on a level too deep for his consciousness to recognize, he had desired to be taken by her, it was not her prerogative to see it done. And how was she accusing him of *prejudice* and *conceit*? What prompted these complaints? Had she heard more of his conversation with Wendlesson than he had previously thought?

"You presume too much, Miss Terrell."

"Do I? Then tell me, how is it your cock cannot stop hardening for me?"

His lips pressed into a firm line, and he felt his anger rise, for what she said was true. It was the lot of his sex to be easily aroused, and it vexed him that he seemed particularly vulnerable to her charms.

"Is it not now hard?" she inquired. "Do you not wish to fuck me?"

His cock throbbed. Eying the lips just below her arse, he thought he saw the glisten of moisture. It made his head swim. Was it possible the paddling had aroused her? She might have been wet from before. He recalled how well her cunnie had fit about his member, how its walls had caressed his length.

She wriggled upon the bed. "I am at your mercy, Master Gallant. Will you not take me? My cunnie or my arse? Or both."

*Bloody...hell.* The thought of plunging himself into her rectum was too much.

"A man's cock is conditioned by primitive nature to respond, but the mind knows better," he replied.

"You'll not admit your lust," she said.

"I admit my sex to be weak in carnal matters, but that does not mean we need be governed by our weakness."

But she was not listening. "You cannot fool me, Master Gallant."

"We have wishes—"

"The cock does not lie."

"—and desires apart from—"

"I know—"

"— the venereal—"

"—you desire to *fuck me.*"

"Silence!"

He needed her to stop talking. He could feel her words in his blood, echoing in his ears, swirling in his groin.

"Fuck me."

She would drive him insane. This was precisely why she could not make a perfect submissive—or a half-decent one. She was incorrigible. Though the challenge—could he teach, discipline and inspire her to perfect submission?—intrigued him.

He shook his head. He should not be entertaining such thoughts. Tossing aside the paddle, he slid onto the bed beside her and fisted his hand in her hair. Yanking her head back, he noticed her eyes glimmered with un-spilled tears, most likely from the paddling.

"I have not yet finished with your punishment."

"Then proceed! Only promise to fuck me when you are done."

He untied the rope from her left hand and spun her around beneath him. He grasped her by the neck with one hand. Why would she not be silent? Never had he given so much of himself to his emotions, raw and seething. Through his rage, desire continued to roar. He felt more beast than man.

"I asked for silence!" he growled.

Her eyes should have blazed with fright, not defiance. "Promise to fuck me first."

*Damnation.* What would it take to make her behave? Walloping her backside was plainly not enough. He reached for her nipple and twisted it through her shirt. She screamed. He had straddled her hips, and they bucked against him. The motion fueled his ardor. When at last he released her, she was mewling. Her eyelashes fluttered. But still she persisted.

"Promise," she murmured, gazing at him through lowered eyelids.

*Damn you.* He grasped the shirt with the intention of ripping it down the middle, freeing her nipples for further torment. Her eyes flew open.

"Wait!" she cried out. "Let me keep the shirt upon

me."

He could hardly comprehend her entreaty. She had made no protest when he had bared her arse and spanked it with a paddle. She had asked him to fuck her. Why would she now concern herself with a shirt?

"You want I should honor your request when you have denied all of mine?" he returned.

"You wanted me *not* to stop."

The possible truth of her words quelled his reply. Frustrated that he could not refute her, he began tearing the shirt instead.

In his earlier haste, he had not secured the ropes as tightly as he was his custom, and she managed to yank her remaining hand free. She grasped his forearms and dug her fingernails into him. Surprised, he released the garment. She tried to scramble from him, but he caught her and kept her pinned beneath him.

"Master Gallant, you may do anything you wish to me," she huffed and panted, "but I will keep my shirt, if you please."

His instincts were to oblige, but he was still too enraged. She had granted him no consideration yet wanted it for herself? He would not allow such hypocrisy. He would not allow her to prevail, not when she had challenged his manhood and disrespected his position as a dominant. The hellcat offered no respect. She deserved none in return.

"It does not please me," he said, grabbing the shirt and yanking it down her shoulder.

"No!"

She cuffed him on the side of the head. Hard. Turning, she attempted to crawl from under him. He recovered in time and seized the collar of the shirt. The fabric ripped between them.

His blood, boiling throughout him from head to toe, turned cold.

He stared at her back, crossed with thick scars where a flogger had torn the flesh. The flogger must have cut deep and often to mangle the skin in such fashion. In contrast to the rest of her smooth and supple body, her back appeared as a rocky terrain, the grooves and ridges forming scars that would last her lifetime.

Stunned and horrified, he stumbled from her. She retreated from him, clutching the torn shirt to her.

"Forgive me," he gasped. He could not tell if the tears brimming upon her lashes were old or new. "Who—How…?"

She would not look at him. When she spoke, her voice sounded small, a far cry from her customary bravado. "I would that you take your leave, Master Gallant."

He did not move. The sight of her mangled back had not left him. The scars were old, thus they could not have been made in her time at the Red Chrysanthemum. Then where and by whom?

"*Now.*"

In sharp contrast to her earlier desires, her current aversion to his presence struck him with the force of a carriage and four at full speed. She looked ready to cry, and for that reason he hesitated to go. But still she refused to look at him. She stared intently but, as if blind, seemed to see nothing.

At a loss, he decided to oblige her and made his way to the door without word. She had not stirred from where she sat upon the bed, appearing as vulnerable as Miss Katherine had her first night. He swallowed with difficulty, wanting to speak to her, but not knowing what to say.

"Miss Terrell," he finally said, hoping the words would come to him.

She turned her head away from him, making clear her disinclination to hear him.

He looked down at the floor, his prior rage hung in abeyance, replaced with sentiments less preferable than anger. He opened the door and took his leave, closing the door gently behind him.

# CHAPTER TWENTY-EIGHT

Terrell heard the door close. Angrily, she brushed the tears that threatened to pour from her eyes. The look of horror upon his face had made her want to retch. She wanted him, of all people, not to see her disfigurement. Her beauty had failed to persuade him, and now surely he could only look upon her with great revulsion. She choked back a sob.

Scrambling out of the bed, she made her way up the stairs to her room and exchanged the torn shirt for her shift. The wounds were years old, but tonight the scars stung as the linen covered them. She dressed in her short stays that laced in front, petticoats, stockings, and her muslin gown. She wanted to bury the scars beneath as many layers of clothing as possible.

She wiped the last of the moisture from her eyes. She refused to cry. In truth, she had brought this misery upon herself. Her arrogance, her impudence, had led her to actions that had lost her Master Gallant. She supposed it a fitting consequence. While she had genuinely believed that enacting the role of a Mistress would titillate him, she ought to have heeded her reservations. But she had pushed onward because of what *she* had desired, because of what she wished to prove. If she had not been so indulgent, so rash, she would not have vexed him. How he must hate her now!

His threat of seeing her expelled from the Red Chrysanthemum echoed in her ears. She had flouted protocol, committed an awful deed. If Madame should banish her, she had no one to blame but herself. But if Madame should spare her, she could not remain while Master Gallant despised her. She would dread crossing paths with him. Regardless of what fate awaited her, she had to ask his forgiveness.

She slid on her slippers and rushed down the stairs. She went straightaway to Baxter.

"Master Gallant," she said, "has he left?"

"His horse was ready but a few minutes ago."

Then he could not have gone far, but she could not waste time by fetching her shawl from her room. She dashed into the coolness of night. Turning right would take her toward the river. She knew not where Gallant resided, but all the superior addresses lay to the left. She hurried down the dimly lit street. She had the luck of a full moon in a sky with few clouds to veil its brightness.

A man on horseback had just turned off the street and into an alley. She scurried after him. The alley was dark and narrow, but it was too short to invite the more dangerous elements of the night.

"Master Gallant!" she called.

The horse stopped. For a moment, when the rider did not turn the animal around, she thought perhaps it was not him. All she saw was the faint silhouette of his head and cloak. He dismounted and turned to face her, but she could not quite make out his physiognomy.

"Miss Terrell."

She emitted a breath of relief. It was Gallant. His tone was not welcoming, but she ought not be surprised by it. He had never appeared particularly pleased to see her, and if she had not allowed her desires to overwhelm her, she might have taken note of this fact.

A stiff silence existed between them.

"Forgive me," she said plainly. "You were right. I presumed too much. I assumed that, because you had been with Mistress Scarlet, you were partial to submitting from time to time."

The words did not come easily, for she had not considered what she was to say. His silence did not aid her. When the horse neighed and restlessly pawed the ground, he turned from her to quiet the steed. She bit her bottom lip at his lack of response. Perhaps he thought she attempted to justify her actions.

"I ought not have made such an assumption. Or I ought not have acted as I did upon my suppositions. And I should not have—I wanted to, selfishly, prove that you could desire me, that you could desire a blackamoor, that I could be as desirable to a man such as yourself as…I wanted to prove you wrong, perhaps even suffer for your words. It was wrong of me, and it was…deplorable."

She paused to provide him a chance to respond. Still, he said nothing. The silence was agony.

"Perhaps you think I speak only to stay you from reporting my behavior to Madame Devereux," she said, not caring if desperation reverberated in her voice, "but I would gladly leave the Red Chrysanthemum if I knew I had your forgiveness."

The horse had calmed, but Gallant did not turn back to face her. She wondered what more she could say? That she would let him suspend her from the rafters for hours? Or suffer any punishment he desired to mete out? Should she promise never to trouble him again? Why did he not look at her?

"Please," she said, attempting a step toward him. "Forgive me, Master G—"

He turned, but with such swiftness that her breath left her. He caught her by the waist, and before she could complete a cry of surprise, he had her pressed against the wall with his body. His mouth descended upon hers.

Her heart leaped into her throat. Surprised, she did move but submitted herself to his kiss, thrilling to the pressure of his lips upon hers, how forcefully they claimed her. His hand cupped her beneath her jaw, compelling her to offer her mouth up for him to feast upon. And he devoured her with a vigor that took her breath away.

Surrounded by him, her body thrilled at the heat rushing through her. She would have responded to his kiss if his mouth did not overpower hers. Over and over, he took her lips and swept his tongue into the depths between. She tried to keep apace but found it easier to simply submit herself. Her hips yearned toward him. The coolness of the night had melted away. He had set her body aflame and only he could extinguish the fire by matching his heat to hers.

He released his hand from her, but she kept her head where it was as he seared kisses down her neck and about her collar. She could not have imagined such bliss! She moaned when he drew the side of her neck into his mouth and arched herself to provide him unfettered access. She wanted to throw herself at him but feared her aggression would startle him.

As if sensing her need, he pressed his body to her. He

propped his left hand above her and circled her waist with his right arm, bringing her hips to his. He returned to kissing her mouth. This time he engaged her participation but guided the pace and motions so that she followed effortlessly. He kissed with palpable fervor but with an *elegance* that left her in awe. He was as skilled at the act of kissing as he was with the ropes, and she relished every moment. If not for the desperate yearning between her legs, she would have been content to lock lips for hours on end.

She gasped when his right hand cupped a tender buttock. The effects of the paddle had not dissipated. As if knowing why she gasped, he slid his hand from her arse to the back of her thigh, lifting her leg to his hip. His cloak shielded them in part, trapping the heat of their bodies. She ground herself at him, wanting him, needing him. Wrapping her arms about his neck, she tried to pull him closer to her. She wanted to be smothered by his body. He resisted and instead brought his left hand down between them. He reached beneath her skirts and found her hot and wet.

She exhaled a moan into his mouth, which still covered her own. He softly caressed the plump, wet lower lips between her thighs. His strokes sent magnificent currents throughout her body. How she had longed for him to touch her there! When his thumb grazed her clitoris, she shivered with such thrill that she would have thought she had never been caressed there before. His touch was divine. There was much she longed to do, but she dared not disrupt his beautiful ministrations.

He captured her sighs with his mouth even while he stroked the fire between her legs without a single misstep. Once more she marveled at his abilities. It was as if he were a musician playing two instruments simultaneously. The effect nearly overwhelmed her. His breath upon hers, the taste of him on her lips and inside her mouth, his hand holding her leg, his warmth enfolding her, the hard wall against her back—there was no escaping even if she wanted to escape.

When he slid a finger into the center of her liquid heat, she nearly whimpered. Her hands dropped to the lapels of his coat, and she dug her fingers into them as a second finger entered her. He stroked the area behind her mound, and she would not have required long to spend, but she resisted as best she could.

"P-Please," she panted, "let me spend upon your cock."

He murmured against her lips, "Request denied."

She took that as permission to spend and let the gates to ecstasy fall. With a cry, she surrendered herself to the delightful convulsions racking her body. Wetness gushed from her, coating his hand and her legs as she trembled and thrashed between him and the wall. She might have fallen to the ground if he had not held her up. Pleasure radiated from her loins. Her cunnie clenched and unclenched the fingers still inside of her.

When at last she returned from where he had catapulted her, she opened her eyes and stared intensely at him. After collecting enough of her breath, she managed three little words.

"Now fuck me."

"Damn your filthy tongue," he groaned.

"Fuck me," she urged, her tone a plea.

He pressed his brow to hers, his breath shallow but not from exertion. "I cannot. I ought not."

"Have I not already compromised you? Is your seed

not already spilt inside of me?"

With a relenting growl, he set down her one leg to attend his fall. In seconds, his cock was freed. She did not require a good look to know it stood hard and stiff. He hoisted her up by the legs, and she gathered her skirts higher. When he thrust into her, the triumph exceeded all prior glory. For now he speared her of his own free will, because he wanted to. He desired her despite her ugliness. Were she not still in the throes of arousal, she might have cried.

Her cunnie had never been this wet, and his cock slid with ease into her. Wanting all of him, she wriggled herself as far down his shaft as she could till the hairs at her mound touched his. With her cunnie, she caressed the prize inside of her.

"My God," he breathed upon her brow.

They each remained still. Perhaps he needed a moment to compose himself. Or perhaps he wanted to relish, as she did, the sensation of their bodies joined in perfect harmony, fitting together as nature intended. His cock throbbed inside of her, sending shivers to her head. She no longer cared if she spent. That he was buried deep inside of her was gratification enough. This narrow alley, the space she occupied between him and the wall, was like a small piece of heaven.

He flexed his cock, stirring her arousal. She responded by clenching her cunnie. He gasped, and his breath grew tremulous. Her arms now rested upon his shoulders, and she wound her fingers into his soft hair. In the dark, she found his gaze.

"Thank you," she whispered.

He groaned. Holding on to her legs, he drew his hips back, then pushed himself into her once more. Pleasure boiled inside her hot, wet cunnie. She grasped his member as if famished, as if his cock had not been inside of her less than an hour before. He could have pounded himself into her, and she would not have protested, but he took his time and found a rhythm and an angle that elicited from her the loudest gasps and most desperate moans.

She could have remained passive and allowed him to make the majority of the effort. He was strong enough. But she wanted to perspire as he perspired, pant as he panted. The muscles in her thighs began to burn. As if sensing this, he propped her more fully against the wall. She braced her upper back into the wall to provide him resistance so that he could thrust into her deeply. She wanted him to spend, but her own ecstasy beckoned, and she could not resist its call for long. The pressure. The pleasure.

"Permission to spend," she gasped.

His pace quickened, every thrust pushing that exquisite agitation closer and closer to its peak. Containing the tension now became more difficult than the attainment of the climax.

"Permission to spend," she huffed. "Master Gallant—"

His hands tightened upon her legs, and he shoved his hips at her quick and furious. If he ground her into the wall with his force, she did not feel it. She knew only that her body was on the verge of imploding and exploding all at once.

Through her cries, she heard him grunt. "Granted."

She had already begun to spend and cared not if he knew or approved. The most rapturous tremors racked her body. She jerked and seized against the wall, against his body. He engulfed her wails with his mouth, perhaps fearing she would wake the tenants of the building against which they fornicated. Pulling her hips into him, he pumped himself into her till his own feral growl threatened to match her cries in volume. He bucked against her several more times before his body trembled and shook. She felt his liquid heat mingling with her own.

After a haggard breath and a final shiver, he eased himself from her and set her gently upon her feet. He leaned against the wall over her as if to shelter her from the night. She heard nothing above the beating of her heart and their labored breathing. The moist evidence of their congress clung upon her thighs, and she reveled in every part of the moment, from his nearness to the lightness of being emanating from deep within her. If she could extend the moment into eternity, she would have done so.

"Does this mean you forgive me?" she asked when she had collected her breath. As soon as she spoke, she worried what the answer might be. Men could have the quickest changes of heart after spending.

"Do you forgive me?" he returned.

Astounded, she looked up at him, searching for his eyes. "For what purpose need I forgive you?"

"I tore your shirt."

"I deserved worse."

"No," he said sternly.

He straightened and replaced his fall. She immediately missed his nearness.

"How did you come by such scars?"

She looked away, preferring not to recall he had seen them, and gave a dismissive shrug. "I was born a slave."

"And what, in God's name, could occasion such atrocity?"

He spoke with anger, and she had no wish to vex him further. Nor did she desire to revisit the more painful years of her life.

"I am not the only slave to bear such marks," she replied, and decided she ought to return to the Inn.

He stayed her. "Upon women? Surely you do not suggest this is common?"

"I consider myself one of the fortunate ones, Master Gallant."

His grasp upon her arm tightened. "What do you mean?"

"You've no wish to know, and I've no wish to recount the horrors of Barbados."

At that, he had no choice but to press her no further. He dropped her arm. However, she sensed his reluctance to leave the subject, and proceeded to walk from the alley out onto the street before he found a way around her objections. Hearing his footsteps and his horse behind her, she paused.

"There is no night watch about these parts," he explained. "I will see you safely returned."

She smiled to herself at his chivalry.

"That is kind of you, Master Gallant."

He placed his cloak about her shoulders and led his horse by the reins. She felt the fine fabric of his garment and pulled it tighter about herself, though not for warmth.

"I will replace your shirt," he said after they had walked a block in silence.

"I prefer a different manner of repayment."

He stopped. "Miss Terrell, what transpired tonight ought not occur again."

"Do you still intend to have me thrown from the Red Chrysanthemum?"

"Have I not forgiven you?"

She took a relieved breath, for he had not affirmed in

words that he had.

"But do not suppose," he added, "that I am always inclined to forgiveness. Do not cross me twice."

"Yes, Master. I am grateful for your mercy."

"Do not patronize me, Miss Terrell."

"Will you discipline me for it?"

"Miss Terrell, there can be nothing between us. You are spoken for by Sir Arthur, and he is not a man I wish to vex."

"No?"

"Sir Arthur and I must deal with each other in other capacities. I am in the midst of seeking the burgess for Porter's Hill. If I should be so fortunate to win election, he and I will be colleagues in Parliament."

"Ah." She now comprehended his reluctance to upset Sir Arthur. Her vanity felt uplifted by this knowledge. "Sir Arthur owns a good deal of Porter's Hill, does he not?"

"How do you know this?"

"He boasted of it."

"We both of us could benefit from Sir Arthur's good graces. Thus, it would be far better if I simply replaced your shirt and nothing more."

"I did not intend to ask for more of your cock if that is what worries you."

He started.

"At present, I merely wish to be your assistant once more in your next lesson with Miss Katherine."

"That would not be wise."

"Why not? She is ready for much more, if you can make proper use of me. I think she is near to what Lord Wendlesson desires."

"Unlikely. We have had but three lessons."

"She has advanced quite far in three lessons."

"Yes, but consider that she started with pure trepidation. She is still apprehensive."

"But she trusts you. Do not underestimate the value your presence and guidance provides her."

He was quiet, then said, "She hardly knows me."

"One does not require a great deal of time to know you, Master Gallant," she replied softly.

"Says a woman who thought I would be interested in assuming the role of a submissive to her."

She grinned. "Are you certain you do not?"

"How fares your backside, Miss Terrell?" he returned.

She grinned. "It be a bit tender still."

"There is a poultice—"

"I know of it."

Though she would have been happy to have him apply it to her smarting buttocks, she would not stay him longer.

"How do you know Miss Katherine is ready for much more?"

"The intuition of our sex. She finds comfort in my presence as well."

"Yes, how did you manage to form such a bond with her so quickly?"

"Because I knew her fears as only a woman could. I could continue to be of service to Miss Katherine."

"And Lord Wendlesson?"

Was that a dash of jealousy she heard in his tone?

"If you make sufficient progress with Miss Katherine, he will not require me," she replied.

He seemed little satisfied. "And if I do not?"

"That is not an affair you need concern yourself with."

"I hope he compensated you a pretty penny."

She thought she saw the muscle along his jaw ripple. "I charged him a full guinea."

His brows shot up.

"But I think for you, Master Gallant, I shall always like to give of myself gratis. But that is to be a secret betwixt the two of us, eh?"

They had reached the Inn. She removed the cloak and handed it to him.

"Grant me time with Miss Katherine tomorrow night," she said. "I will ascertain if she is indeed ready for more. If I am wrong, you may dispense of my services."

"Why do you wish to lend your time to this cause?"

"You do not trust that I act out of charity?"

"I do not."

"If I am right, perhaps I redeem a little of myself in your eyes. If I am wrong, perhaps I will find myself another guinea richer."

He bristled, and she could see he regretted asking his question.

"Good night, Master Gallant," she said as she went up the front steps.

"Good night, Miss Terrell," he said.

Baxter opened the door, and if he was surprised to see Master Gallant again, he showed no evidence of it.

"Miss Terrell," he greeted.

She entered without looking back. Baxter was a seasoned servant at the Red Chrysanthemum and was never known to gossip. But she thought she had glimpsed a shadow in one of the windows as she and Gallant had approached the Inn.

"One suitor not enough for you?"

Terrell turned into the hallway to find Sophia smirking, her arms crossed over her bosom.

"Alas, it would seem he is not as endowed in the purse as Sir Arthur," Terrell replied.

"But far tastier. I wouldn't mind a bite of that one meself."

Terrell stifled her jealousy before replying, "It be true I am a greedy wench, but I do favor my cocks to be made of gold when possible."

She knew it was on the tip of Sophia's tongue to accuse her of avarice, of the corporal kind, and it satisfied her to take the opportunity from her. Sweeping past Sophia, she headed upstairs. The splendor of being in Master Gallant's arms had not dissipated, and she knew she would relive the moment over and over again. Indeed, she wondered that she would sleep tonight. She had his forgiveness when she thought she might have made of him a permanent enemy, but her instincts had proven true. The man had desired her.

But his hesitation to cross Sir Arthur would be hard to overcome. She did not wish to exasperate Master Gallant, but now that she had spent in his glory, she knew one night would not be enough. Her desire for him had only grown, and her biggest fear was how to quell the flames before they should burn the both of them.

# CHAPTER TWENTY-NINE

Sitting at his breakfast table, Charles threw back the shot of ginseng before washing it down with a cup of coffee—very strong coffee. He wondered that he would ever take to the taste of the Chinese root, but after a long day yesterday, followed by a prolonged evening, thanks to Miss Terrell, he needed the effects of the ginseng, which the Chinese believed to include improved health, alertness and vitality.

He took up the paper, but his mind wandered straightway to the events of yester evening before reading a single headline. He had already replayed the memories, but he went through them again for he could not make sense of his emotions. A part of him was still in shock, mystified by all that had transpired. He had gone from rage to forgiveness in but a few hours. That had never happened before. Was it pity that had moved him? He could not recall the vision of her scarred back without cringing. By all means, pity played a part. No creature need suffer such violence. He wondered who had administered the flogging. What had Miss Terrell done to provoke the harsh flagellation? How old was she when it had happened? His stomach turned at the possibility that she might have been much younger than she was now.

It was astonishing that she could adopt flippancy

toward such an outrage. How could she consider herself one of the "fortunate ones"? He remembered reading the accounts of slavery penned by Thomas Clarkson, but the worst abuses seemed to fall upon the male slaves. Charles did not believe female slaves managed to escape maltreatment, but till he had seen the evidence of it before his own eyes, he had harbored some hope that the worst of it did not fall upon the gentler sex. He would have it out of Miss Terrell.

Which meant seeking her out. Less than four and twenty hours ago, he had been on the verge of seeing her tossed out of the Red Chrysanthemum. What if he had not torn her shirt? How far would he have gone to punish her for her deed? He could not know because he had not meditated upon what he would do. He acted only in the moment, but, now that he had the capacity of reflection, he found the force of the emotions guiding him last night vexing. He could think of no one who had ever riled him so.

And aroused him.

Despite his anger and abhorrence for her actions, the lust in his body had not waned. He'd wanted to possess her. On his terms. And it had been as glorious as ever he could imagine. Trapping her to the wall, hearing her pant beneath him, caressing the supple flesh between her thighs, he'd known he had to claim her. It had mattered not that they stood in a dark alley, barely able to see each other, risking the more dangerous elements of the night finding them. His desires would not be denied.

Her cunnie was magnificent. How it clutched his shaft. How the walls rippled along his length. He'd felt the effect all the way to his toes. Her strength, both times, when she had ridden his cock in the chair and when she had received his thrusts against the alley wall, amazed him. In a different position, perhaps upon her back with her knees to her head, he could penetrate her deeper. He would like to see her brow furrowed in ecstasy once more.

*No, he would not.*

But the growing bulge at his crotch belied his conviction. He took up his cup of coffee as a distraction from his hardened cock, but the beverage was no longer hot. He sought to adjust his trousers, but, remembering how her moist heat had encased him, he cupped his erection instead. Perhaps it was time to be done with breakfast. He could read the paper after he attended to—

"Mr. Warren is here to see you."

Charles straightened and leaned toward the table. *Damn Wang,* he thought to himself. The slender Chinese servant always managed to steal into rooms with hardly a whisper. A former sailor for the East India Company, Wang had lost half his right arm when the rigging for a load of cargo had failed to hold. It was Wang who had taught Charles the Chinese language and facilitated his travel beyond the factory in Canton.

"The Returning Officer?" Charles replied.

"Yes. Shall I advise him to return at a later time?"

Wang maintained his customary stoic countenance, as if he had only the blandest of reasons for his proposal, but Charles knew better. Nothing escaped the notice of those eyes, darker than even those of Miss Terrell.

"Let him know I am not yet done with breakfast, but he is welcome to join me," Charles answered.

If he needed an antidote from the sort of lustful desires Miss Terrell engendered, the square-faced and podgy Returning Officer fit the bill.

"Mighty considerate of you, Mr. Gallant," Jonathan Warren said when Wang had shown him into the breakfast room.

After shaking hands, Charles said, "Please, partake of what you will. There is far more here than I can finish."

Mr. Warren sat his rotund frame into a chair and began piling several slices of ham onto a plate. "Having come here as fast as I could, I did not take my customary breakfast."

"Something amiss, Mr. Warren?"

"Something I thought to bring to your attention, Mr. Gallant. Spoke with two men who expect to be voting. Each let on that Mr. Laurel is paying them no less than 20 shillings a man for votes."

Charles watched Mr. Warren cover his ham with a ladle of beans. "I did not know Mr. Laurel to possess that kind of funding."

"He must have a wealthy benefactor. I know not your situation, Mr. Gallant, but I always thought you would make a right good MP, as your father would have before you. Of course, I will oversee the election with the utmost propriety."

"I should hope so, Mr. Warren."

"Which is why I refused an offer from an anonymous person of some two hundred shillings to skew the votes in favor of Mr. Laurel," Mr. Warren said with a mouthful of ham and beans, "though my wife fair threw me out of my own house for refusing. You see, I have a brother in a poor way, and we do what we can to help him. This leaves my wife and I rather thin."

"Given this situation you describe, you are a most virtuous man to have declined the inducement."

Mr. Warren slowed his heretofore zestful chewing of his food. Charles suspected it was not praise the man was truly after.

"You flatter me, Mr. Gallant. I am more a simple man, and I profess no love for the color blue, but my wife can be most insistent. Wives can be quite the nuisance. When you are married—although, I do not mean to suggest the future Mrs. Gallant will be anything but delightful—"

"I could not be party to a bribe, Mr. Warren."

"'Course, 'course. I always thought you and your father to be honest men. Honest as they come."

"But I do believe in rewarding those who do right in the face of temptation and corruption."

The man brightened.

"I would not wish to win in a false election," Charles continued, "but perhaps you can apply to me for assistance with regards to your brother *after* the election, which, in your hands, I trust will be conducted without fraudulence."

"'Course, 'course, Mr. Gallant."

Satisfied with his prospects, Mr. Warren turned his full attention upon his food. Charles, feeling the Returning Officer consumed enough for the both of them, took only a fresh cup of coffee. His schedule for the day included several hours canvassing voters and tea with the widow of a former MP of Porter's Hill and her more influential friends. He had also received an invitation to attend a dinner party at the Dempsey residence. After that, the Red Chrysanthemum awaited him.

And Miss Terrell.

# CHAPTER THIRTY

**"O**w!"

Terrell winced as the needle pricked her finger. The ribbon of her bonnet had begun to shred in a most inconvenient spot. The whole bonnet needed replacing, for the straw had thinned in two parts, but she decided she would replace the ribbon first. She allowed herself a sigh for the beautiful bonnets she'd once possessed.

No. She never had possession of the bonnets. From shiny baubles to undergarments, these were always the property of the man. *She* was once property, no different from the inanimate accessories that she prized.

"Done early with Sir Arthur tonight?" Sarah asked as she entered their room with George. Sitting upon her bed, she undid her stays and settled the little boy upon her lap to nurse.

"He was content to have my mouth," Terrell replied, setting aside her bonnet and needle. She knew she ought to reinforce the stitching once more, but she had little affinity for needlework. "And I am content to provide it for I can make quick work of a man with it."

"How quick?"

"With Sir Arthur tonight, I think it five minutes."

"Five minutes!"

"I've finished a man in as few as two before."

Sarah's mouth dropped. "You are truly skilled! I would that I had such a talent."

"I think not. I've had to swallow many a cock. They are not all as fine as—"

She stopped. *Not all as fine as that of Master Gallant,* she had nearly said.

"What?" Sarah prodded. "As beefsteak?"

They shared a laugh.

"In truth, I try not to look in the direction of *that,*" Sarah said. "I know not why their sex reveres this appendage. To me, it is not at all an attractive part of the body."

Terrell said nothing, for she could not stop thinking of Master Gallant's cock. She thought it a very attractive, very delightful appendage. She would take it over beefsteak any and every day. She could not have been happier that Sir Arthur's visit proved a short one. All day, she had replayed her moments with Master Gallant. After returning to the inn last night and creeping into her bed, for Sarah and George were already asleep, it had taken her some time to fall asleep for the giddiness and anticipation in her. Counting the hours, she wondered that she could wait to see him again.

"A penny for your thoughts."

Terrell looked up. "Hm?"

Sarah observed her friend. "You came to bed late last night. Did you have to service another patron?"

"In a manner."

"I wonder that Madame is aware of Sir Arthur's disposition and his jealous nature?"

"It was not at Madame's request," Terrell admitted, feeling ill at ease with prevaricating to the only person she might deem a friend.

"I shared my reservations with you concerning Sir Arthur."

"And I do not mean to disregard your well-intentioned advice, but I do not know that Sir Arthur's interest in me will last. I must weigh the risk with the reward."

She surprised herself with just how much she was willing to risk to have Master Gallant. She hoped that Miss Katherine would not need to attend her mother-in-law tonight. Despite his forceful show of passion in the alley, Gallant still refused to accept her for his submissive.

"If you must," sighed Sarah. "Who was the lucky gentleman last night?"

Terrell did not immediately reply. The answer might only distress Sarah, though the woman was aware of her interest in Master Gallant. A part of her did want to confide in Sarah.

"I would not burden you," Terrell responded before further delay would rouse suspicion. "It is of no consequence."

"Burden me? Why would you think it a burden?"

Realizing she might have misspoken, Terrell said, "Because you fret of Sir Arthur and how he might react."

But Sarah did not seem placated. "Do I know the gentleman?"

Not wanting to lie, Terrell relented. "Yes."

She offered no more and picked at a hole in the bedclothes. Sarah, too, was silent.

"Pray, tell me it is not so!" she said at last.

"Of what do you speak?" asked Terrell, though she kept her gaze averted.

"You sly skirt! Master Gallant!"

Dread and relief battled for primacy, but she could not stymie the grin that spread her lips.

Sarah's mouth dropped a second time. She disengaged George, who had grown drowsy from the nursing, and curled him in her arms.

"I can't believe it!" she exclaimed softly. "After what you told me…but how…what will Madame think? Will she allow it?"

"I have no intention of informing Madame," Terrell said firmly. "As for Master Gallant, I should not be surprised if he woke with the greatest regrets over what had happened. I doubt I could succeed a second time with him."

"Do you? I rather doubt that. You always seem to possess such assurance with regards to their sex."

"Yes, but Master Gallant is different."

"In a way I respect and admire."

"Yes," Terrell replied, pensive. She understood how his recalcitrance might fuel her sense of sport. She wanted to prove herself. But there was more than vanity, competition or curiosity at play.

"In truth, it quite surprises me that he is a member here," Sarah added. "But tell me, if you will indulge in some detail, how did you manage to seduce him?"

"I forced myself upon him."

"Indeed? How so?"

"You've no wish to know," Terrell murmured, and was glad that Sarah accepted the wisdom of her caution.

"And he did not resist?"

The memories flashed through Terrell's mind, and she felt the stirrings of a familiar warmth. How marvelous his cock had felt inside her mouth, how arousing his groans and grunts, how intoxicating to have this formidable dominant surrendering to the pleasure her body wrought upon him. And the thrill of being taken by him, pressed against the wall in that alley, his strong arms holding her up as he thrust into her over and over again.

"He resisted, but…"

"You prevailed."

"I only hope he does not hate me for it."

Terrell recalled the blaze of anger in his eyes and his rough handling of her after she had freed him of his bonds. Her heartbeat had quickened for several reasons. Though she did not fear a coarse hand, she had never witnessed it in Master Gallant. But she had exalted in the spanking, in having unleashed the dominant in him. Her arse had smarted for some time afterwards.

"I cannot envision Gallant to have such ungracious feelings toward you for his own weakness."

"Mine was not a noble seduction, if such a thing exists."

"Gallant is a grown man, intelligent, and able to fend for himself."

Terrell shook her head. "I forced his hand."

Sarah looked at her in surprise. "It sounds as if you are the one filled with regret."

"Of my actions, yes. Of the outcome, no."

"He proved a good tumble then," Sarah grinned.

"M'lady!" Terrell responded with mock horror.

"I would that I had your fortune!"

Terrell smiled, marveling for the first time at her own accomplishment.

"But I am not as bold as you," Sarah continued. "You would have him a second time. That is clear as day."

'I would have him a hundred times," Terrell blurted before thinking.

"He is as good as that then?"

"He is…unlike the others."

"Yes, and for that reason, he is a danger to us."

"How can that be?"

Sarah looked wistful. "Because we shall only torture ourselves with longing for a man whose company must surely come to an end sooner than we wish."

"By company, you intend something more than venereal."

Sarah studied her. "I suppose you might be in less peril than those of us with a more tender inclination."

"If you fear I might fall in love with Master Gallant, I am far too practical to succumb to that sort of infatuation. I would venture to say that I am incapable of tender emotions."

Sarah shook her head. "You've not such a cold heart."

"It's true I'm not completely devoid of benign sentiment, but, in my situation, I cannot allow for affection. It does me no good."

"I will take inspiration from such pragmatism. It—and faithfulness—have not done me good either."

Terrell smiled in encouragement. "I cannot know love, but I can know pleasure, corporal pleasure, to the fullest."

"Yes! I know too many women who have neither love nor the pleasures of the flesh in their marriage. At least I may know the latter."

"Does Captain Gracechurch come tonight?"

"He set sail this morning for Lower Canada and will be gone at least two months. I do not mind the reprieve. Tonight I will care for Georgie on my own and wish you well in your endeavors."

"If all goes well, I will find you and Georgie fast asleep upon my return," Terrell acknowledged. She reached under her pillow for *Fanny Hill*, which she had retrieved last night from the scene of her crime.

"If I were a betting man, I would lay the odds in your favor. If he submitted to you once, he will do it again. Men are predictable creatures."

"Thankfully so."

Book in hand, Terrell took her leave of Sarah and Georgie. She had two objectives tonight. First, for many reasons, she wanted Miss Katherine to make significant progress. Second, she wanted Master Gallant to accept her as his submissive. The events of last night had hardly quenched her desire for him. Rather, she knew now, beyond doubt, that she wanted Master Gallant in the fullest way possible. And she would not rest until she had him.

# CHAPTER THIRTY-ONE

"This matter with Miss Terrell concerns me greatly," said Madame Devereux. "I mean to speak with her but wished to consult you first."

This was the meeting Charles had dreaded. He had learned from Baxter that no note from the Wendlessons had arrived. Thus, Miss Katherine, and likely the viscount as well, would be expected. It was possible Miss Terrell had once again intercepted any communique, but Charles sensed enough contrition in her last night to believe she would behave herself better tonight.

Joan reached into the bowl of confections upon her writing table. Chewing a chocolate confection, she expounded, "As you may know, Wendlesson approached me the other night requesting—practically demanding, I should say—the assistance of Miss Terrell. As you can imagine, it is hard to refuse him. He has been such a devoted patron."

"And a generous one, I should think," Charles added. Seated opposite Joan in a settee, he reserved further comment to himself. While he had not the wealth of Wendlesson or Arthur, he was situated well enough in the way of funds that he could bandy money about to further his own purposes. It was simply not his habit or his inclination.

"You understand me too well, my dear Charles. I have no wish to upset Wendlesson, but while Sir Arthur is new to the Red Chrysanthemum, I have no wish to upset him either, and one of his conditions in seeking the company of Miss Terrell is that she not entertain the attention of any other man."

Charles was loath to keep secrets, but, despite his avowal to do so yesterday, he did not wish to betray Miss Terrell to Joan.

"Was Sir Arthur's stipulation made known?" he asked.

"I explained as much to Wendlesson, and Miss Terrell is well aware of her restrictions, but I do not trust the girl. Where money can be had, she will not turn away."

"Perhaps she hopes to purchase better accommodations. The room she shares with Miss Sarah is barely comfortable for one person, let alone two."

"They have no complaints, for it is far easier for them to receive their room and board here."

"You could let them use one of the rooms upon the third floor without impacting the activities of the membership. If she felt better provided for, she might have less need to seek out every possible coin."

"Her compensation, especially with Sir Arthur as one of her suitors, is more than decent."

"She gives little appearance of it. I wonder she has more than one shift."

"What she does or does not do with her funds is her affair. Perhaps she is partial to gin or gaming."

He considered the possibility. While he did not know Miss Terrell well enough, he saw no evidence to indicate she squandered her money on such pursuits.

"I wonder that their kind have the forbearance to resist simple temptations," Joan added.

Charles raised his brows. "Their kind? Whatever their vices or failings, which seem to differ little from those of any other mortal, they have proved among your most profitable members."

Joan raised her brows in turn.

"I doubt any of your other members could claim a prize as rich as Sir Arthur. And then there is Mistress Primrose. She may not have the complete appearance of a blackamoor, but it is plain she is of mixed blood. Her two submissives are Edeltons, and from what I gather, absurdly devoted to her. It would not surprise me if she could milk their last penny from them."

"Your acumen is impressive. Yes, well, it would seem I've had a bit of luck with their kind. But Miss Terrell could easily jeopardize her situation with Sir Arthur. I have a mind to forbid her any further dealings with Wendlesson."

"The viscount is interested primarily in his wife." As he spoke, Charles hoped this to be true. "Miss Terrell's presence affords Miss Katherine comfort."

"Yes, I understand, for Wendlesson said as much. In truth, this surprises me much about Miss Terrell."

*Much about Miss Terrell is surprising,* Charles thought. Aloud, he said, "I think, if we grant one or two more nights with Miss Terrell's assistance, we may reach enough progress that her presence will no longer be required. Without doubt, my task with Miss Katherine would have been much more difficult, near impossible, were it not for Miss Terrel's assistance. Lord Wendlesson cannot grant me more time. Without Miss Terrell, I fear I cannot accomplish the objective we all wish for."

He had not intended to defend Miss Terrell's participation in the education of Miss Katherine as strongly as he did, but he granted that the Viscountess benefited from the blackamoor. He had, of course, his own selfish interest in seeing Miss Katherine advance as much as possible. If he succeeded, his servitude with Joan would be at an end. It was the only motive he would permit for himself to entertain.

Joan sighed and reached for another chocolate. "I suppose I must allow it then. But you will see that she behaves herself?"

"I do not think she intends to seduce Wendlesson."

"Nevertheless, you will ensure that Wendlesson's attention remains fixed upon his wife?"

"Gladly."

He did not confess that his own attentions needed guarding. He meant what he said to Miss Terrell, that there could be nothing betwixt them. But she had a way of confounding his statements. He was not a capricious man, not a man who made idle threats, not a man given to harsh statements or treatments toward the fair sex, yet it would seem he was all these things when it came to Miss Terrell.

"I should like to see Sir Arthur become a full and continued member of the Red Chrysanthemum," Joan said. "Perhaps I can persuade him to take an interest in Miss Sarah or one of the other members in place of Miss Terrell."

Charles made no reply. Having tasted of Miss Terrell, Sir Arthur might as easily be persuaded to give up Bordeaux for rot-gut gin.

"At least I can trust you will handle the situation," the proprietress continued, giving him a large smile. "Indeed, I feel much relieved of the dilemma after speaking with you. I wonder that I was not too hasty in offering your freedom?"

He cringed inwardly at her declaration of trust. He wanted to say he was not as worthy of her trust as she believed, but said instead, "If I fail to protect the interests of the Red Chrysanthemum, you may reclaim my servitude."

"That is kind of you, Charles, but I will do right by you, not merely because you are a valued member here, but because I value our friendship. As Miss Katherine may be here already, I will detain you no further."

Standing, he readily took his leave. He vowed to strengthen his forbearance where Miss Terrell was concerned. Last night was an exception, complicated by her outrageous deeds and his own miserable actions. He could not have known that she wished to hide her gruesome disfigurement from him, but he would have expected better of himself to refrain once he had heard the panic in her voice, which, without the haze of anger clouding his head, echoed plain in his ears. Though he could only wish that tonight would hold no surprises, he was determined, for all their sakes, not to succumb to Miss Terrell.

# CHAPTER THIRTY-TWO

Still giddy and nervous from the events of the prior evening, Terrell allowed herself to dream of another night with Master Gallant. He had said there could be nothing more betwixt them, but there might come a time when she could renew her request for him to make her his submissive for a night. One night would seem less daunting to him. And if she could secure one night, he might be inclined to more afterwards.

"You are exceptionally alluring tonight," Terrell remarked to Miss Katherine as she removed the pins from the viscountess' hair. It was a quiet night at the Red Chrysanthemum and they had the dressing room to themselves.

"Am I?" Miss Katherine responded as she looked at herself in the vanity mirror. "I purchased a new shade of rouge. You do not think it too bright?"

"It is very pretty."

"It is called Rose of Venus. I thought the name appropriate for the evening."

Miss Katherine blushed, and Terrell thought she saw a sparkle of eagerness in her eyes. Terrell inquired into the health of the countess.

"Better," Miss Katherine replied. "The countess suffers from bouts of insomnia, but his lordship offered to sit by her side till she fell asleep. She did so in ten minutes! When I am there, she must first lament her condition for at least half an hour."

Terrell smiled as she brushed Miss Katherine's long locks. How easily the brush slid through the soft, thin hair!

"What say you we surprise the gentlemen tonight?" Terrell asked.

"What do you mean?"

"Is it said that ours is the weaker sex, but in venereal matters, their sex is often the weaker because the eros reigns supreme for them. They lust for our bodies. Let fall the garments from your shoulders and bosom, and they fall to their knees."

Miss Katherine shook her head. "I could not bring my husband to his knees."

"You can. And you shall." Several thoughts went through her. "If he be on his knees already, you will bring him to his feet."

Miss Katherine's breath grew shaky at the prospect.

"Would you like this?" Terrell asked.

Miss Katherine nodded.

"And would you be willing to press yourself further to accomplish this?"

"How?"

"Follow me lead. Worry not. I will not have you do that which you are not ready for. And you always have at your disposal the safety word. Do you recall it?"

Finding that she sounded like Master Gallant, Terrell smiled to herself.

"Jean," Miss Katherine answered.

"Good. Then let us finish undressing upstairs."

Gallant had left only brief instructions for the women to await him in their appointed room. He and Lord Wendlesson had been requested to attend upon Madame Devereux, who wished a word with the gentlemen. Terrell could not help suspecting that she might be the subject of their discussion.

Once in the familiar room, she was reminded of all that had transpired the previous night. She could not look upon the chair without recalling how Master Gallant had been bound to it, his cock at her mercy. Looking to the bed, and in particular the edge her arse had rounded, she felt a tingle where his paddle had landed. Heat began swirling between her legs.

It was also, there upon that bed, where her deformity had been revealed. Inwardly, she winced. Doubtlessly, he had never seen anything so hideous. As much as she had desired him before, at that moment, she had wanted him gone with every fiber of her being, gone before he ran from her as one might flee from the presence of a leper.

Only he had not fled. That most unsightly part of her had not dampened his desires. He had taken her there in the alley as if she was still beautiful, unmarred by ugliness. For that, she was grateful. She hoped it was not pity that moved him. He had thrust into her with too much passion for her to think that pity alone compelled him. Surely he would not have don so if he found her merely *tolerable,* if he disdained her blackness. She would know better when he fucked her again.

Terrell undressed Miss Katherine to her shift and decided to do the same for herself. She could not resist a little envy upon seeing the contrast between the two shifts. Though both undergarments were simple, with similar shapes, Miss Katherine's was white as snow and the hem edged with small lace.

"We ought assume the proper position of greeting when they come," Terrell said. "I think to request the flogger tonight. Do you trust that Master Gallant will use it gently with you?"

The viscountess bit her lip but nodded.

"But first, we will place his lordship in a proper frenzy. Will you allow me to touch you?"

"If you must."

They knelt upon the floor. Terrell untied the drawstring at Miss Katherine's décolletage and arranged a single curl of hair to rest upon a breast.

Hearing footsteps, the women placed their hands behind their heads. Terrell kept her gaze dutifully downcast, but she knew the sight of them had had an impact when the door opened and the tread of the men stopped upon the threshold.

After the pause, Master Gallant entered first. "Well done, Miss Katherine, Miss Terrell."

"Thank you, Master," Terrell replied.

"Thank you," Miss Katherine echoed.

"Permission to speak, Master."

"Granted," Gallant replied after a brief silence.

"Will his lordship take a seat? We wish him to sit and enjoy the lesson."

"I mean to participate in the lesson," Wendlesson replied.

"Of course. I am certain your lordship will not be able to resist rising from your chair for long."

"Do you mean to challenge me?"

"I promise you will like what you see."

Wendlesson looked to Gallant, who said, "It would

seem Miss Terrell has designs for us. I've not known Miss Terrell to disappoint."

Terrell believed he spoke as much to her as to Wendlesson.

"Very well," the viscount relented. Flaring the tails of his coat, he took a seat in the chair.

"Permission to rise," Terrell requested.

"Granted," Gallant said.

Rising, she assisted Miss Katherine to her feet.

"May I continue?" she asked of Gallant.

He nodded. She went to the sideboard and retrieved a red scarf. After guiding Miss Katherine to stand before one of the bedposts at the foot of the bed, Terrell raised the woman's slender alabaster arms and tied the wrists to the bedpost above her head. Wendlesson grunted in approval.

"I will now worship your body with caresses," Terrell told her. Leaning toward Miss Katherine's ear, she whispered, "And observe his desire for you burning in his eyes."

Kneeling upon the bed behind Miss Katherine, Terrell brushed the back of her hand down the length of one of Miss Katherine's arm. Miss Katherine shivered. Terrell swept her fingers lightly across the collarbone before dropping her hand below the décolletage to grasp a breast. Her other hand embraced Miss Katherine about the midsection before cupping the hip and traveling down the side of the thigh. Both men watched with fixed gazes.

Terrell slid from the bed and knelt upon the floor before Miss Katherine. Her hands traversed Miss Katherine, gently manhandling the breasts through her shift, grasping waist, hips and thighs. With echoes of their first lesson together, she slid her hands beneath the shift and caressed the legs. Miss Katherine emitted a soft moan, and then a gasp when Terrell nestled her thumb at the bud of sensitivity hiding between the folds. Terrell stroked the nub softly. Miss Katherine was quick to respond, her breath soon growing uneven. Behind her, Terrell heard Wendlesson shift in his chair.

After fondling Miss Katherine till she panted and moisture began to collect between her thighs, Terrell reached both hands to the lace-trimmed hem of the shift and slowly pushed the fabric up the pair of slim white legs, past the hips, and to the waist.

She glanced up to see Miss Katherine stared at her husband. Terrell would have liked to have seen his expression, and that of Master Gallant as well. She remembered well his response to her previous efforts.

Wanting to hear his voice, she asked, "May I taste her, Master Gallant?"

"You may."

Wendlesson added, "By all means."

Terrell parted the legs and reached her tongue between them. Miss Katherine gasped, then quivered against the bedpost as Terrell applied herself in earnest. Miss Katherine must have bathed recently, for she had the scent of soap mixed with the musk of her womanhood. Terrell flicked and swirled her tongue. The viscountess moaned. Her legs tensed as the fondling intensified. With her fingers, Terrell parted the folds to allow the swollen nub greater emergence.

"May she spend?" Terrell asked between licks.

"Do you wish to spend, my dear?" Wendlesson asked of his wife.

"If it pleases you," Miss Katherine answered.

"It would, but you must ask it for yourself."

"May I spend?"

"May I spend, *Master*."

"Not yet, but Miss Terrell is to continue her efforts nonetheless."

Still nuzzled between her thighs, Terrell, her nose tickled by the soft down above, did as bid, but when she sensed Miss Katherine nearing her edge, she slowed.

"No, no, Miss Terrell," Wendlesson cautioned. "Only your best effort will do. Anything less will earn you a sound punishment."

"M-May I spend, Master?"

"If Miss Terrell applies herself with proper industry."

She pressed her tongue and lips to Miss Katherine, who gave a little cry and strained against the bedpost.

"Ah! Ah!" Miss Katherine gasped.

Within minutes, she began to shudder as her body succumbed to pleasure's paroxysm. Her hips bucked and her cunnie momentarily muffled Terrell, who stayed where she was till the climax faded and Miss Katherine slumped against the bedpost with a satisfied sigh.

Terrell dropped the hem of the shift and observed the serenity upon Miss Katherine's flushed features. She took some pride in having brought Miss Katherine to this point. She hoped Master Gallant would be satisfied, too.

"I did not grant permission to spend."

Miss Katherine's lashes, which had come to rest upon her cheeks, flew up. "Wh-What?"

Terrell, too, turned toward his lordship.

"I did not grant permission to spend," he repeated as he rose from his chair. "And now you will have to pay the price of your insubordination. Master Gallant, a flogger, if you will."

# CHAPTER THIRTY-THREE

Charles looked to the viscount and saw the man did not jest. He did not agree with Wendlesson. The man had made a statement that implied permission had been granted, and from the reactions upon the women, they had assumed as much. If he did not so intend, he should have been more explicit.

Looking to Miss Katherine, Charles saw the whites of her eyes surrounding the iris. He waited for Wendlesson to soften his words. By God, did the man not see the alarm in his wife?

Before he could address the viscount, however, Miss Terrell had risen to her feet.

"I will take her punishment, if you please," she said. "I failed to understand your intentions."

Wendlesson shook his head. "That will not serve. She will not learn."

"Perhaps a demonstration then."

"Yes," Charles interjected before Wendlesson accepted. "I will demonstrate upon Miss Terrell what may be expected. Your lordship will then execute the same for Miss Katherine."

Moving quickly before anyone could object, he went to the sideboard and pulled out the other red scarf. In another drawer, he found a short and simple flogger with about twenty wide straps of soft leather. The man who mutilated Miss Terrell's back would not have used so simple a flogger. Charles shuddered to think what manner of flogger the monster might have employed.

"Miss Terrell," he said when he had returned to the foot of the bed, standing at the corner opposite Miss Katherine. After removing his coat, he tucked the flogger beneath an arm and stretched out the scarf in his hands.

She knew what he required without further word or gesture and went to him. He gazed up at the bedpost where he would tie her wrists. She stood before the post and raised her arms. Perhaps she would make a good submissive. With the scarf, he bound her wrists to the bedpost and stood back to admire the two women adorning the bed like figureheads of a ship's bow.

His blood, heated by the sight of Miss Terrell upon her knees servicing Miss Katherine, swirled in his groin. He was reminded of how her mouth had felt upon his own body. He wanted nothing more than to apply the flogger to her supple curves, but taking the implement in hand, he hesitated.

"Can you tolerate the flogger, Miss Terrell?"

She looked slightly insulted. "I can tolerate anything you wish to bestow, Master Gallant."

He would have thought such a statement mere exaggeration, but, given what she had suffered, he believed her. Nevertheless, he reminded her, "Your safety word is 'obedience.'"

She appeared to swallow what impudent retort may have been on the tip of her tongue, saying instead, "Yes,

Master."

"And yours, Miss Katherine?"

"Jean," the viscountess replied.

"Good."

He took a step toward Miss Terrell and stood much closer to her than he intended. She met his gaze, her eyes bright with anticipation. A dutiful submissive would have kept her eyes downcast, but he liked to observe the emotions that went through them.

"Are you wet, Miss Terrell?" he asked, his voice growing husky at the thought.

Unable to keep her impishness at bay, she replied, "Will my Master not see for himself?"

A rising tide of heat waved through his body. He would have liked nothing better, but it was wiser not to. With her hands tied to the bedpost, however, she could not lift her own shift.

He presented the flogger to her mouth. "Hold this."

She parted her lips and he fit the handle of the flogger between her teeth. If not for the presence of the Wendlessons, he might have been tempted to claim her mouth first. But she did look lovely with the handle of the flogger between her lips. He wanted to stand even closer to her but feared her intoxicating scent would arouse him too much, though he was glad she had not donned the perfume of last night.

With one hand, he gathered her shift slowly till the hem reached her thigh. He sensed the unevenness of her breath and marveled at how her eyes sparkled with desire. Slipping his hand beneath the shift, he reached between her legs to where he had ventured not four and twenty hours ago. His fingers brushed against the thick curls at her pelvis before finding that sweet target. She made a small gasp when his digits slid against the moisture there, and his own breath hitched. He grazed the nub of flesh between the folds, and she nearly dropped the flogger.

His hand wanted to stay, wanted to stroke her till she spent, but the blood pounded too heavily in his head already.

With his free hand, he relieved her of the flogger. Slowly, he withdrew his other hand from its paradise. His cock stretched against his trousers as he noted how his fingers glistened with her arousal. He brought them to her lips and she took them into her mouth immediately, swirling her tongue about the digits, sucking them, tasting herself. The sensation upon his fingers was provocative enough. Imagining the same upon his cock made his legs weaken.

From the corner of his eyes, he beheld the widened stares of Miss Katherine and Lord Wendlesson. He need not worry of the arousal of the latter, but he hoped to keep Miss Katherine titillated. He curled his fingers upon Miss Terrell's tongue and grazed the inside of a cheek. She moaned and sucked harder. As if it were the recipient, his erection lengthened. He sawed his fingers in and out of her mouth in the motion his cock would have desired.

Gradually, with reluctance, he slid his fingers from her mouth, leaving moisture upon her lower lip as he withdrew.

"Thank you, Master," she said softly.

He cupped her chin and brushed his thumb over her bottom lip. Such succulent rosiness. He wanted to partake of it, tug at its suppleness with his teeth, and taste it upon his tongue. Dropping his hand, he lightly passed his knuckles down her throat and under a collarbone. Her bosom heaved to meet more of his hand. He obliged and pushed the décolletage down to cup the side of a breast. He weighed the fullness of the flesh in his hand before squeezing it. She groaned. Her nipples were already protruding against the shift. He clasped one between his middle and forefinger and gently tugged. She groaned more forcefully. Gripping it with his thumb and forefinger, he rolled and twisted the nub till she began to squirm against the bedpost. He wanted to capture the nipple in his mouth, but it was best not to attempt too much. Best not to venture too far down a road from which he could not return.

"Will I find you more wet, Miss Terrell?" he asked, returning his hand to the breast as he studied dark-brown areolas. The coloring reminded him of cocoa. And as enticing. More enticing.

"Yes, Master."

"Good."

She pouted in disappointment when he withdrew instead of verifying the truth of her answer.

Stepping back, he prepared the flogger. "I will now kiss the flogger to your legs."

He swung the tails gently against a thigh and down one leg, then the other. Against the shift, the tails made a soft swishing sound.

"Do you like the caress of the flogger?" he asked for the benefit of Miss Katherine.

"Yes, Master. You may apply a harder blow, if it pleases you."

He whipped the tails against the side of her right thigh, the touch still too light to cause pain.

"Thank you, Master."

He swung the tails a little harder against the same thigh.

"Mmmm," she purred.

After lashing the tails upon the right thigh, he whipped the left thigh as he returned his arm.

"Thank you, Master."

Her body warmed by the softer blows, he let the flogger fall harder. "Did that hurt?"

"No, Master."

With the flogger, he drew the figure of an eight in the air, striking her right thigh, then her left thigh, the right, the left. After several minutes, he paused.

"Thank you, Master."

Wendlesson crossed his arms. "I have seen her endure far worse."

Charles gave the man a hard stare. "She is not being punished."

Turning to Miss Katherine, he asked, "Are you ready to experience that which I applied to Miss Terrell?"

Miss Katherine gave a shy nod.

"Exactly as I had done and no more," Charles said to Wendlesson as he handed over the flogger.

"But I *do* intend a punishment," Wendlesson said.

"Let us see how your wife fares. She has not as much flesh as Miss Terrell."

Wendlesson grumbled as he took the flogger. To his wife he said, "You will advise me if the pain is more than you can bear."

"Yes, Master," she replied.

With misgiving, Charles watched as Wendlesson landed the flogger against her thighs. His touch was not as light as Charles' but it was not harsh enough to elicit more than a small gasp, mostly of surprise, from Miss Katherine.

Wendlesson glanced at Charles as if to say, "And you would doubt me." Charles made no reply.

To his credit, the viscount kept his strikes on the

gentler side. Charles discerned the man more than competent at wielding the crop and knew the areas of the body to stay away from.

"Thank you, Master," Miss Katherine said when he had finished.

Wendlesson presented the flogger back to Charles with raised brows. Miss Katherine appeared in comfort still. Only twice had she gasped when her husband whipped the flogger with a little more force.

"Was there any pain for you, Miss Katherine?" Charles asked, taking back the flogger.

"A brief sting once or twice, but nothing of consequence," she answered. "I was once stung by a bee. I could endure at least as much pain as that."

He turned back to Miss Terrell. "Now I will apply the flogger harder."

She nodded. He saw the enthusiasm in her eyes. He wondered that she did not abhor the instrument.

Bringing back his arm farther than before, he lashed the tails at her thigh. She gasped sharply.

"Thank you, Master."

He snapped the tails at her other thigh.

She jumped. "Thank you, Master!"

"I will use the tips, which produce more of a bite."

He snapped the tails against the side of her breast. She yelped. He rained several more blows upon her body before giving her a reprieve.

"Thank you, Master."

"How do you find the lashes I administered this time?"

"Pleasurable, Master."

"Indeed? Do not lie, Miss Terrell."

"I do not."

"What of the pain?"

"The smarting lasts but briefly and barely exceeds a mild discomfort."

"And you say it is pleasurable?"

She pinned him with a smoldering stare that went straight to his groin. "I do indeed. If you doubt me, I pray you seek confirmation."

She lowered her gaze to indicate *where* he would find substantiation. His cock throbbed. It was too tempting.

"Miss Katherine," he said without taking his gaze from Miss Terrell, "do you believe it possible for pleasure to be derived from pain?"

"I do not think Miss Terrell to lie," the viscountess replied.

"That does not answer my question, Miss Katherine."

"I suppose, as she is experienced in this, er, these situations, she could find arousal."

"You do not sound entirely convinced."

"I…"

"Then let us see what proof we may find."

He approached Miss Terrell and thought he could feel the heat of her arousal radiating from her body. Seeing the flames of desire in her eyes, as provocative and alluring as her most intimate parts laid bare, was nearly his undoing. How she must yearn to touch herself.

"Do you wish to touch yourself?" he asked.

She pulled against her bonds. "Very much, Master. I've wanted to for some time, since I began pleasuring Miss Katherine."

"Did you enjoy pleasuring Miss Katherine?"

"Yes. She tasted quite delicious and has a most quaint cunnie."

"You enjoyed bringing her to spend."

"I would do it again if I could, and especially if it

pleased you, Master."

"Enough talk," Wendlesson interrupted. "I do not wish for my mother to wake and find Miss Katherine gone. We have expended enough time as it is."

Charles felt his jaw tighten at the man's impatience. Miss Terrell lifted a knee. It brushed his leg, scorching him. Grasping her shift, he lifted the garment to her hips and reached his other hand between her thighs. She gasped at the sudden invasion.

*My God.* She was sodden.

"Am I not more wet?" she asked, triumphant.

He brushed his digits against her clit, making her pant. He pushed a finger between the folds, into that tight opening of bliss. She groaned when he began to caress the walls inside. He found a spot that made her gasp and tremble. He stroked it. Her body writhed as if wishing to be free one moment and savoring the bedpost the next. Her lashes fluttered, and she could no longer look at him with that penetrating stare.

When she was beyond agitated, he withdrew and lashed the flogger against her several times. She squirmed and rubbed her legs together.

"Thank you, Master. Harder. Please."

He obliged and slapped the tips of the tails to her.

"Yes!" she cried. "Yes! Thank you, Master!"

"My turn," Wendlesson said, taking the flogger.

Miss Terrell took in a deep breath, though she seemed not in the slightest relieved. Charles was aware that his own breath had become ragged. Hearing the thud of the flogger, seeing the tails strike against her body, he wanted the distraction of pain for himself.

Miss Katherine exclaimed, and Charles worried that Wendlesson was too impatient to go gently with his wife.

But she withstood the assault of the flogger with more stamina than he expected. She cried out with each strike but remembered to thank him each time. This reassured Charles, but he continued to watch them with care.

"Th-Thank you, Master," she said with furrowed brow.

"I wonder if she is as wet as I," Miss Terrell asked of the viscount.

Wendlesson stopped and reached underneath his wife's shift. His expression revealed the answer. He rubbed her till she moaned, her head falling back against the bedpost.

Pulling back, he applied the flogger once more. The veins in his neck protruded. Miss Katherine cried out, but this time she did not thank him. She squirmed and twisted her body away from the flogger.

Just as Charles took a step toward Wendlesson to intervene, the viscount dropped the flogger. He unbuttoned the fall of his trousers, hoisted her legs about his hips and plunged into her. Miss Katherine continued to exclaim, but the nature of her cries differed.

Charles turned to find Miss Terrell staring at him. She shook with the bed every time Wendlesson thrust into Miss Katherine, shoving her into the bedpost. The room filled with the sounds of Wendlesson's grunting and Miss Katherine's cries, and the bed scraping against the floor. Charles could not tear himself from Miss Terrell's gaze and returned it with equal intensity. He could see desire writ upon her countenance and was certain she could see it writ upon his. He knew what she wanted, and he wanted the same.

But he could not.

He had surrendered to temptation last night, but he required more forbearance—for the both of them.

Picking up the flogger, he whipped it upon her to

relieve the distress of her arousal. Her cries soon matched that of Miss Katherine. Wendlesson bucked harder.

Suddenly, he roared and shook as if he might fall to pieces. He shut his eyes and rammed his thick body into the small frame of his wife. After several more grunts, he disengaged and dropped her legs. He stumbled back, his breathing labored, his cock drooping toward the ground.

He had spent.

# CHAPTER THIRTY-FOUR

It did not appear to Charles that Miss Katherine had spent, but she smiled as if in triumph.

"Will my lord release me?" she asked. "My arms are sore."

Nodding, Wendlesson stumbled toward her and untied the red scarf that bound her to the bedpost. Her legs weakened, and he caught her in his arms. He pressed a kiss to the top of her head.

Charles released the breath that he had held.

After setting her back on her feet, Wendlesson replaced his fall, then retrieved her robe for her. "Come, we ought not tarry."

Charles stayed them. "Before you go, I would like to know what you thought of the lesson tonight, Miss Katherine."

Her countenance glowed. "I think it went well, Master Gallant."

Though he would have preferred to see her spend, he believed her truly satisfied with the results.

"I am glad to hear it," he said. "I will ring for Tippy or perhaps Miss Terrell can—"

"I will see to her toilette," Wendlesson said. Offering his arm to his wife, he led her toward the door. At the threshold, he turned. "Thank you, Master Gallant."

"Miss Terrell deserves more the credit," Charles replied.

"My thanks to you as well, Miss Terrell."

"Thank you," Miss Katherine added.

When they had gone, closing the door behind them, Charles turned to Miss Terrell, who remained tied to the bedpost. If she had smirked or attempted one of her impudent remarks, he might have been better able to resist. Instead, she only looked at him, patiently waiting, her cheeks still flushed with arousal, her eyes bright with uncertainty and longing.

As Wendlesson had done, he dropped the flogger and covered the distance to the bedpost in one step. One hand went to the back of her head, the other grasped her jaw, tilting her face up so that his mouth could cover hers. With her head trapped in his hands, he claimed the lips he had coveted, delving his tongue between the generous suppleness, taking greedy mouthfuls of her, interrupting her breath and making her pant through her nose for air. When she had recovered from her surprise, she met his ferocity with her own, as intent upon consuming his mouth as he was of hers. Being tied to the bedpost limited her efforts, but it was enough that she could press her hips to him.

Mad with desire, he dropped a hand to cup a buttock and hold her thigh against his hip. She ground herself at him as his lips moved from her mouth down to her neck. She craned her neck to allow him better access. The fragrance of the pomade she used in her hair filled his nostrils. He wished she would use less of it, but he could still smell *her*. He could not describe it, but it stirred his blood, as the scent of a prey might rouse a wolf.

While feasting upon her neck, he reached up and pulled the end of the scarf. It unraveled from her wrists. He swept her into his arms and placed her upon the bed. He returned to kissing her upon the mouth. She grasped his head with both hands, threading her fingers through his hair, and held his head in place as they took turns ravaging each other with lips and tongue. When she bit him gently upon a lip, he growled and clamped his mouth about her, kissing her with a desperate fierceness. Somewhere in his head, caution advised him against such actions. He had been careful throughout Miss Katherine's lesson. Why put all that forbearance to waste?

But all misgivings were overruled by desire to take her and make her spend, to give her the ecstasy she had waited for. It would be unfair of him to make her witness both Miss Katherine and Lord Wendlesson attain that rapturous end without achieving her own glorious finish. He wanted that ecstasy for her. For himself.

His hand gripped and caressed the length of her body from shoulders to waist to leg. Every touch elicited from her a gasp, sigh or moan. Reaching beneath her shift, he grasped her arse. Remembering that he had walloped her good last night, he turned her toward him to better view her backside. It bore no marks and was as fresh and smooth as that of a babe. His cock stretched at the sight of such shapely orbs gleaming in the light of the lamp. He dug his fingers into the flesh before giving it a playful smack.

She was planting kisses along his jaw, and he gasped when she thrust her tongue into his ear. One of her legs slid along his, and he felt his attention pulled in several directions. She clenched his hair till it pulled upon his scalp while kissing him voraciously, pressing her tongue at the soft spot beneath his chin.

He took both her wrists, and she allowed him to pin them above her head. Holding them in place with one hand, he loosened the drawstring of her décolletage. There was one other part of her he had desperately wanted in his mouth. Pulling her shift down, he scooped a breast. The nipple pointed hard at him. Too overcome with desire, he dispensed with more gentle ceremony. His mouth swooped down upon the bud. She exclaimed and writhed, but he had her wrists pinioned and half his body pinning her to the bed. He suckled and licked the nipple. She arched her back. She thrust her hips. She yanked her arms. Her movements fueled the fire in his veins, and he knew there was no hope of desisting now.

Knowing her cunnie wanted attention, he moved his hand between her thighs. They were soaking wet between, making his head swim. He stroked her folds, then nestled his thumb at her clitoris. She whimpered. He petted the little bud, coaxing it to engorge. His mouth was still locked to the other bud, and he alternated between licking the one and caressing the other before bearing down on both. Her body bowed off the bed.

"Please!" she cried. "Please...I want your...fuck me..."

No siren's song could equal those two little words. *Fuck me*. What mortal could resist such a plea? With a groan, he sat up and nearly tore the buttons off his fall. His erection freed, he positioned himself atop her. Glancing at her, he found himself pulled into the brightness of her eyes. It was the one thing that made him pause when every fiber of his body yearned to sink into her.

"Now," she whispered, lifting her pelvis to his. "Please."

He met her and pressed his hardened shaft into her soft, wet folds. The heat encasing him was utterly divine, and he could not refrain from pushing more of his length into her. Exquisite. Marvelous. Wondrous. There were not words enough to describe how she felt.

She flexed about his member, making him shiver, then ground her hips at him, her desire perhaps more impatient than his. Her hands reached into his hair once more, pulling him down to her lips. He took them into his mouth as he buried himself to the hilt. She gave a satisfied grunt and wrapped a leg about his, her cunnie grasping at his cock while she devoured his mouth.

Her aggression astonished him, but he was excited by her unabashed hunger. Her body strained against him, wanting to spend, needing and using his body to reach her objective, but her motions were a bit haphazard in their zeal. When, in her fervor, she pulled too hard upon his hair, he grabbed her wrists and pinned them once more above her head. He shoved into her forcefully.

With a gasp, she gave him her attention. Though he would have been glad to pound her cunnie in wild abandon, he forced himself to thrust with a controlled rhythm. He wanted to ensure she spent. On his cock.

She followed the rolling of his hips and gave him not the soft pants of Miss Katherine but deep, ravenous groans. In unison, their bodies rocked the bed. He drank in the sight of her physiognomy. Every furrow of the brow. Flutter of the lashes. Pouting of the lips. For a while, she held his gaze, but as she neared her climax, she began to close her eyes. The blush upon her cheeks spread, and light perspiration gleamed upon the tip of her nose and the cleavage of her breasts. He quickened his motions to shorter, faster thrusts, smacking his groin against her.

With a cry, she trembled and bucked beneath him. He surged toward his own apex as the beauty of her spending filled his senses, but he withheld himself. He was not without gratitude for her assistance with Miss Katherine and Lord Wendlesson tonight, and he would show his appreciation by making her spend again.

He managed to stay his own urges till the convulsing of her cunnie about his cock quieted. Allowing her a moment to bask in her finish, he brushed a tendril from the side of her face.

She opened her eyes and curled her lips. "Thank you, Master."

His heart warmed at the radiance in her face. He returned her smile. "You forgot to ask permission."

"Oh." But the lapse in her smile was fleeting. "Was it agreed that I am your submissive?"

"Do not feign ignorance with me, Miss Terrell."

Dropping his head, he pulled aside her shift to bare a

breast and took the nipple into his mouth. He sucked till the whole of her back arched off the bed. As he nipped and bit her, she squealed, a little too loudly for comfort, for the door to their room remained unlocked. He reached for the scarf that had landed upon the bed and stuffed it into her mouth upon her next cry.

He stared into her eyes. "You must always ask permission to spend. Even a novice submissive knows that."

The scarf stifled her response, but he imagined her to be asking how she would do this with the scarf in her mouth. He withdrew and flipped her onto her stomach. Pushing aside her hair, he feasted upon her neck, then kissed her lower.

She inhaled sharply when his lips brushed against the top of a scar. He would not repeat his error of last night. Instead, he threw the lower part of her shift up over her arse and admired the backside he had bared. Such curved succulence. Such pristine buttocks. His heartbeat quickened at the prospect of remedying that. He sank his fingers into one orb, then smacked it.

She wriggled her arse, inviting him to slap it some more.

He accepted. He rained several blow upon one cheek till a rosy glow formed.

Already hot and uncomfortable from before, he decided to remove a few articles of clothing. Straddling her to keep her in place, he swiftly removed his waistcoat, cravat, collar and braces. After pulling off his shirt, he resumed the walloping of her derriere. The sharp sound of his hand connecting with that firm, full flesh was made more melodious by her muffled grunts and cries. He pushed his erection at her rump. Had she not said he could claim her back paradise? How many men had received a similar invitation from her?

His cock strained against his trousers, but he would not permit himself the sweet invasion of her arse. Not yet.

But he would take her cunnie again. He reached a hand below her buttocks and found her thighs newly wet. She moaned and said something into the scarf. He could not decipher the words but thought he understood the tone. He pushed his trousers down. Laying his body atop hers, he speared himself into her.

She exclaimed and mumbled into the scarf. His cods were at a boil the instant he was inside of her with his groin pressing against her derriere. Taking in a deep breath, he brushed his lips once more along the nape of her neck. He pinned her wrists once more above her head as he slowly sawed his shaft in and out of her.

In this position, with her arms locked in place, there was little she could do but submit to him. She could widen her legs to provide him better access, but from her anxious groans, he surmised the angle of penetration suited her. He saw her fingers digging into the bedclothes below. Her speech quickened. It sounded as if she said, "Master…please." After that, he could not discern if she even spoke words.

To pleasure her further—and make matters worse—he dropped a hand and insinuated it under her pelvis, searching for that accessory to her undoing. He found the still engorged bud and stroked it. Her hand grasped his arm, pulling at it, but with only partial conviction. She struggled, knowing she ought not spend without gaining his permission but wanting to surrender to the delight.

He provided her a moment of relief when he ceased his caress and pinched the bud. Hard. Her hand tightened upon his arm. He released the bud and returned to stroking it. She shivered and raised her hips as if to escape his hand, but she was trapped beneath his body with nowhere to go.

She grasped and pulled at his arm. Shaking her head, she tried to speak through the scarf. He suspected she cursed him. She bucked as if to throw him off or interfere with his penetration, but he only hastened his thrusting, slapping his groin against her rear. Realizing he was too strong, his weight too much for her, she relented. She squeezed her eyes shut and held onto his arm, the concentration writ upon every inch of her face as she did her best to hold the dam against the flood of rapture.

Not without struggle to stem his own growing tide, he pulled the scarf from her mouth.

"P-Permission…" she stuttered, her voice dry and raspy.

"Granted."

Shoving himself at her, he pushed her over the edge into a pool of paroxysms. As if attempting to swim upon the bed, her limbs flailed beneath him atop the bedclothes. Her cunnie convulsed about him, sending ripples of pleasure down his legs. He drove himself into her with greater fury to achieve his own end, which erupted inside him with such force he wondered that his body could contain it. His body bucked uncontrollably against her, his roar mixing with her continued cries. He slammed into her several more times, as if the only means of saving himself was to bury his cock as deep inside her as possible.

Spent, he allowed his body to settle atop her while he gulped for air. He could feel his seed mixing with her nectar about his shaft. His cock throbbed in the comfort of her heat. Her cunnie would flex briefly about him, making him gasp. When the pulses up and down his legs began to abate, he lifted some of his upper weight off her and kissed the crook between her neck and collar and across the top of a shoulder. She purred and relaxed into the bed.

"Thank you, Master."

He slid off her and pulled her to him. His heart beat strongly still, but holding her had a calming effect.

"It is I who should thank you," he replied. "I do not think Lord Wendlesson would have been as pleased if the lessons had continued as I originally intended."

"Then you do not regret my intrusion?"

Not knowing what to make of it all, he made no reply at first. Did the end justify the means? He supposed that, if the Wendlessons were satisfied, he ought have no complaints.

"I do not condone your interference into my affairs," he said, partially to warn her against future thoughts of the same. "As I have said before, your behavior is far from that of a perfect submissive."

She turned around to face him and propped herself upon his chest. "Instruct me then. I can be taught to become the perfect submissive."

Touched by her earnestness, he cupped the side of her head, his fingers threading through her curls. Like the hair of Oriental women, it was thick and coarser than that of English women.

"I can instruct you, but your wayward nature does not predispose you to well-behaved submission."

"You would enjoy instructing me."

He said nothing. Doubtless he would take great pleasure in it. His hand remembered how fine her arse had felt. He would like to see it quiver once more. But it was useless to entertain such prospects. He tucked his free hand behind his head.

"It would be a fruitless endeavor," he told her, marveling that her mouth lost none of its sensuality when she frowned. He ran his thumb against her lower lip.

"Are you not up to the challenge?"

He started, then gave her an admonishing look. "I will not be cajoled by your wiles."

She looked at him through lowered lashes. "Do you fear failure?"

He forced her head to look him more fully in the face. "The amount of discipline required to turn *you* into the perfect submissive would be more than you could bear."

"You're wrong. You forget I have endured much in my past life."

His jaw tightened. "What was this past life?"

She looked down at his chest and traced the muscles with a finger. "The life of a slave."

When it was plain she would say no more, he said, "I will know it.

"If you please," he added when he realized he'd spoken sternly, "lest telling of it brings you pain."

She glanced tentatively into his eyes, then returned her attention to his chest.

"I consider myself beyond blessed that I was brought to England, where I may be a free woman. I mean never to return to Barbados."

"How long were you in Barbados?"

"I was born there."

"And into slavery."

"Yes."

"And it was in Barbados that you acquired the...scars?" She nodded.

"At whose hand?"

"An overseer."

"I hope he came to some justice for his deed."

She looked at him as if what he said bore little sense. "That is the way in Barbados. What I received is merely a consequence of upsetting the white man."

"Lest you killed a man out of malevolence, I fail to see what you could have done to merit such a hateful flogging. This overseer is a brute of the worst kind. What prompted such savagery?"

"I had a half-sister. Younger and far prettier than I. She was twelve years of age, and Mr. Tremayne, the overseer, took an avid interest in her. One day, he asked where she was. I knew why he sought her. I replied I didn't know, but he had seen us together but twenty minutes before. When I would not tell him where she was, he reached for the flogger."

Charles felt sick to his stomach. His hand tightened upon her. "This is true?"

She met his gaze but only briefly. "There have been far

worse consequences for lesser crimes."

"How did you come to England?" he asked, hoping to steer the dialogue to a less painful period in her life.

"My master wanted my company far too often for his wife's tolerance. One day, when he went into town, she sold me to another."

"Good God," he responded as another nauseating wave hit him. He knew he would regret the answer to his next query, but he asked it nonetheless. "How old were you?"

"Six or seven and ten. For a Negro, the years do not matter."

He sat up. "Six or seven... When did you start keeping the company of the master of the house?"

"A year before perhaps. Before that, I entertained Mr. Tremayne."

He was aghast. "What? The man who beat you?"

"Mr. Tremayne is not a man to cross."

"He wields the flogger often?"

She nodded. "If he be in a proper rage, he would apply salt pickle, bird pepper or lime juice to the wounds. And flogging was not the only form of punishment."

Charles felt the color drain from his face. "What else did this monster employ?"

She paused before saying, "He had Jonah, caught stealing a banana, naked in the bilboes and rubbed with molasses. During the day, the flies swarmed him. At night, the mosquitoes."

"My God."

Her gaze assumed a vacant quality. "Mabel died of the dysentery for Mr. Tremayne had plugged up her arsehole with a corn-stick."

Charles could not speak. Wang had once told of how a cousin of his had been dismembered by horses. Charles had not thought he could hear of anything more gruesome till now.

"How could the master or the owner permit such

atrocities?"

"The master was not a better man. When he thought Nathan, the stable boy, to have maimed one his prized colts, he had Nathan buried alive."

Charles could not suffer to hear more. He thought of her mutilated back and shuddered to think she might have received a worse fate.

"You see how fortunate I have been," she said.

He had many more questions but asked only, "Did the man you were sold to bring you to England?"

"That man was a drunkard and a poor gambler. He was sometimes flush in the purse, but there were times he had but pennies upon him, which went to gin as often as could be had. Once, I went five days without eating till I came upon a mulatto who spared me part of her breadfruit."

Charles ran a hand through his hair. If he were to ever cross paths with the man or with Mr. Tremayne, he would be hard-pressed not to cane them to within an inch of their lives.

"But here I was blessed," she consoled. "After but a few months, he sold me to Mr. Terrell, who treated me kindly, almost as if I were a daughter or a niece."

"But one he fucked," he replied with a wry grin.

"Yes, well, that was to be expected, but as he was much older, he did not require my favors as often as others had. It was he who brought me to England."

"Were you married to him?"

She shook her head. "He had acquired malaria in his time in Barbados and passed away within a year of our arrival in England. I had to start a new life for myself in an unfamiliar land. I wanted nothing to do with my past in Barbados, not even the name I bore as a slave. I feared I would be found somehow and returned."

"So you became Miss Terrell. You have no other name?"

She gave him a wry smile. "The men who take an interest in me care not what name I bear."

He refrained from wondering how many men she might have lifted her skirts to, but she seemed to know his thoughts.

"It is true I have lain with many men. That is how I know I am barren. I would surely have conceived by now if not."

"After the treatment you have received at the hands of white men, why should you wish to submit yourself to another? I wonder that you can tolerate the implements we use at the Red Chrysanthemum without their provoking the pain from your past?"

"At first, they did, though my first instruction came from a woman. Mistress Brownwen. She gave me a gentle introduction into the *arts* here."

He lifted his brows. "She was my instructor as well."

"You were a submissive?"

"One cannot be a good dominant without fully appreciating the other half."

"You have had no Mistress since her?"

"Not one who demanded my submission...till you."

She had the decency to flush.

"And if you reprise such a stunt, I will have your hide," he warned.

"From my backside, I hope?"

He stared at her. There was no winning with her.

"I know not that I could submit to anyone if I had endured what you have," he diverted.

"But, at the Red Chrysanthemum, we submit for corporal pleasure. Submission is not slavery."

"But there are members here who treat it as such. Even the language can be the same, the instruments of punishment the same."

"There is a fundamental element of difference betwixt the two: choice. The members here *choose* their bondage, as I ask it of you, of my own free will, Master Gallant."

He could not escape the clarity of her gaze as her last words echoed in his ears. There was no passiveness to her tone. He realized there never would be with her. Despite the nature of the words, she spoke them more to affirm her own will than to convey deference. Though she professed to wanting instruction and wanting to be the perfect submissive for him, as he had countered to her, she would never truly submit all of herself. She was too willful, too wayward, too wanton.

And yet he could not help but admire her. A lesser man or woman would have had their spirit broken by all that she had suffered. He knew there was far more she had not disclosed to him. That she would trust him when she ought to have fled with revulsion from every one of his kind was more than flattering. It was inspiring. He found himself curious to know how well he could tame the she-panther.

"Will you instruct me as your submissive?" she asked. "I ask only a sennight."

He rose from the bed and pulled up his trousers. If he tarried in the bed, he might find he would not leave.

"Have you forgotten Sir Arthur?" he reminded her. "Or do you intend to forsake him?"

"Would you take me if I did?"

He reached for his shirt and pulled it overhead as he pondered his answer. "No. You can fetch far more with the likes of Sir Arthur, and I am not seeking a submissive at present."

"Why not?"

Because he had hoped for the return of Miss Greta. Aloud, he replied, "I have an election that requires my full attention. It is an opportunity that will not come to pass for many years."

"But I ask only a sennight. When you are finished with Miss Katherine."

"You could not be instructed in the ways of a perfect submissive if given a fortnight."

She sat at the edge of the bed and pouted. "That is unkind."

He smiled. "I fear it true."

"Let me prove you wrong."

He tucked his shirt into his trousers and secured the braces. "I am certain of the outcome, Miss Terrell. You may indulge me at first, but your true nature is not that of a submissive."

"Do you fear to be proven wrong?"

That was at least twice, if not thrice, she had accused him of being afraid. Grasping the back of her neck, he angled her head up toward him. Her mouth dropped open.

"Your accusations grow wearisome, Miss Terrell."

"If you did not desire me, I would not trouble you again. But you do."

Sensing a dangerous area coming upon them, he released her. He picked up his collar.

"I do not deny you are a very alluring young woman, but we do not suit."

"We suit in the way that matters for the Red Chrysanthemum. My cunnie suits your cock perfectly, and your cock craves my cunnie."

"That is not all I seek at the Red Chrysanthemum."

Seeing that he struggled with his collar, she knelt upon the bed and fixed it for him. "What is it you seek?"

"If—*if*—I sought one to be my submissive, she would be nearer my age."

"I could not be much younger than you, and I have fucked men twice your years."

That was hardly what he wished to hear.

"And she would be proficient in the ways of submission," he added.

Taking up his neckcloth, she wrapped it about his neck. He allowed her to arrange the cravat though he felt himself responding to her nearness. If her hands should wander...

"I am no novice," she said.

"You are worse than a novice. You are intractable."

She yanked on the neckcloth. He grunted as the linen tightened about his neck.

"That is the second unkind statement you have made," she remarked with aplomb.

While he valued truth and honesty, he would not have been so blunt if he thought her constitution too delicate. And with her, subtlety was as effective as a light spanking. She required something more forceful.

"Forgive me," he said, "but you deserve the truth of my thoughts."

"Then grant me three days. If I show no promise in that time, we may go our separate ways, and I will plague you no more. But I think you will find you want the full sennight with me."

Silent, he believed he shared in what Eve felt when faced with the forbidden apple. He put on his waistcoat. The more layers of clothes he had on, the better.

"Miss Terrell, we have had this discussion before."

She responded as if nothing could be simpler, "Take me as your submissive and we need discuss it no further."

The saucy minx.

"Three nights," she reiterated as she began to button his waistcoat. "You owe me a shirt and may repay me with your time."

By design or not, she played upon his guilt over the incident.

"I prefer to replace your shirt with a new one. Of better quality."

"You may offer me a dozen new shirts. I prefer *you*, Master Gallant."

She had reached the final button of his waistcoat, and he was conscious of how near her hands were to his crotch. She placed both hands upon his midsection to smooth the waistcoat. Her hands traveled down to the buttons of his fall. His breath grew uneven. He caught her hands before she could touch him more intimately.

"*When* you are finished with Sir Arthur, *when* I have completed Miss Katherine's instructions, and *if* I have an interest in taking a submissive, I will consider your request," he told her.

Dropping her hands, he went to the sideboard to pour her—and himself—a glass of wine. He wanted a stronger drink, but given that he had to ride the streets at night, it would not be wise. Approaching, she accepted the glass he presented her.

"Why these stipulations?" she inquired. "Have we not already ventured down the path you persist in eschewing?"

"It was unwise. And wrong. We allowed—I allowed compulsion to best judgment."

"If the dye be cast, why worry of it now?"

"Having erred once—"

"Twice."

"You think it of no consequence to repeat the folly?"

"We cannot undo the crime."

"We can make it worse and expose ourselves to discovery."

"We have done so already."

He found her robe, which was heavy with something, and offered it to her. She slid her arms into the sleeves. Her eyes were downcast in thought, and, for the first time, she appeared a little disheartened. He cupped and lifted her chin.

"Terrell—Miss Terrell, you are a most desirable and enticing beauty. But I have no interest in taking a submissive."

"I would not require much of your time. You cannot be every minute on your election. The harder you work, the more you require a reprieve."

With an exhale, he realized he would have to give her the other answer. "Because another occupies my heart."

"Ah. I had suspected as much. But I do not seek a place in your heart. I only wish for your time…and your cock."

"I am certain there is a member here who can substitute—"

She shook her head. "I am certain there is not."

"Then approach me in two fortnights. After the votes for the burgess have been cast."

She frowned. "Two fortnights? Can you truly wait that long? Will your cock not pine for my cunnie terribly?"

It would, but he was determined to overcome his baser inclinations.

"If you behave yourself in that time," he provided, "I will be more disposed to granting your request."

She sighed. "Very well."

Relieved that she was relenting, he planted a chaste kiss upon her brow.

"If you will not take me as your submissive," she said, pulling out a book from the pocket of her robe, "will you grant me your time and read from this?"

She held *Fanny Hill* in her hands. He had wondered where the book had gone.

"Merely read?" he asked in skepticism.

She nodded. "We may read in the dining hall or an open park if you worry I may attempt mischief."

He did not respond that he thought her capable of mischief anywhere. Recalling that she did not know how to read, he found it hard to refuse her request.

"It would serve in place of the shirt," she added.

"I will replace your shirt," he replied firmly. Despite his reservations, he said, "And I should be pleased to read for you."

Her countenance brightened, and he felt a corresponding glow spread within him. It was a dangerous response, but he was glad he could offer a small source of joy for her. He could not imagine the life she had led till now and dreaded that it was far worse than what she had described. Yet he wanted to know more.

"Will you have time tomorrow night?" she asked.

"I have two more lessons to provide Miss Katherine."

"Then the night following your final lesson with her."

"Why do I suspect you will hound me daily till I yield?"

"If Mistress Scarlet should return tomorrow, I think

you will forget all about me."

It was possible, but he greatly doubted he could forget Miss Terrell.

"If I give you my word it shall happen, it will," he assured her. He went to open the door for her. "Till then, good night, Miss Terrell."

She stood in the doorway, holding the Cleland novel against her. When she looked up at him, he thought she intended one final attempt to entice or harry him, but she said only, "Good night, Master Gallant."

Turning from him, she headed into the hall. He watched her until she descended the stairs. Once she was out of view, he leaned against the frame of the door. He let the back of his head fall against the wood. He could not decide if he could claim any victory in holding off her advances. One could argue he had only delayed matters. But a great deal could happen within two fortnights. Perhaps Sir Arthur would be done with the Red Chrysanthemum by then. Miss Terrell might find another member to prey upon.

Or, if the proper circumstances were in place, he might indulge in taking Miss Terrell for his submissive.

# CHAPTER THIRTY-FIVE

"There you are. I had sent Miss Sarah for you, but she returned saying she could not find you."

Madame Devereux gestured for Terrell to enter the room. Stepping inside, Terrell noted how much the bedchamber of the proprietress differed from her own accommodations. In contrast to the stark furnishings in her own room, Madame's furniture served dual purposes of utility and decoration. Wallpaper and sconces adorned the walls. A fire crackled brightly in the hearth.

"Where could you have gone off to at this hour?" Madame asked as she settled herself onto the sofa.

"I have been here the entire night," Terrell replied.

Madame narrowed her eyes. "Not trying to ensnare a new admirer?"

"I did survey the new members, for I do not expect that I can retain the favors of Sir Arthur for long."

"You might be surprised. He is no simpleton or I could speak with more certainty, but without doubt he is taken with you. I think we may be assured of his presence for a little while."

Terrell could not decide if she found comfort or not in Madame's assessment. Surely she ought to. How many men of Sir Arthur's wealth frequented the Red Chrysanthemum?

But what if he were gone? Would her chances with Master Gallant improve? A part of her still could not believe that Master Gallant had not agreed to three nights with her. He had fucked her when he could have simply untied her from the bedpost and sent her on her way then. Was it gratitude that had prompted him to pleasure her?

No. He had fucked her with passion. Nor did she think she had imagined the flames of lust in his eyes when he flogged her. Why did he still resist? Did Mistress Scarlet truly weigh upon him?

A rare sense of sadness gripped her. Perhaps if she were not a blackamoor, if she were pale of skin, if she had softer hair, if her body was not marred, she might command his acquiescence. She thought of Mistress Scarlet, with her straight reddish hair and slim body. Terrell knew her to be the daughter of an apothecary. The woman could be the daughter of a shoemaker and still she would possess better breeding than a former slave.

"Then I am fortunate," Terrell said. "If, in another sennight, he still calls upon me with frequency, the rate must need be higher. For certain, I will have other requests by then."

Madame smiled. "Your thoughts could not be more similar to mine."

"He may not like having his hand forced. Would you say the man could afford a harem?"

"I know few men richer than he. Yes, he could afford a harem, but there is only one Miss Terrell. You must make that clear to him."

"I intend to keep him a happy patron—an exceedingly happy patron."

"You would have two happy patrons to your credit. Lord Wendlesson came to see me before he left. Praised Charles and yourself. I've not seem him this pleased before. Offered to contribute a hundred guineas to the Red Chrysanthemum, then promptly made it two hundred."

Madame ended with a sigh of satisfaction.

"That is a goodly sum," Terrell said.

"He said that you had befriended his wife."

"Our paths crossed in the dressing chambers."

"Then it was not Master Gallant who had prompted your assistance in the instruction of Miss Katherine?"

"I merely offered my company to Miss Katherine at first. When she was more at ease, I offered my hands and mouth."

"Indeed? And what of Lord Wendlesson? He surprised me the other night with his appearance. I had not thought he would involve himself in his wife's instruction."

Terrell could not discern if the queries stemmed from curiosity or something more. She lowered her voice as if in conspiracy. "What man can resist the sight of two women together?"

"True. And how were you compensated for your part? Did Master Gallant pay you? Or Lord Wendlesson?"

"I had hoped you would be pleased enough to consider a perquisite in order."

"Hmmm. I did not ask that you assist Master Gallant."

"Then I hope my actions will stand me in good stead in your eyes, which is not without value."

Madame was silent in thought before finally saying, "There are a few rooms that see little use. Perhaps you would prefer accommodations upon the third floor?"

"Would Lady Sarah accompany me?"

"Miss Sarah would benefit from the new arrangement, for she and the babe would have your current room to themselves."

Terrell considered that even the smallest room on the third floor would be preferable to the room in the attic. Having her own room would be quite the luxury, and she could make use of the privacy, but Sarah and Georgie needed more space, and she enjoyed their companionship. "But if she preferred to share the new room?"

"I suppose it matters not to me. I leave the decision to

you."

"Thank you, Madame. You are generosity itself," Terrell said with the proper amount of exuberance.

"In the future, however, I prefer you consult with me before involving yourself in the instruction of new members."

"Yes, Madame."

"And do put forth your best effort with Sir Arthur. Please *him*, and a liberal bounty will surely come your way."

"Thank you, Madame."

Sensing the conversation at an end, Terrell withdrew.

She knew she ought to consider the evening a grand success. Madame had granted her a new room. Master Gallant had agreed to read to her. She could still feel her moisture—and his—between her thighs. It would flow for a while longer, and she savored the evidence of his presence inside of her. She knew she would relive the moments of their congress many times, recalling how his body had slammed into hers, how his cock had filled her full and deep, how they had lain together afterward amidst the rumpled bedclothes. She wanted to reprise it all and more.

As she mounted the stairs, she was certain her hand would be between her legs within moments of reaching her bed. She was certain, too, that despite his refusal to take her as his for now, she was not done with him. She would prove to him that she was worthy of being his submissive. She would earn his regard. She would seduce the Master.

# THE END